2018

IN THE
BELLY OF THE
HORSE

IN THE BELLY OF THE HORSE

a novel
Eliana Tobias

inanna poetry & fiction series

INANNA PUBLICATIONS AND EDUCATION INC.
TORONTO, CANADA

We gratefully acknowledge the support of the Canada Council for the Arts and
the Ontario Arts Council for our publishing program. We also acknowledge the
financial support of the Government of Canada through the Canada Book Fund.

Cover design: Val Fullard

In the Belly of the Horse is a work of fiction. All the characters and situations
portrayed in this book are fictitious and any resemblance to persons living or
dead — with the exception of historical personages — is purely coincidental.
Names and incidents are the products of the author's imagination and historical
events are used fictitiously.

Library and Archives Canada Cataloguing in Publication

Tobias, Eliana R., 1945-, author
    In the belly of the horse / a novel by Eliana Tobias.

(Inanna poetry & fiction series)
Issued in print and electronic formats.
ISBN 978-1-77133-429-7 (softcover). -- ISBN 978-1-77133-432-7 (pdf). --
ISBN 978-1-77133-430-3 (epub). -- ISBN 978-1-77133-431-0 (Kindle)

        I. Title. II. Series: Inanna poetry and fiction series

PS3620.O25I5 2017   813'.6   C2017-905377-9
                                                   C2017-905378-7

Printed and bound in Canada

Inanna Publications and Education Inc.
210 Founders College, York University
4700 Keele Street, Toronto, Ontario, Canada M3J 1P3
Telephone: (416) 736-5356 Fax: (416) 736-5765
Email: inanna.publications@inanna.ca Website: www.inanna.ca

To the children in the world
who are caught in the terrors of geo-political conflicts
and are denied a just and healthy childhood.

Prologue

P ERU, ONCE A PART of the great Incan Empire, was conquered
by the Spanish in the sixteenth century. The Spaniards
established their government body in the city of Lima, which
then became known as The City of Kings. From there, they
ruled their South American colonies until the *criollo* Peruvians,
who had obtained political and economic strength, proclaimed
their independence from Spain on July 28th, 1821. Decades of
political instability and a war against Chile over deposits of
sodium nitrate followed. Peru lost the combat and was forced
to cede territory to its enemy.

During most of the twentieth century Peru's government
was marked by a series of military dictatorships and coups.
In the 1980s, the guerilla warfare group known as *Sendero
Luminoso*, or the Shining Path, waged a terrorist campaign
against the central government. The Shining Path derived its
name from the motto of the 1920's founder of the Peruvian
communist party who stated: "Marxism-Leninism will open
the shining path of the revolution."

In the late 1960s, the philosophy professor Abimael Guzman
revived the communist party and drafted a political military
document inspired by the ideas of Maoist China to establish a
dictatorship of the proletariat. As the years passed, "*Presidente*
Gonzalo"—Guzman's *nom de guerre*—began to gain a large
and loyal following.

Throughout the 1980s, the movement grew in strength, especially in areas of the country that were greatly impoverished and where the population had been grossly neglected. Calling for its militias to engage in an armed struggle, Guzman began to harass farmers and peasants in the countryside. At first these acts gained little notice. When strikes were mounted in the capital of Lima, the conflict got some attention in the press. The government did not respond to the uprising right away. By the time they did, they did so reluctantly.

Geography is destiny.

1

OTILIA PEREZ SOBBED uncontrollably as she watched her husband, Manuel, lift their son to his chest, tightening his hold as he prepared to run up the hill with the child.

"Don't worry, *mujer*," Manuel hastened to say, conveying a pained tenderness. "I'll take him up to Rodrigo's place and hurry back. I promise I won't be long. You must stay calm. Guard our property. If nobody's here, they'll seize our land."

Otilia was incensed. When had her husband planned this escape?

"You've got to think rationally," Manuel continued. Things have changed; we must protect ourselves from this ghastly group before things take a turn for the worse. We must save the child. Let me get him to safety while we can. You'll be with him soon enough."

She was shocked. Their son was so young, only seven, and it was hard to believe that there was an imminent threat. "Why must we be caught up in this madness? I know there are concerns, but why overreact?" Otilia touched Manuel's arm in sympathy, but she looked away, anxious to hide the desperation in her eyes. At times, when Manuel exhibited overbearing behaviour, she knew it was best not to pressure him.

"They act without restraints. They shoot first, ask questions later; the clashes are coming our way."

Otilia quickly rose up to her tiptoes, her hands stretched

out to caress their son's head. Salvador tried to lean down to kiss her, but Manuel was already on his way. Hanging to one side and looking back, the boy's scarred upper lip reddened as he offered her an apologetic smile. "If you think we should leave, I should go too," she yelled as the lump in her throat grew large. But Manuel did not look back, only walked away more purposely and more swiftly.

Stunned, she stood in the doorway, her mouth open in silent protest, watching them fade away into the expanse. Why? she asked herself. What could have caused Manuel's sudden decision to go into hiding today?

For years they had heard about the fanatical assailants roaming the countryside—a gang of bandits, some said—while the authorities' pledges to curb them went unheard. Most people expressed their disapproval of the revolutionary group calling themselves *Sendero Luminoso*, the Shining Path, laughing them off, playing them down, and saying they had no clout to turn the Peruvian political situation around.

"This is foolish," she managed to mumble; Manuel had acted too hastily. Looking up and down the street, she saw no evidence of the elusive enemy. Their presence was known in the southern part of the country, but even there, they were considered a fringe element at best. Unconvinced of a menace, she turned and went inside her house, shutting the door firmly behind her. She had clothes to wash, ironing to be done, a chicken to pluck, and beans to soak for supper.

But bothersome thoughts began to fester as soon as she started her chores. What if the Shining Path were not so weak after all? Poverty afflicted a great number of people in her country and the government wasn't helping the economy push ahead. Perhaps this insignificant Peruvian organization was becoming stronger than many assumed. Maybe they were *levantando cabeza*, gaining ground fast, making strides in their fight to bring justice to the poor. What if the Sendero was growing, with substantial numbers joining their rank and file? No, it wasn't possible—the government kept them in check, she reminded herself, of that she was sure.

Mulling over the facts from last night, she thought about how Manuel had returned from his business trip—tense and sharing few details about his concerns. He'd been quieter than usual, saying only that his business dealings had been frustrating. He'd been to see a farmer and was close to making a deal for a customer wanting to buy some of his cows, when the farmer suddenly became extremely uncooperative. There'd been no room for negotiations. Cocky, he'd stood firm on his price. Manuel invited him for a couple of beers so they could chat at ease, but their conversation turned into a heated argument, the farmer saying that he would no longer tolerate being pushed around by some rich guys who thought themselves better than him. Livestock, after all, deserved a fair price. He struggled to make money and at long last, there were others out there fighting to protect his rights, people who were going to help him make a better life.

Who were those people? Manuel had asked, but no answers were to be had. When Manuel left to convey to the buyer that he hadn't been able to negotiate a deal, the buyer backed out, saying he feared that things were starting to heat up and it was best he held on to his cash. Cash would be paramount when the guerillas attacked.

Manuel had gone to bed earlier than usual and, before he retired, he made sure he had closed the front door's heavy latch. He was asleep before Otilia joined him, but she noticed him tossing and turning all night. He was up in the early morning and seemed anxious, racing around between the barn and the house, tuning into the radio, trying to find out if there was trouble nearby. Few words passed between them and when she had endured enough of their silence, she finally asked, "What's going on?"

"What do you expect?" he'd answered harshly.

Later, apologizing for losing his temper, he told her there

were too many subversives roaming around. It was then that she began to worry as well, but she was sure the talk of conflict was just idle rumour-mongering intended to scare and intimidate them.

Otilia switched on the television but only *telenovelas* were playing. Soap operas dominated the channels they got at this time of the day. She'd have to wait for the news to come on at one o'clock. She turned on the radio by the kitchen sink, fiddling with the knob, anxious to get some information, but couldn't find a station with any reports.

At around three, she listened to the sudden roar of a truck's engine passing by with a sinking feeling in the pit of her stomach. Eager for conversation, she decided to call her friend Marita. She picked up the receiver from the rotary phone and dialled the number. She did not mention her worry once her friend had said that all was quiet and fine as usual with her. When she hung up, she thought about visiting her neighbour to ask if she had heard about any disturbances, but decided against it. She was sure Manuel wouldn't appreciate her talking to people he considered *metidos,* nosy, and who would embellish her story, turning it into juicy gossip.

She shuddered when she looked up at the clock, alarmed that it was already five and Manuel still hadn't returned. She was acutely sorry that she had let them leave without her. Why wasn't he back? What could have happened?

At the height of the summer the days were long, but now everything around her turned dark. She heard strange noises coming from outside, but she didn't dare turn on the lights. Rhythmic screeching sounds, a thumping foot on the ground, the bark of a dog—did something explode? A blast? Were the guerillas on their way to her village tonight? Were they deliberately harassing people, trying to scare them? They'll get me, she thought, but then she recalled her recent chat with another friend, Laura, who, after travelling to visit her mother, had said she had no concerns for her personal safety while on the road.

She listened with care once again. She thought she heard the thud of boots. She moved toward the window and tentatively pushed the end of the curtain aside, and took a peek outside. Everything was dark. There were no lights; not even the row of houses on top of the hill showed any sign of life. Had the guerillas sabotaged the electric power plant?

Otilia pulled a woollen shawl from her dresser drawer and wrapped it tightly around her shoulders to control her furious shivering. She slid into a squat on the floor and huddled in a corner, pressing her back to the wall. She held her breath; from outside, she heard sharp cries and what sounded like guns being fired nearby. She was so tired she couldn't think straight and remained tightly swathed with her knees against her chest.

Rising abruptly, she made her way to the coal storage one floor below. She faced the ladder and with light steps she tentatively descended one rung at a time. This was the perfect spot to take cover while waiting for danger to pass. She felt for the flashlight they kept on a ledge, then sat on the stool facing the black cast-iron furnace. Her mind filled with desperate thoughts, Otilia forced herself to think of the warm glow that would come from the red coals after she'd lit the fire in the early mornings during the cold winter months. She thought of the trucks delivering the load once a month, and the men carrying the sacks of coal down the ladder on their backs. It warmed her heart to remember when Salvador was still a toddler and they had made designs with coal chunks on the cement floor in their backyard. How he had laughed.

Only once did she go back upstairs in the middle of the night to use the bathroom. When she descended again she decided to try a different tactic to clear her mind from the unnerving worries. She started to count her inhales and exhales as she took in deep breaths, but the smell of coal-ash made her cough and she began to fret again. With her head throbbing, and hardly able to breathe, she lay on the damp ground, counting the hours for dawn to arrive. She wished she'd insisted that all three of them remain together at all times. Sleep didn't come and neither did her husband and child. Where were they now?

Tired and chilled, she finally believed enough time had passed and she climbed back up. Holding her breath, she listened carefully for sounds. All was silent. Her hands were shaking, and she felt a prickly pain in her knees and soreness in her back. She heard her stomach rumble. With different versions of the same story crisscrossing her mind, she forced herself to stay calm. She'd get something to eat. She went to look outside, but all she could see was the stark daylight of the early morning, and clear skies. She looked at her hands and realized they were caked with black dust. She removed her clothes to wash up and resolved to wait for another hour. If they were still not back, she'd head out, go up the mountainside.

She found a bag, packed some shirts, an extra pair of pants, and then threw in some food. What else should she take? The money that she'd stashed away, of course, and a jacket for the rain. And some clothes for her son, a toy truck? But she put the toy down; it was silly of her to be thinking of carrying it around. She tucked it under Salvador's bed for safekeeping until they got back, and picked up a small plush toy instead.

Why hadn't Manuel sent someone for her if he hadn't been able to come back himself? There were lots of people he knew and could count on. Why so much delay? Something was wrong. She had a horrible feeling that Manuel was in deep trouble. It was hard to make sense of what had happened in the past twenty-four hours. Why hadn't they seen it coming? Prepared themselves. Was Salvador—her precious boy—somewhere up on the hills all alone? No, Manuel had said he would leave him with his friend. Would they have gone to one of the caves on the side of the road or the one more secluded, higher up?

She walked out of her house, locking the door behind her, and wondered if she should stop by to see her *comadre*. Would a visit be prudent? She might be taking a risk.

Only last month, when she had prepared a *sancochado* for Alba's family dinner, rather than thanking her, her neighbour, in a hushed voice, had told her it was not a good time to talk. "My son's just arrived from the south." Alba's face seemed unusually pale; she had watery eyes that darted from side to side as if fearing that someone was lurking nearby. Otilia had heard rumours that Alba's son had joined the Shining Path—she didn't ask.

What if, last night, government soldiers had come looking for guerillas and had picked up Alba's son? What if they had hauled the whole family away? She would not stop at Alba's place nor would she go to the local police. It was best to go looking for Manuel and Salvador herself. She remembered a radio broadcast where they reported that in some isolated southern communities, when trouble loomed, the local police were fearful to engage and opted for a hasty retreat, leaving the community to cope as best they could.

As gusts of wind blew dust in her face, she turned toward the imposing mountains in the distance and propelled herself down the path she had taken so many times. Stories of arrests and investigations rose in her mind as she wrapped her head with her light cotton scarf, her dark hair long and heavy showing in the back. Apart from the sound of trees swaying in furious motion under grey skies, all was still.

Walking by adobe dwellings with terracotta tiled roofs, she noticed rebar and sacks of concrete sitting alongside piles of bricks. She thought she'd see people outside, at least a few men building their homes and women cleaning the raw wool from their sheep, but there wasn't a soul around. Not even the chickens were out. Had people gone into hiding? Had soldiers cleared corpses overnight? She shivered as horrendous images bounced around in her mind. These villages were peaceful, inhabited by hardworking people who had their papers in order, could show proof of legitimate deeds to their lands. Why were they not working the farms? Why would anybody want to harass them?

As she hastened her footsteps through the jagged rocky terrain, the more disquieted her mind became. Images of Manuel and Salvador flashed before her as she spun scary explanations of their whereabouts. She'd go up to where Rodrigo lived. If there was no sign of them, she'd go to the nearest police station to list them as missing persons and express her indignation at the offense perpetrated on her village the night of February 23. Her eyes continued to sweep the expanse as she maintained her brisk pace up to the gusty moors where sheep and cattle grazed. Why was the countryside so deserted? And what if the police doubted her story, proclaimed her a rebel—no, an accomplice—and she ended up being locked up? What good would that do? Nauseous from the nagging thoughts occupying her mind, she pressed on.

Walking steadily on the hillside road, she came to a low stone wall surrounding a house perched on an overhang. Her breathing had become laboured and she stopped for a moment to clear the film of sweat on her brow. Then she knocked on the door. There was no response. A screeching hawk flying above was the only sound she heard.

The entrance to the small horizontal cave, invisible from the road, was just across from Rodrigo's stone house. It had been a while since she and Manuel had climbed to this point. They'd come here occasionally on an outing, bringing along some lunch. This was a good place to hide, and Manuel would have asked Rodrigo to keep a close eye on the child, while he went back to fetch her.

Slowly making her way deep into the rocks, she walked in silence as a few rays of sunlight seeped in through the cracks.

Shadows enclosed her as she moved around in the cave, calling Salvador's name. Excited to finally see him, her voice grew loud and shrill, reverberating in the rocks. Running from one place to the other, searching behind the stalactites, she realized Salvador wasn't in sight. Heartbroken, she hurried outside and went back to knock again on the windows and door of Rodrigo's house. Drained, Otilia sat down on the ground under the roof's overhang to wait for someone to show up. It began to turn dark. She had no appetite but made herself chew a handful of nuts. She put on her jacket and placed her head on her bag, hoping sleep would set in for a while.

Early the next morning, she left. Manuel and Salvador were not there. Where had they gone? Stupefied, she began her descent toward the valley below. Burying her feelings, she went on, but fatigue slowed her down. She still couldn't eat. Otilia breathed hard and fast, so fast she felt dizzy, and had trouble walking. What if she fell? Would she be left to die all alone? She couldn't leave an orphan behind. She couldn't have that. She sat for a while and forced some bread down her throat. She fervently regretted letting them go, and was annoyed for not having responded differently. She should have run after them. The image of her son looking into her eyes from his father's arms haunted her and tears poured down her face.

Walking by acres of rich soil growing rows of vegetables, she reached down to grasp the top of a bunch of carrots. Tugging firmly, she pulled them out. She sniffed the sweet scent, shook off the dirt, and tucked them into her bag. Meandering through the field, she wondered if she should reach for another bunch but decided against it, since her small bag was already jam-packed. She stopped in her tracks when she noticed a wrecked barbed-wire fence lying on the ground. There was damage to the crops inside the fenced area. Squash had been pulled out. Beets and spinach were crushed. Men with machetes must have cut the wooden stakes and trampled the fields as they advanced. They'd left heavy footprints behind.

She walked along the path for a few more miles until she reached an asphalt-paved road where she waited under the blazing sun to catch a bus going into Cajamarca. After some time, when there was still no bus in sight, Otilia waved down an oncoming truck. Stopping a few yards ahead of her, a driver wearing dark glasses rolled the windows down. She darted up to the truck to talk to him, but before she could say anything, he removed his glasses, made eye contact, and smiled, "*Mamita*, do you need a ride?"

"I'm going to Cajamarca, *señor*," she panted.

"Hop in."

Weaving his way up and down the hills, the driver steered carefully around piles of rocks accumulated on the side of the road. Fearing unwelcome inquiries about the motives for her trip, Otilia was grateful when the driver switched on the radio. She sat back to gaze at the rolling, green pastures where animals grazed and the tiny, quiet villages nestled around groves.

Potholes made the next stretch slow going. The driver began to curse. "Doesn't anybody here take care of the roads?" he bellowed.

She was dozing when a series of squeaking brakes startled her awake and she spotted a group of soldiers at a checkpoint. They were stopping all the cars and questioning the drivers. She made herself small, and leaning her head against the passenger door, she pretended to sleep. Their truck moved slowly along the lineup and the driver was quickly waved through. An hour later, they pulled into the parking lot of a truck stop. The driver switched off the engine and opened the door on his side. "Come on," he said, "let's go get something to eat."

"Don't worry about me, sir."

"Come along, it'll be my treat."

Otilia was beginning to feel hungry and thought it best to keep her meagre supplies for hard times ahead. She jumped out of the truck and was enveloped in a cloud of dust as another truck pulled out of the unpaved lot.

The truck stop was busy, mostly with men eating and drinking and talking loudly among themselves. They found a place to sit and ordered their food, which arrived quickly. Otilia gulped down the bottle of water the driver offered her before she looked down at her lunch plate. He was a tanned, muscular man with large hands, short with words. "Oscar's my name," he grunted. "We should be in Cajamarca by three."

She nodded, and suddenly famished, she polished off the food in front of her. When they had both finished their lunch, the driver started talking again. "Where do you come from?" he asked.

Otilia hadn't realized how much she needed to talk. The words spilled out. She told him about the harrowing nightmare she was going through. "I don't know what to do," she said, wiping away the tears streaming down her face. Then she apologized for bothering him with her story.

Oscar lit a cigarette. Turning his chair to face her, he crossed his legs and said, "*Mamita,* you better not go into town. Let me take you somewhere else."

"I can't. My husband and son…" she whimpered.

"It's dangerous."

"I need to make a report to the police."

"You'll do nothing of the sort," he replied firmly. "If you witness disturbances, they don't like it. They have this decree now. Anyone can be detained incommunicado for up to thirty days for questioning. I think you should stay away."

"But I didn't see anything. I only heard shots in the distance. I don't even know if they were shots, or if it was my imagination," Otilia said, her narrowing black eyes filled with grief.

"Well, it's up to you," he shrugged.

Feeling slightly carsick from the turns and twists of the road, Otilia had an inner debate about where she should go and what she should do next. She tried not to look at Oscar, not wanting him to ask any more questions.

"What's going on?" she heard Oscar mutter as the traffic came to a sudden halt.

"Another road block?" she asked.

Oscar reduced his speed as they approached a rusty sign: *Control*. "Security is getting worse by the day," he said, coming to a full stop in another long line of cars and trucks.

Otilia thought of jumping out, running away.

Sensing her discomfort, Oscar said, "Say very little; you've done nothing wrong, understand?"

Letting out a sigh, she reached for her bag to look for her identity card.

"The circle of suspicion is tightening," Oscar said, rolling down his window.

"*Celulas por favor*." The armed guard barked and commanded Oscar to step down with his identity card. "Open the back." He pointed a flashlight at the cargo. "Provisions, you say? Let's make certain of that."

A spark of alarm rushed through Otilia as the guard searched the truck, taking his time. Petrified, she waited for her turn to be questioned.

"And you," the guard said, stepping up to her side to look at her identity card, "get out. Where're you going?"

"To visit a relative," she mumbled as she descended from the truck.

"Excuse me, sir," Oscar interrupted, trying to distract him. "How come the road's closed?"

"A car bomb went off this morning. The *senderistas* are targeting members of the city council. We are in a state of high alert. You're free to go, but be watchful."

Oscar jumped back into the truck and started the engine. He looked pointedly at Otilia who had climbed in beside him. "So, you still want me to drop you off at the intersection?"

"Yes, *por favor*."

"It's terrible what people are up to. Believe me when I tell you, right now it's not safe. Come up to the mine with me. I'll talk to Teresa and she'll get you a job. Stay there for a while. From there you can begin to send word out."

"I can't abandon my husband and child."

"You'll be taking care of your family by protecting yourself. Right now there's a lot of turbulence."

"I don't know, *señor* Oscar, I should stay in Cajamarca," she said, staring out the window. "I have to inquire if they have information on my Manuel and Salvador."

"*Mamita*, be careful. Inquires can turn to interrogations. They aren't interested in finding one child. Once you disappear you become nothing—you don't exist for them. Trust me, I travel the country and see things no one reports about."

Otilia grew anxious and swallowed with difficulty. She couldn't do anything rash—she needed time to reflect.

"The country's a mess. You have the guerillas and the soldiers chasing after them. All cons—they've been hijacking buses, taking bribes from us, even raping and killing innocent people. You are a young woman with a beautiful smile, dark eyes; be cautious—small people like us can't fight either side. Don't be stubborn."

Otilia broke out in a cold sweat.

"Give it a little time," Oscar said, keeping his eyes on the road.

2

A S THE TRUCK PASSED fields of matted grass, alarms blared in Otilia's mind. She spent hours churning the question of where she should go. A few times she had been tempted to ask Oscar to be let off, but her instinct for self-preservation kept her in the passenger seat until the truck reached the mining camp. She suspected that Oscar was right; having travelled the land, he knew what was going on. If she could hold out in this remote place for just a few weeks, maybe the danger would pass.

A bulldozer forging its way up the mountainside, digging through rock and dirt, was the first sign of life she noticed in the glumness of the landscape. Oscar pulled up the truck next to a series of modular buildings and said, "Here's the kitchen where Teresa works."

Otilia rubbed her face with her hands and brushed the wrinkles from the front of her shirt. Swinging her handbag over her shoulder, she jumped out. Oscar opened the door to the building and she heard the sound of a blender. Florescent lights shone over big stoves where young women stood stirring large pots, while the head cook, a chubby woman in a white apron, her hair tucked under a net, stood at the far side, chopping vegetables. She raised her arm and waved. "What a surprise, *compadre*; what brings you here this time of the day?

"*Comadre*, I have a favour to ask. I don't mean to take you away from your dinner duties, but I'd appreciate it if you can spare a moment at this time."

"*Pase, si como no*, of course come this way."

Once they were in a small room in the back, Oscar explained the predicament Otilia found herself in, and it took Teresa no time to make up her mind. Without hesitation, she stepped out to ask one of the girls to show Otilia to the women's residence.

Lying on her narrow bunk bed in the women's dormitory the morning after, Otilia woke up to the sound of rain pounding against the prefabricated walls. She'd been given a spot in a small room that she shared with seven girls. Clothes hung from pegs on the wall and personal articles were piled on the beds. Closing her eyes and pulling her sheets above her head, she thought about her terrible bad luck. She'd never imagined she'd be living with strangers. Haggard from too little sleep, she managed to sit. Hugging her knees to her chest, she pulled her long hair back as thoughts of being caught in a trap entered her mind. Floating images of Manuel carrying Salvador came back to her and she hoped her actions hadn't produced dire consequences she would regret, wreaking havoc on her loved ones. She put on her jeans and turned to two women who were whispering, applying lipstick, and looking at themselves in the mirror on the wall.

"Are you off to the kitchen?" Otilia asked.

One of the girls nodded and said, "Take your time, we can wait."

On the way to the kitchen the lively girls started to chat, giggling as they gossiped, never stopping through their hasty breakfast of coffee and toast. When Teresa showed up and gave each one orders about what they needed to prepare for lunch, they separated. Otilia was told her first job was to mop floors and empty rubbish cans.

With her life as she knew it shattered, it was hard to go from one day to the next. It had been two weeks since she'd been trapped in this remote place and the restless thoughts moving through her head had increased. At times she found herself haunted by images of her family and was deeply demoralized. How would she ever find her husband and son from this far away? She was becoming extremely anxious and couldn't focus on anything. She wished there was someone to share her concerns with. There were days when she wasn't even concentrating on the tasks at hand. Yesterday, for example, she had broken some plates and felt full of shame. She hadn't a clue how it occurred—they had suddenly slipped out of her hands.

She'd had a lovely family and it had been torn apart; all she felt like doing was crying. By the time she'd see Salvador again, her son would have turned into a stranger. Over and over she questioned how they had failed to see trouble coming their way. Why hadn't they moved away from their village for a while? Why hadn't she talked to Manuel? There were so many unanswered questions and she remained lost in her feelings.

Could her husband have been targeted by the guerillas? Is that why he hadn't returned? Could he have been hiding information, involved in a matter he hadn't disclosed? No, he wouldn't have been on their side—she knew Manuel didn't sympathize. What was wrong with her? She was losing her mind trying to set things straight. She mourned the loss of Manuel and felt angry about being forced into separation by threats. As the flashback of Manuel fleeing into the hillside with Salvador entered her mind, she grappled with the unimaginable.

Otilia wasn't convinced that she'd made the right decision to come up to the mine. She was self-reliant, but feelings of loneliness were overwhelming her, keeping her paralyzed. She felt confined in this forlorn spot, surrounded by guards in black masks, with guns in their holsters, all keeping a watchful eye. She longed for her home and her land. This rugged terrain was a sorry sight; there was scarcely any plant life, with the hillsides exposed to carved-away patchworks of barren rock.

The ceaseless beeping of the tipper trucks going back and forth, and the giant diggers gathering rocks, were driving her deeper into madness with each passing day. She would have to leave this horrid place, end the anguish of waiting, and begin her serious search.

The weeks stretched out endlessly and most of the time she kept to herself, with her co-workers' chitchat becoming background noise as she went about her work. It was at night, when she huddled beside the radio to catch the news, that she slowly became aware of the conflicts in the rural zones, even if the details were patchy. Last night she'd listened with interest to a commentary about the increase in Shining Path guerilla hostility toward the peasants. They were entering villages without warning, overthrowing existing government institutions and replacing them with their communist revolutionary command. She became scared when she heard that their ideology made violence an integral part of the movement. "There's an aura of unnatural, evil power about them," the announcer had said.

Otilia showered, dressed, tied her kerchief around her head, and made her way to the dining hall, trying to avoid the rain blowing into her face. She weaved in and out between trucks carrying loads of building materials and lurching along the muddy road. She crossed the road and hurried toward a cluster of low buildings that were off to one side. Two labourers in hard hats greeted her; the one with disproportionately large hands held the heavy door open for her to go inside. She heard sounds of blasting dynamite detonating in the distance and automatically ducked as she entered. She hastily brushed raindrops from her dress as she made her way to the kitchen. Grabbing her plastic apron, she turned to face the stacks of dirty dishes left from the night before, waiting to be washed.

Later that morning, her vision becoming blurry as nausea rose from her gut. She ran to the bathroom and vomited; then she passed out. Next thing she knew, Nilda was at her side.

"*Hermanita*, sit up," Nilda urged her. "I'll take you to the infirmary so you can be checked out."

Otilia hooked arms with Nilda as they trudged up the hill. When they heard the crunch of gravel behind them and a small truck approached, the women moved to the side. They stepped into the infirmary and the strong smell of disinfectant made Otilia feel queasy again.

"You can come this way," a receptionist said, showing them into a small examining room after Otilia explained why she was seeking help.

A few minutes later the door swung open and a nurse with a stethoscope hanging around her neck asked, "What brings you here today?"

Otilia remained silent and Nilda responded instead. "She fainted," she said.

The nurse retrieved a thermometer and a blood pressure monitor and asked, "How long has this been going on?"

Tears rose in Otilia's eyes.

The nurse wrapped the blood pressure cuff around Otilia's arm and, looking at Nilda, said, "She'll be here for a while. You better go back."

After recording her vital signs, the nurse stepped out of the room and came back with a warm cup of coffee. "Do you want sugar?" she asked. "When you are ready, you can tell me what is happening in your life. Perhaps I can help."

Otilia didn't want anybody knowing her business, as she feared for her husband and child. Why should she put them in jeopardy? People would talk; it was best to be circumspect, to keep her thoughts to herself.

"I can't sleep and I have no appetite," Otilia said, then closed her eyes. Her face felt flushed. Her eyes felt swollen and she was hollow inside. *My world is upside down*, she wanted to shout. "I've been having bad thoughts from so much looking back," Otilia confessed.

The nurse looked at her kindly with warm almond-shaped

eyes and waited patiently for Otilia to continue.

"They disappeared in front of my eyes."

"Who did?" she asked.

"My husband and child."

"A cruel fate," the nurse said, her eyes and the tone of her voice sympathetic and kind.

Otilia looked at her sheepishly.

"You're going through deep grief," the nurse continued.

Otilia was mortified, and afraid of what the nurse would think of her, but she opened up and spoke at length about her tribulations.

"I'm so sorry for what you've gone through," the nurse said. "You're spent, and your energy's low from so much worry." She reached out to hold Otilia's hand. "You're fortunate to have come here, where you're safe," the nurse said, gently stroking the length of her patient's arm.

Otilia continued to unburden herself. "I was blind to what was going on around me. There are destructive forces.... I didn't want to believe it. Now, my dreams for my boy have been swept away."

"It's difficult to imagine what you're going through. I'm not so sure I could live through what you've experienced."

"*Señora,* losing one is terrible enough, but I've lost two. I cry for them day and night. If only I could know where they are! At least if they were in a cemetery, I could visit their place of rest, or perhaps kill myself."

The nurse's jaw fell. "You have the right to be angry. I can understand how powerless you feel; but listen to me, you need to take care, trust all is well with them."

Otilia's hands began to shake.

"I will give you some *pildoritas*; take these pills before going to bed," the nurse said as she reached into a cupboard. "Take one every night just before you lie down. You've got to sleep, and you've got to eat. You have decisions to make."

"Thank you," Otilia said.

"Come back and see me next week. Take good care and please don't do anything rash."

The nights Otilia took the sleeping pills, she was able to switch off her worries for a while, and on the following mornings she'd have renewed energy with *ganas*, a little more lust for life. She became a bit more talkative at work. It was during one of those mornings, while Otilia leaned over the sudsy sink scrubbing kitchen utensils, that Teresa came over and suggested they take a break.

Teresa was a bit brash and liked to share stories about her life. Otilia discovered that Teresa had a storehouse of narratives to divulge, but intimate subjects unnerved Otilia and she wished Teresa would converse with the other girls instead. But earlier this morning Teresa had stood by her side and, with a note of distress in her voice, said, "I worry that you're unhappy. You're withdrawn and when you fainted the other day I became concerned."

So Otilia decided to follow her out of the kitchen and into the room in the back where Teresa went regularly for coffee and a smoke. They sat down on the scratched leather couch and after Teresa cleared her throat, she asked, "Tell me, honestly, are you all right?"

Otilia looked at Teresa and without faltering told her everything.

"Bastards," Teresa said, sternly. "You need a plan to fight back."

Otilia said she'd wanted to go to police headquarters but had not dared leave the camp. She thought it best to wait for a while, for fear of being implicated in a crime. "If you were in my shoes, what would you do?"

Teresa shrugged, thought for a moment, then said. "Why don't you compose a message to be read on the radio? Then it might reach a family member somewhere."

"How would I do that?"

"I'll get you an address. I'll help you word it, if you want. I've heard tons of them lately from people trying to connect with loved ones."

"I wrote my older brother, who moved to Cajamarca years back, but we've lost touch—I don't even know if he's still at that address," Otilia said.

"And?"

"No answer yet."

Otilia gradually took a liking to Teresa. She had a sense of humour and a sure sense of self. So, when Teresa asked her to go to church with her on Sunday to pray for help, Otilia went along. When they walked into the modular building that served as a chapel on Sundays, two women were lighting candles and unfolding a picture of the Pope. A large wooden crucifix hung on the wall behind a makeshift altar, and a young priest in a black cloak was turning to face the small group of attendees dressed in their best clothes. The priest, his missal in hand, gave a sign that he was ready to initiate the devotional acts, and the congregation stood up.

Otilia closed her eyes and followed along to get her thoughts on the right track. Faith was her only protection at this time. She asked God to keep watch over her husband and son. After prayers, Otilia felt more at peace. Perhaps she should make prayer a daily routine, she thought, to help her deal with her anguish and find the strength to continue the search. On her way out, she became aware that her mood had changed. She shook the priest's hand and felt content hearing his words, "May you go in peace." Afterward, she stopped to smile at a young mother cuddling her child, rocking her back and forth on her lap, and once again she became overwhelmed by the great sadness and guilt she carried inside.

3

IT WAS DARK when Salvador woke up and realized he was still crouched inside the warm cavity of the stallion his father had sacrificed. "He's the tallest and oldest of them all; we must kill him so you'll survive," his father had said in a tone full of anguish, before he performed the unpleasant task.

His father had swiftly carried him up the steeply rising mountain, through the rocky barren hills and down a ravine to the valley below. He hung tightly onto his father's chest until they reached the familiar terrain dotted with pine and eucalyptus groves, where his father put him down. This was the spot where peasants from surrounding villages brought their herds of horses and cattle to graze, and where Salvador had accompanied his father many times to fetch a cow. But today was different—his father seemed pressed for time.

"Can't we play superhero?" Salvador asked.

"Yes, we can." His father seemed to lighten up.

"Too bad I didn't bring my mask."

"Today my Superman will have to hide—no flying around."

"How come? Superman doesn't hide from the bad guys."

"We're going to play a trick on them; we'll wait for them to carry out their orders, keeping out of their way. You're going to disappear, tucked inside this belly," his dad said, giving the horse a pat.

"Oh, wow!"

Manuel deposited Salvador under a tree and told him to stay back with his eyes shut tight and to count to one hundred and nine. Salvador didn't obey. He opened his fingers wide and saw his father move toward the animal with a knife ready to stab its spinal cord, bestowing the fatal incision. The paralyzed creature shuddered and fell to the ground instantly. Slitting the underbelly open, his father proceeded to remove the entrails, laying them to one side. Then, coming to get him, he led Salvador by his hand and gently helped him climb into the cavity. "I'm glad you're small for your age. This is your new pal, he'll keep you company tonight. You'll fool the bad guys."

"But I am seven, not so small anymore," he protested.

"You are strong and you are shrewd—they'll never find you. Try to sleep for a while until I come back."

His father kissed him on his head, inserted a reed to provide an air hole for him to breath and have a bit of a view, then placed a piece of hide loosely over him. It smelled like raw meat and he thought of the time his father came home with half of an animal that he had butchered—it was the same smell. He wiggled around, out of the way of the ribs pressing against his side, to place his head on a chunky part. He closed his eyes. The wind blew hard, but he was a superhero; he was brave, and tonight he had a special job to carry out.

Salvador stretched out from the fetal position he'd been folded into; his feet and legs felt prickly and numb when he woke up. Elongating himself, he tried to crawl out; he was wet, covered with some kind of slime. The foul smell that enfolded him was pungent and he felt like throwing up. Nauseated, he pushed himself out and jumped. He landed tremulously next to the animal's gut and then ran.

His father had promised he would be back once he got his mother to safety, but they still hadn't shown up. He'd better wait close to the site. He touched his damp pants and shirt, then ran his hands over his caked legs. He was drenched in blood. A wave of queasiness rolled up from his throat as the dead animal's stench reached him. He heard a dog bark in the distance, then another taking it up. He cautiously walked a few feet away until he came to a shallow stream. Crouching down, he put his hands in the chilly water just as dawn appeared in the sky. Removing his shirt to dunk in the water, he washed his face and rubbed clean his blood-spattered legs and arms. He laid his clothes on some stones and dried his body in the wind, under the faint sun. He looked around—the valley was deserted except for some horses and cows. After a while he became frightened and made up a game, repeating the phrase, "I'm Superman." Twirling around and around until he was hypnotized, he remembered his mother saying that when he was scared he should think of words that would bring him courage. "I'm Superman," he repeated again.

His jet-black hair was cut short and dried fast. Rubbing his hand through it, he recalled his mother always fussing with it after his bath. With a stick he dug a hole by the side of the stream and filled it with small stones. As he looked for some pebbles to toss into the water, he spotted a bullfrog sitting on a log and he observed it for a while. He remained close to the slow-moving stream most of the day, picking up twigs and small sticks, twisting leaves and turning them into tight rolls. At one point he stumbled and fell, skinning his knee. It was then that it hit him that he was alone in this world, with no parent to console him. He lay back to watch a flock of warblers foraging in the branches overhead and told himself to be brave. Sitting on a stone, he stared into the mountains around him as the sun was sinking low in the sky; he felt famished. Dizzy with hunger, he got up to walk toward a cow with its teats hanging low. Salvador patted her side. Looking around he found a tin can amongst some discards. He ran to the stream to give it a rinse and rushed back. Standing close, talking to the animal in soft tones, he recalled his mother saying, "It's not what you say, but how you say it that makes the animal cooperate." Holding the front teat he squeezed hard, pressing until milk began to flow. After drinking a couple of cans he lay flat on his back, close by. The cow, curious, sniffed and licked him and then crouched down, letting Salvador place his head on her backside.

The next morning Salvador woke up to a woman's voice. She had a full bosom and a full skirt, and was rocking his body close to her chest. "Where have you come from? What are you doing here all alone?"

When he looked up he saw her black teeth and a bulge in her cheek. Bits of white saliva clung to her lips. "Are you hungry?"

She pulled out an ear of cold corn from her bag and said she would take him to her home.

"I can't go with you," Salvador said. "I'm waiting for my mother and dad to come back."

They followed a path between two ridges, with many undulations and dips. "We're nearly there," she said, after they'd climbed a steep slope.

One more push of energy was needed. His mouth was dry and he could hardly talk. He could see a small brick house surrounded by a plot of land that had been tilled and worked. A bunch of T-shirts and colourful skirts had been left to dry, draped over the grass. Once they were inside the woman's house, she lit a fire while he sat in a corner of the smoky room.

"First, a good wash," she said, removing her felt hat.

She put on an apron and went to fetch a plastic tub. She poured cold water from a bucket then added some hot water from the large pot she had placed on top of the burning logs.

He told her how his father had left him that night to run away from "some bad guys."

The woman said, "You'll go into the city to get news about your parents. My eldest son, Ramon, will take you to town tomorrow."

The next day, after eating his eggs and some corn, he followed

Ramon into town. They walked through the fields until he spotted the red city below. Ramon did not want to walk down all the way into town—he wanted to get back and play—so he told Salvador to go on alone. Ramon handed him the bag with food and bottles of water his mother had prepared for them, and turned back. Salvador felt lost, but he walked for a while and then sat under a tree to devour his lunch.

As he approached Cajamarca, still up on the hill, he heard music playing. Following the trail, he noticed a man draped in a woollen poncho, wearing a wide-brimmed hat that covered his face from the sun. He was playing the pan flute for some people who had gathered on a landing that offered a panoramic view. As Salvador looked down, he could see the narrow streets and a splendid church, made of volcanic rock, rising high in the distance. Then he noticed a path. Taking one step at a time, he walked down the stairs to the city below.

When he arrived at the plaza, a number of kids were hanging around. Salvador sat on a bench across from the cathedral. He stared at the cathedral's facade, wondering how they carved out those enormous arches and columns by hand. He watched the children around him; some were shining shoes to earn a few coins, while others were begging for money from passersby.

The afternoon stretched before him and he'd not left the bench. When a group of youth started herding a boy to the edge of the square, handling him roughly and prodding him with insults, a girl came to sit next to him. "Come with me," she said. Her tone was urgent. "This way—watch out for them."

The girl had dark, observant eyes; she seemed tough, despite her wiry frame. "I'm Lucia," she said, grabbing his hand as the sunlight disappeared from the sky. She wore a dirty dress over faded pants, and he noticed her hands were covered with scars.

"I've been watching you. You've been here for a long time." She let go of his hand to pull up the sleeves of the red moth-eaten sweater that hung long on her frame. "Do you have a place to spend the night?"

"No," he whispered, shaking his head.

She took him through the streets of the busy core of the city, crossing in front of honking buses to get to the other side of the road. They passed stores whose metal shutters were closed for the night and by restaurants and seedy bars until they reached a dusty street, quieter than most, where only a few streetlights were on. "We're here," she said, approaching a high metal gate with a large padlock, as two skinny dogs stirred in the dirt. "This way," she motioned for him to follow.

They crawled through a narrow opening in the barbed wired fence, and he followed her through a row of tombstones, some with fresh flower arrangements and ribbons on them.

"If it's not raining, this is where I sleep," she said, pointing to a patch of grass toward the back of the cemetery. "It makes for a soft bed."

Grass surrounded the tall mausoleum where they would lay. The marble tile floor shone in the dark. "That slab's much too hard," she said when she noticed him looking at it.

The rooster's crow at daybreak woke him up the next morning and the first thing he saw was Lucia sitting at a fountain with a statue of Mary and the baby Jesus, washing herself.

"I'm hungry," he said.

"Then wash up and we'll go to the market to see what mood the vendors are in. It's hard to find things to eat in the morning, but we'll try. The better pickings are at closing time."

Crossing the square toward the market, delicious smells came from the steaming food stalls. Music pulsated steadily down from the speakers as shoppers made their way through the crowd. Lucia guided Salvador's hand to snatch a banana, in case the merchants weren't handing out food.

"A few vendors have soft hearts for us kids. Maria, for one, will give me some caramels and gum to sell and let me keep a few cents. But she says she has to be fair, and give all of us a turn, but I have been getting none. Sometimes I'll find a rich housewife who'll tip me for carrying her bags to the car. That's when I'll buy stuff."

This morning nobody was in a charitable mood. Lucia told Salvador he would have to fetch something to eat on his own. As he made his way to nab an apple from a basket, the vendor clamped his earlobe, pinching it hard. Gripped in fury, spit flying from his lips, the man kicked Salvador in the butt, yelling, "*Carajo*, stay out of my shop!"

Salvador ran out of the market as fast as he could and found a place to sit on the curb a few blocks away. Lucia found him looking forlorn, slouched over with tears rolling down his cheeks. "Come quickly—the tears are good—go up to that restaurant and tell them you haven't eaten for days," she said, pulling him up, thrusting him forward.

Passing by a mangy dog lounging lazily, he walked through the open door in the back of the restaurant, while Lucia climbed into the dumpster to look for scraps. Salvador got some fresh food while Lucia found some cans with remains of soda inside. They went down the street to eat, taking refuge in a nearby park, sitting next to some hookers at a picnic table.

That night, back at the cemetery, Lucia fetched her belongings, which she kept in an empty gravesite in the back. Newspapers, glass bottles, pieces of soap—all went into plastic bags in the hole. Crossing her legs and sitting upright, she pulled out one of the bags and put a small bottle to her mouth. She pressed her mouth to the jar and inhaled, drawing the fumes into her lungs.

"Listen up, stay clear of those gutter rats."

"Who?"

"Those snot-nosed little fuckers."

That afternoon they'd been surrounded and taunted by a bunch of street kids. "They hide in the gutter and jump on you when you least expect it."

She inhaled more glue fumes and went on, "They have no

mercy. They say they'll protect you, then gang up and beat you, take your things, and force you to join them."

"What are you doing?"

"Try it, have a puff, it'll make you happy."

He held the jar in his hands, inhaled, then coughed; he couldn't stop coughing, feeling a scratch in his throat.

"Like this," she said, laughing at him, demonstrating once more. "Then they'll rape you."

He didn't ask what she meant. He drew some more air into his mouth and lay on his back on the grass. Feeling floaty and not able to talk properly, he covered himself with a rag. He was not sure where he was; everything started to look blurry. Trying to hold on to the picture of his mother and dad that he kept in his mind, he closed his eyes.

Two months after Salvador met Lucia he developed a fever and diarrhea. He slept most of the day until a man standing tall in a brown uniform and cap woke him up. "Now, now, what the hell do we have here?" he said in an angry voice, tapping his foot with a stick. "*Carajo*, what's up?" Tensing his jaw and raising his voice, "Are you deaf or what? You better get out, make it fast."

Salvador shifted his body lightly to his side, and moving in slow motion, he sat up and threw up right on his boot.

"*No jodas*. This is disgusting." He jumped back. Walking away at a fast pace, he yelled, "Scoot. Don't let me see you here when I make my next rounds. I'll be watching out for you, kid."

Salvador buried his face in his rags—he couldn't do much.

When Lucia returned early that evening, she was sweaty and out of breath. Salvador noticed her swollen face. "What happened?"

"I got in a fight. Take it, it's for you," she said, giving him the soup she'd gotten for him in a plastic tub.

"I can't."

"Now listen, drink up. He nearly took it; I held on to it for dear life."

Salvador couldn't refuse it. He forced down the broth, a sip at a time.

Lucia was eleven or twelve—she wasn't sure of her age. She'd said she didn't know much. She could read a little and she'd learned how to count, but hadn't been to school for a while. She knew how to be a good friend and to be motherly. Lucia stayed at his side. She offered him a stick of gum to settle his tummy and helped him walk to the empty grave in the back to hide from the security guard. She stayed close, holding his hand, and he slept most of the day.

When he awoke the next day, Lucia was still sitting at his side, cleaning her nails, filing them down. When she saw him, she straightened up; she placed her hand on his forehead and said, "You're okay. Go wash up."

4

THE THREE-STORY BUILDING, which Lucia had eyed on a quiet tree-lined street a few days before, had its front door opened wide. Salvador followed Lucia inside and they climbed through the dim narrow stairwell right to the top. Lucia tried the door to the patio and found it unlocked. A rope, stretched between two walls, was weighed down with half-dried clothes. Colourful shirts, jeans, underwear, towels, and sheets blew about in the wind. "Quick," said Lucia, "grab the laundry on that side."

Salvador pulled off jeans, socks, and shirts to stuff in his plastic bag. Once Lucia had filled hers, she yelled, "That's enough, let's get out of here."

They ran down the stairs and out of the building through the back, sprinting fast. They only diminished their pace when they noticed two women sitting on the doorsteps, knitting and chatting away. Not to arouse suspicion, they walked until they reached an empty lot where they stopped to lay out the wet clothes. In the midday sun they inspected their loot, trying on stiff jeans and oversized shirts. They laughed as they folded up the pants legs, tucked in the shirts, and hopped around like performing clowns. "I'll need to find someone with a sewing machine," Lucia said.

Spurred on by thoughts of finding his family, Salvador roamed the city daily, eager to find a familiar face. He'd been alone for a number of months—how many he couldn't tell, but he sensed that if he didn't locate somebody soon, he might end up tucked away in an orphanage or living forever on the streets. He was tired of begging and was spending more time trying to keep out of the cold now that early winter temperatures had arrived. He and Lucia had even started to sleep head to foot to keep their bodies warm.

They endured standing outside the churches on Sundays with no coats, hoping to collect alms, trying to evoke feelings of compassion from the people going by. But since they were older, they didn't fare well; people were more charitable to the younger kids, who were cuter and melted their hearts.

Squatting on the sidewalk, Salvador stopped to rest from roving the downtown streets. Tears ran down his cheeks, which he dried with his sleeves. Head bowed, his eyes fixed on the pavement, he spotted a bunch of small stones. He picked them up and began to make a mound. If only his uncle would surface. How else would he ever find him? He recalled his mother mentioning that she had an older brother who had left the village to make a living in town before Salvador was born. He'd never met him—just seen photographs of Tomas with his mother when they were growing up. At noon the downtown core was teeming with people and Salvador walked to one side of the plaza where cabbies waited for rides. His mother had said his uncle Tomas had learned how to drive, with hopes of owning a cab. He was a rebel, she'd said, desperately wanting to grow up and get away from the farming community where they lived.

A man with a heavy mustache, wearing a cap and holding a key in his hand was standing by his cab. "*Señor,* excuse me, do you know a driver by the name of Tomas Campos?" Salvador asked.

"No kid, *no jodas.*" The man pushed him aside. "And by the way, has anybody told you how stinky you smell? Go take a bath before you go bothering somebody else."

Salvador blushed and stepped to one side, looking back at the cab as it took off toward the traffic roundabout. Making his way back to the cemetery, he went past the movie theatre to try his luck begging for a few coins. Nobody paid any attention to a vagrant kid. In anguish he edged up to a field where he stopped to look at some boys in shiny soccer uniforms, playing ball. He watched them make a pass. He couldn't bear it; he, too, wanted to play ball and go to school.

That night, as he lay on the grass shivering, crouched down in fear, listening to the quiet with his arms wrapped around his chest, and hiding under the plastic tarp Lucia had recently fetched, he started to cry. *I don't want to stay ignorant, someone who knows nothing at all. I'll have to pull myself up and out*, he told himself, closing his eyes.

The next day he was inside the market at lunchtime, walking by open bags of dry lentils and beans, when he was stopped by a matron who requested he hail a cab, then come back to help her with her bags.

"A *patrona* needs you to take her home," Salvador said to the first driver in the lineup at the curb. "And sir, would you know a driver by the name of Tomas Campos?" he ventured to ask, taking a close look at the man. He was constantly keeping an eye on the drivers, examining the faces behind the wheel.

The man shook his head. Salvador ran back to help the lady and found her at the butcher's counter waiting for her meat to be wrapped in newspaper sheets. While they waited, she offered him a sweet bun and he wolfed it down before carrying out her shopping bags.

A few days later, Salvador found a driver willing to engage in a conversation with him. He sent him to speak to his taxi company's dispatcher, saying, "He knows everybody; he might be able to help."

Salvador made his way to the other end of the city, where the dispatcher was arranging for a pickup. He seemed surprised to be approached by a child. He frowned for a while, but he removed his earphones and listened to Salvador's appeal. Then he shook his head and got back to his work. But before Salvador was out the door, the man yelled, "Kid, try Tomas down the street, he might know the guy you're looking for."

For months he'd been waiting for someone to give him a tip—maybe the time had come. He kicked at a stone he found on the side of the road and pushed it downhill, following it until he stood in front of a tall gate.

"Hey, Tomas, there's a little guy here to see you," the security guard yelled.

"Tell him to come over here," he heard a voice say.

Salvador went to stand by some tools fanned out on the ground at the rear of a truck as a man with a sharp face, covered in grease, slipped out from under and asked, "*Si?*"

Salvador explained.

"That's not me. Seem to be many with the same name. I've heard there's a cab driver that lives down in Otuzco; go see if that could be him." As he slid back under the truck, disappearing from view, Tomas shouted directions where he could find the other Tomas. "At the entrance to town on Calle Primera, a green house."

Salvador arrived at the bus station the next day and walked through the door, jostled by a crowd on either side. Out of sight, concealed by people's umbrellas, amid their heavy coats, he avoided being spotted by the security guards. They wouldn't be kind to a waif, Lucia had said. He went up to the counter and cocked his head; using his most polite tone of voice, and asked the ticket seller how he could get to Otuzco that day.

"We have no buses on Tuesday," she said. "You could hitch a ride—try the trucks parked outside."

He ran out to ask a driver if he was heading south and would be willing to give him a ride. The first one he approached was agreeable. "I'll be leaving in a few minutes. Get in."

When they arrived in Otuzco, Salvador asked to be let out. As the driver pulled away, leaving a rising trail of dust behind the truck, Salvador stood on the road, contemplating in which direction to walk. He spotted a flat-roofed house with a taxi parked outside and ran toward it. Traces of green paint were visible on its weather-worn lumber frame. The few chickens that wandered the fenced-in yard scattered when Salvador unlatched the gate to go inside. He walked up to the door and knocked hard several times before an unshaven man with an unbuttoned shirt hanging loosely over his pants answered, wincing in the bright sunlight. "Yep?"

"I'm looking for don Tomas Campos," Salvador said.

"That's me." His voice was hoarse. Scratching his scalp and clearing his throat, he said, "What do you want?"

"Are you from the village of El Milagro, señor?"

"For God's sake, what is it?"

Salvador lowered his eyes. "Then you're my *tío*, my mother's brother."

"What'd you say your name was?"

Salvador repeated his name. His uncle didn't seem to understand. He couldn't figure out what he was doing there, alone and without his mother.

"Where is my little sister?" he asked.

Salvador was mute.

"So where is your mother?" the uncle asked impatiently.

"She's gone," Salvador whispered.

"What are you saying? Come in this way, we'll talk inside." Tomas turned around and shuffled in.

He hiccupped as he picked up a couple of empty bottles of beer from the floor, then got another one from the fridge. "You want an Inca Cola? Hold on, so—I am a *tío*?"

He giggled in his slightly drunken state, handing the boy his soda. "I never knew my little sister was married with a kid." Tomas burped. "So did you say you're all alone? You caught me on my day off. How did you get here?"

Salvador didn't respond.

"I work long hours all week; it's my day to relax," he said, taking another gulp.

When his uncle went to the bathroom Salvador tiptoed to the kitchen to lift the lid of a pot on the stove top. His gut hurt. "Can I have something to eat?" he asked when Tomas returned.

"Help yourself," he said, lighting up a cigarette. "Do you need a place to stay? Of course you do. Hey, tell you what, I have lots of space. You'll spend the night ... we're family."

Salvador woke up the next morning with a pillow over his face. His uncle was snoring, lying fully clothed on the bed next to his. Staring at him for some time, he felt bewildered and concluded that Uncle Tomas didn't resemble his mother at all. Neither his eyes nor his mouth were set like hers. There was nothing familiar—no gesture, not even his diction, was similar. It was truly odd. Perhaps this wasn't his relative, merely another guy with the same name, and this wasn't the place for him. Moving away from the room, he closed the door behind him.

5

TOMAS GOT OUT of bed, had a shower, and shaved. He opened all the curtains and started picking up beer bottles from the floor to tidy up. For a few moments, he stood in the centre of hallway separating the kitchen from the dining room, studying the child. "So you're Otilia's boy," he said, scratching his head.

Salvador, who had been watching the chickens walking around the porch, turned to look at his uncle. He felt relieved to see Tomas looking so changed. He wore a clean plaid shirt tucked inside his pants. "Tell me, where did you come from? Where did you say your parents are?"

Salvador shrugged his shoulders, gazing at the barrel-chested man who was showing concern. Should he be fearful of telling him his story?

"Why are you here by yourself?" Tomas asked.

Tomas sat him down at the table, and said, "Let's try piecing your story together while we have some breakfast, shall we? How do you like your eggs?"

Salvador told him what little he knew.

"*Pobrecito*," Tomas said. "Poor child."

Tomas shook his head. "You hid in a horse? You're joking; how can that be? So you haven't seen your parents for a while?"

Salvador started to cry.

"You've been able to live on your own—you're quite a kid,

real brave," Tomas said, patting the boy's head. "There's no doubt; you can't trust anyone these days," Tomas muttered, as if to himself. "I don't quite know what we should do. We'll figure it out. In the meantime, come," he said, taking Salvador by the hand after he'd drunk his milk. "Tell you what—this room will be yours. We'll make up the bed, get it ready for tonight."

Salvador would have his own bed with sheets and warm woollen blankets; he'd be clean every day and be able to get plates of food any time he was hungry without having to beg. Finding food had been one of the hardest things he'd had to learn how to do. There were no others living with uncle Tomas. He had a wife, he said, who'd gone to work in Chile and hadn't returned.

"Now that you're staying with me, young man, I'll show you a few things," Tomas said that afternoon. "I'll take you to where I want you to go buy bread in the morning and my bottles of beer at night. There's a corner store a few blocks away where I carry a running account. Ernesto will let you have whatever we want. But first, you need a good haircut."

Tomas took him to a barber, who gave him a military cut. Since he'd never been to a barber, he didn't know what to expect. He remained motionless for a very long time, trying not move when the barber took the razor in his hand. At home, his mother would get the scissors and cut his bangs. She would only cut the hair on the back of his neck when his father complained that his son was starting to look like a girl.

The next morning, when Tomas informed him that he should get ready for school, he felt excited. Salvador climbed into the taxi, wearing a new warm jacket and long pants. Fascinated by the vehicle his uncle drove, Salvador looked out the window with a smile. When the car came to a full stop and Tomas said, "Here we are," his heart started to flutter with nerves.

A fleshy man in a pressed suit with pens protruding from his breast pocket came out to greet them when they arrived.

Tomas shook hands with him, and explained the reason they were coming at this time.

Salvador, tilting his head upward with a feeling of curiosity and hesitancy, watched the man straighten his tie. The principal looked at him and smiled.

"What grade were you in?" he asked, as he bent down to look into Salvador's eyes.

Salvador didn't speak.

"He's not been to school yet," Tomas said.

"We'll put him in first grade. You must work hard to catch up—the school year is already halfway through."

The three of them walked down the corridor until the principal came to a stop in front of one of the many closed doors. "Please wait here for a moment," he said. He came out with a young, pink-faced woman wearing a frilly blouse.

Crouching down to his level, the young teacher said, "Welcome, I'm *señorita* Ina, come with me."

The next minute, his uncle was gone and Salvador was standing in front of about forty students, all staring at him. He blushed as he stood, paralyzed, waiting for further directions. "Class, we have a new student," Miss Ina announced. "Now, no more wasting time, get back to your work."

As *señorita* Ina turned her back to the class to clear a spot for him, one girl with buck teeth waved her hand then stuck out her tongue at him. Another girl in a sharply starched apron moved to the end of the bench and Salvador went to sit next to her. He ran his fingers along the edge of the table, looking down at the deep scratches made long ago in the wood, and waited for instructions for what to do next. Not daring to look up, or to either side, he remained with his eyes cast down, holding his breath. Suddenly a sense of dread rose up from inside. How was he going to get back to his uncle's place? They hadn't made plans. His uncle had not said he would pick him up. Maybe he should forget about school and go back to Lucia, lead an unbound life.

When *señorita* Ina approached him with a bundle of papers, she said, "Try to do these." He looked at the letters and numbers and started to trace them with coloured pens.

A loud buzzer sounded and Miss Ina announced it was time to break for lunch. "Stay with Pato," she told him. "He'll show you around."

The children lined up and marched to the dining area where two cooks were serving bowls of stew. After lunch he was asked to join the others who were kicking a ball on the field; when they tired they sat on the grass, where Pato reached into his pants pockets and shared his sweets.

Uncle Tomas was waiting for him by the school entrance when class was dismissed. Salvador smiled shyly as soon as he saw him and his uncle winked back.

Uncle Tomas took time to teach Salvador how to behave properly. He talked about manners, how to sit and eat with a fork and knife, and reprimanded him when he became slack. He told him he should engage grownups differently than kids, for to get ahead in this world he would need to speak to them with respect. He enforced the use of terms such as *sir* and *madam*, for this was the appropriate way to address those in positions of authority, and to speak only when he was asked.

At home, Salvador was assigned responsibilities and he began by cleaning the kitchen and emptying the trash. It was early to bed and early to rise and he had to complete his homework every night. As Salvador was bright, he caught on fast and had no difficulty mastering new tasks.

Tomas was not one to praise much, but one day he said, "You'll grow up to do good things."

After having been at his uncle's for a few months, Salvador dared to ask Tomas if he could see Lucia. "Please?"

"I'll drive you," Tomas offered. "Where did you say she lives?"

On his day off, Tomas drove him up to the cemetery in Cajamarca, pulling into the empty parking lot. They walked through the gates and Salvador led the way. For a moment he felt disoriented weaving his way through the graves, trying to find Lucia's favourite hiding spots. He stopped for a moment to read the names of the deceased, carved into the headstones, excited to have come a long way since months before when he wasn't able to figure out any of the words. But *Tío* Tomas was getting impatient and yelled, "Come along."

"I'm looking for a statue of the Virgin and Christ."

"Over there." His uncle pointed it out, after spotting it in the distance.

Salvador ran over to the large mausoleum where he and Lucia had spent many nights. It was odd to think he had lived here for a while. Slowly he recognized other familiar spots and walked on, but Lucia was nowhere in sight. Leading his uncle to the empty grave in the back, he saw that there wasn't even a trace of Lucia's things.

"She's not here," he said, shrugging his shoulders, feeling sad.

They stood on the damp grass as light rain started to fall. Salvador's eyes filled with tears as Uncle Tomas pressed his hand on his back. "Time to go."

Salvador whimpered all during the drive back.

"No need to be disappointed; some way we'll find her."

Back home, Tomas left Salvador to himself and headed out to fix a dent in his taxi. Salvador went to his room and plunged onto his bed. He thought of his parents and wondered why important people disappeared from his life. How could he impress upon his uncle that they had to make a greater effort to look for his parents when, every time he brought up finding his mother and father, his uncle balked? Why did he have to say they should wait for things in the country to calm down? That they were going through dangerous times. Wasn't that even more reason to look for them right away?

The last time he begged Tomas to take him to the police

station, his response had been, "Salvador, my boy, the least said the better off we will all be. One day your mother will come and she'll be happy to see you content."

Why didn't his uncle understand that he needed them?

That evening, Salvador stepped out of his room and found his uncle on the couch, reading the evening paper. He went to sit by the lamp with tasseled shades hanging down, and picked up a section of the paper to read as well. He tried to understand an article but became flustered when some of the words were too hard to decipher. He'd have to learn how to read and write properly, fast, so he could find the newspaper account of what happened in his village of El Milagro that miserable night.

"I've been thinking we could go to the market and ask if somebody knows where your friend Lucia is living now," Tomas said, putting his paper down.

"No," Salvador said. "First, I want to find my mom and dad.

That night before they retired, Tomas ruffled his hair and gave him a hug. Once in bed, Salvador clenched his body and shut his eyes. He wanted to think of all the memories he had accumulated throughout his short life. One thing was clear, he couldn't forget them; he wanted to recall every detail he had of his mom and dad.

6

"**Y**OU SMART little whore, I got you." The cemetery's keeper snickered as he shone a light on Lucia's face. He yanked Lucia by her shoulders, pulling her up and out from the vacant grave where she lay.

Lucia, startled, instinctively struggled with all her might to free herself but was easily overcome by his strength. He ripped off her lightweight dress. Straightening her shoulders, she lashed out at his face. Grinning, he muttered under his heavy breath, "Little piece of shit. You're just ripe for a fuck."

He had alcohol on his breath. She yelled and his anger surged. Holding her firmly, he commanded, "*Puta*, take off your pants."

She swung her arm with great force, clawing his body with her fingernails. But he took her breath away with a stroke, hitting hard. "*Coño*, do as you're told."

As her eyesight blurred, she howled and she kicked.

"Shut up! Enough with the hysterics, you little bitch!"

All she saw next was the deep scar on his face turning purple as he trapped her beneath his weight. As he drove his body hard into hers, all she could feel was *asco*, disgust—and what pain!

When he finished, he lifted her body to carry her out the cemetery gates and deposited her by the side of the road on the dirt. Her body burned. The taste of blood came from her split lips. Giving way to exhaustion and numbness, she blacked out.

It was just before daybreak when a truck driver passed by

and stopped to ask if she needed help. She saw his face bending down toward her body before she turned her head away as a sharp, shooting hatred rose from her chest. She was in too much pain to even lift her head. Her soreness ran through her stomach and down the length of her legs. She managed to turn onto her side, away from him, her body curled up, her knees bunched to her chest.

The truck driver, a tall lanky man, lifted her up gently and placed her on the back seat of his truck. "You're hurt, I'm taking you to the clinic," he said, in a matter-of-fact tone.

Lucia, limp and dazed, noticed blood running down her legs. Ashamed and in agony, she folded her arms, hiding her face.

Watching the sleeping girl moan, the nurse in charge was smitten by her angelic face. She felt sorry for what the poor girl had gone through. What horror she had faced.

Lucia coughed, opened her eyes, and closed them again. Sweat broke out on her brow as the nurse checked her blood pressure and pulse. "You've had some sedation; you needed a few stitches. "You're safe," the nurse explained.

Lucia's breathing was shallow; she didn't speak.

"Try to rest. I'm Rosa. If you need anything, ring the bell." Retrieving the cord from behind the railing, Rosa placed the switch in Lucia's palm, then gently patted the top of her hand.

Throughout the day, Rosa brought her food trays, but Lucia wouldn't eat. Trying to engage her in conversation, Rosa asked a few questions during each visit she made, but Lucia lay rigidly on the bed. She didn't move. She just stared at the ceiling above, grimacing. Rosa administered painkillers, massaged her bruised legs, and, before her shift was over, tenderly placed a kiss on her forehead.

"*Jesucristo*, I'll get to the bottom of this disgrace," Rosa said in a whisper to the doctor tending the patient next to Lucia's bed. "I'll send the police after the sonofabitch."

"We're living in troubled times, so many more people

44

coming in for help. I saw a lady this morning, suffering from second-degree burns to her face, half-blind. She wasn't talking; I couldn't get out a word from her."

"They're scared to tell their stories; it'd be good if they'd set the record straight," Rosa said.

In the hall outside of the room, Rosa and the doctor talked about his patients a moment longer. "I went to talk to the chief of police the other day and told him about the vulnerable patients coming in, but he said that since the incidents were not taking place in the city, it was not their concern, damn them."

Rosa just shook her head. "Good night," she said.

On the morning of Lucia's fourth day at the clinic, Rosa came to her bedside with a toothbrush and a glass of water. "I hear you had no breakfast, perhaps your mouth will feel fresher if you brush," she said with a smile.

Lucia looked up with contempt.

"Brush and swish, like this. Your mouth needs to be clean, so your body can heal fast."

Once she was done, Lucia lay back and said, "I have a headache and a stiff neck."

"You'll have a warm bath, that'll help; it's time to get out of bed."

Lucia placed her delicate frame on the edge of the bed, dangling her feet while waiting for Rosa to get slippers. Her face drawn with pain; she gave a sharp cry when she stood up. Rosa held out a hospital gown and said, "Don't worry, child, take your time."

Linking arms, taking small steps, Rosa guided her down the hall to the bathroom. Rosa filled up the tub halfway. "One foot at a time."

"What is your name?"

"Lucia," she said, as she squatted slowly spreading her knees.

As her bottom touched the water, one hand went up to her mouth to stifle a moan.

"It'll be fine," Rosa said.

When the warm water covered Lucia's belly and chest, she lay back and closed her eyes. Her nostrils flared as she inhaled the scent of the eucalyptus oil that Rosa had dabbed in the water.

A few days later, right after Lucia was told by the doctor that she was good to go home, Rosa came up to her bedside. "I've been thinking you could spend a few days at my place. You need proper care and what better place to recuperate than in a nurse's home."

Lucia closed her eyes and lay still as if waiting for danger to pass. Her own space had been shattered and the only certain thing was that there was no adult out there to take care of her. She had to fend for herself. She wouldn't go back to the streets to live with the gutter rats, sharing the money she got and rationing her food. Those snot-nosed little fuckers would gang up on her and she wasn't about to let anyone violate her once again.

Rosa stood at the foot of her bed, pulling clothes from a shopping bag. "These are for you."

Lucia's face froze. Averting her eyes, Rosa turned to look at the wall.

"I'm leaving them on the chair. When you are ready, get dressed," Rosa said, and walked away to attend to somebody else.

When Rosa returned, she said, "Lucia, I'm off in an hour. Come spend the weekend with me—we'll eat ice cream and watch TV."

While Lucia tried to sort out her thoughts, nausea started to build at the back of her throat. Here she was tucked into a raised bed between two clean white sheets for the first time in her life. She'd never had much. Her family had lived in a mud house, sleeping two to a mat, close to a wood-burning fire stove with smoke stinging her eyes, until the day horror struck. Then she'd navigated life, able to get out of harm's way until the prick at the cemetery found her hiding place. Enraged, her mind raced.

A long time ago, was the story she'd been told, her family had made their way from the coast to the mountainous region for work. There was plenty to do in the hacienda but no one, except for the wealthy landowner, got ahead. Not her grandfather, who was expected to provide free labour for the use of the land, nor her father, who in spite of the property reforms that granted him land, was unable to grow and sell enough crops to move ahead. "We are the *olvidados*, too remote, the forgotten ones," her father would say. That was until the guerillas appeared one day out of the blue, first raiding their harvest and livestock, then killing the rest of her family, destroying her way of life for good.

"Lucia, get dressed," Rosa said, handing her the pink sweatshirt.

Lucia nodded. She'd give it a try.

"We're good to go then?" Rosa asked. Lucia smiled weakly.

Red, yellow, and orange dahlias arranged in vases on low tables at either side of the couch were the first things Lucia noticed when Rosa opened the door to her home. Would she be trapped inside? She'd be pissed off if she was supposed to follow fucking rules. She wanted none of that.

"Heavens, *mijita*, don't stand there. Come and sit by my side."

Lucia felt irritation surging inside. She stood rigid, scorn on her face. This was a warning her life was about to change. She had too much hate in her heart to be appreciative. She suspected she'd have to act politely, but couldn't avoid staring angrily at Rosa as she stepped in through the front door.

Rosa reached out for Lucia's hand to walk her through her orderly apartment. They stopped in front of a shelf where Lucia picked up a delicate ceramic sculpture that intrigued her and examined its fine shape.

"That was done by my father," Rosa said.

Rosa was kind and she had a calm manner, and at that moment Lucia thought she'd try to be like her one day. They sat on the velveteen couch and remained quiet for a while until Rosa clicked on the television. News reported that police were blocking the road and stopping a boisterous crowd in great force. Rosa changed the channels until a cartoon flashed across the screen and Lucia became mesmerized.

The weekend passed fast with Rosa indulging Lucia, keeping her entertained by playing games. "Don't force yourself to do things. Eat well and rest until you've regained all of your strength," Rosa said, when Lucia offered to help.

On Tuesday night they sat side by side and had a chat. Rosa told Lucia she had to go back to work but Lucia could remain in her place. "Stay for as long as you want."

7

THE DAY OTILIA was scheduled to serve the evening meal in the lounge, it snowed. She had gone for a short walk and seen the shepherd boys bringing their flocks down from the mountaintops. Autumn was turning into an early winter; Otilia had been living in the camp for four months and still had no word of her loved ones. After wiping her boots on the mat before entering the administration building, she went straight to the mailroom. She eagerly waited in the lineup for her turn. When she reached the counter she eyed the clerk with great expectation.

"Your name?" the clerk asked

"Perez."

The clerk sifted through batches of mail while Otilia berated herself inwardly for not having kept in touch with her only brother. How she wished they'd initiated a letter exchange years ago, but after their disagreements, Tomas hadn't shown any interest in continuing their relationship. Otilia stared at the clerk who separated an envelope from the bunch. She was stunned.

"Thanks," Otilia managed to say excitedly. The writing on the envelope was surprisingly familiar handwriting. She did a double take when she looked at the envelope again and realized it was the letter she'd sent Tomas. It had been stamped "address unknown."

She was flooded with apprehension. Distraught, she realized she had no one else she could turn to. Walking toward the job waiting for her in the kitchen, a torrent of panic crept into her mind. Disconcerted, she came to a sudden stop. She struggled to calm her racing heart and she felt dizzy. Bracing herself, she crouched down. Head reeling, she thought about Manuel and Salvador and her family in ruins; her body felt heavy, then so light that she thought she would faint. When, a few minutes later, she managed to stand, her throat tightened. Her teeth began to chatter and she felt cold, but she forced herself to walk on, heading toward the infirmary where she would check in with Rosa, the nurse scheduled to be in the mining camp today.

Otilia was told that Rosa would see her in a few minutes and she took a seat in the empty waiting room. With agonizing thoughts swirling in her mind, she didn't notice the nurse appearing at her side. "Come on in," Rosa said, and Otilia followed her to an examining room.

Sitting on the edge of a chair, having difficulty speaking, Otilia put her hand to her heart and whispered, "I feel ill, a tightening in my chest."

"You are awfully pale." Rosa reached for her stethoscope and gently placed it on Otilia's damp chest.

"When did this sensation start?"

Otilia's body stiffened and she felt terror rising within her. "About half an hour ago."

"I think you are experiencing a panic attack. Your body is in a state of high alert. What's the cause for your distress?"

Otilia remained silent.

"Your mind is racing. You must be exhausted. Where were you when your symptoms began?"

Otilia's body began to shake. "I feel nauseous."

"It's okay. Let's breathe in and out together, nice and slow.

"I'll never see them again," Otilia cried.

"You're grappling with the unforeseen; it's to be expected

that your body would react this way." Rosa sat beside here and listened as Otilia described what had happened at the post office. There was a knock at the door and the receptionist popped her head in to let her know an ambulance was on its way over. "Your condition is not dangerous," the nurse added. "I will give you some medicine to relieve your anxiety."

Otilia walked into the kitchen where Berta was peeling potatoes and Aya was cutting fine pieces of lettuce with a sharp knife. "*Hola*," both girls greeted Otilia at the same time.

"Are you working the kitchen?" Berta asked.

"No, I'm serving in the lounge."

"You're early then. We were just going to sit down for a cigarette," Aya said, wiping her hands. "Come along, you have time."

When two other younger girls saw the threesome entering the room in the back, they pouted but remained seated for a little while. Carla moved her chair closer to the table to make room for Otilia, Berta, and Aya.

"Will you go away this weekend?" Mirella asked. Thursday was the day the subject came up, although not all of them had the same two days off, as schedules rotated and changed according to the needs of the camp. "Will you be seeing Juan?"

Carla blushed.

"Carla's in love," Mirella announced with a smile. Glancing at the clock on the wall, she quickly got up. Both girls hastened out.

"These young people—men is all they have in their heads," Aya said.

"Such a fantasy," Berta said. "I have to go home tomorrow. Got a call from my sister, my baby is ill again. He's sick all the time. It's been so ever since he was born."

"Some kids are that way," Aya said.

"But mine, I can count his healthy days on the fingers of one hand. Perhaps it was the difficult labour. They pulled and pulled and it felt as if they were pulling out my gut. Who knows what damage they caused him at the time; they said he had green stuff in his lungs."

"He needs your motherly love," Otilia said.

"Yes, *comadre*, I feel sad not being able to be there with him all of the time."

She'd never mentioned a husband and Otilia assumed there wasn't one.

"If you're wondering about my child's father, well, he was a sonofabitch," Berta said. "I met him in Lima, we moved in together and *ya esta*—that's it. He stopped working, drank too much, I was his cash cow."

"So you left?" Aya asked.

"Here's the thing, he was no good. When I got pregnant, he left me, so here I am. Lima is no place for a single mom."

"Where is your boy?" Otilia wanted to know.

"In the *sierra*—the highlands—not too far. I'm grateful I found a good-paying job to support us."

"I was lucky my husband was hard-working and kind," Aya said.

"He's no longer with you?" Otilia asked.

"He died four years ago. We'd bought a space, right on the main square in Alberra, to run a restaurant. All was going well, but he worked too hard; then he had a heart attack. We couldn't save him."

"You have any kids?"

"Two girls, married. They moved away."

"He must have worked hard, saved his money," Berta said.

"He worked for a woman who ran a boarding house. When she died, she left him the property."

"*Que bien*, wonderful," Otilia said.

"We sold the house and with the money bought the restaurant. That was our dream. With the Shining Path around, the business shrunk. Now all the money is gone."

Otilia became aware that her roommates were also tormented

by their own pasts and the events of these hard times. It gave her a measure of comfort to know they were all in the same boat, trying to find ways to cope.

The lounge was quiet, still empty in the early part of the evening. The professionals had their own bar and dining room, separate from that of the labourers, who ate in the cafeteria. In the lounge, people ate at small tables decked in white tablecloths, and conversations were kept hushed. It was customary to find guests lingering after dinner with drinks, discussing the problems at hand, while in the cafeteria no liquor was sold; workers ate at communal tables, had their meals quickly, and then retired for the night.

By seven o'clock, the diners began to trickle in and it was her job to show them to their tables. Most formed parties of two or three, but a gentleman, older than the rest, came by himself and asked to be seated alone.

When Otilia approached his table to take his order, he stated that he had a special dietary request: a simple pasta, no sauce, with shavings of parmesan cheese and no salt.

"Here you are, as you requested, sir. May I bring you anything else?" Otilia asked when she brought him the dish.

"No thanks." Removing his glasses, he looked up at her face. "Are you new? I've not seen you before."

"I'm assigned to the lounge whenever they are short-staffed, *señor*. I've been working in the kitchen for a while." She was surprised that she was being spoken to by a professional of high rank. But he was a foreigner; they were different, not concerned about class.

He offered her a smile.

She'd never had a word with a gringo. She noticed his accent and how gently he folded his napkin with his well-groomed hands. "Pull up a chair and let's have a chat." Lighting a cigarette, and sitting back, he asked, "How long have you been here? Making good money?"

"*Señor,* I'm so sorry, I have to attend to my tasks."

"Well, next time perhaps," he said, taking a sip from his wine glass.

She thought he was drunk, much too upfront. Before he departed he said *adios* quite loudly, but by then most of the patrons had already gone.

From then on the gringo made small talk every time he saw her; sometimes he joked, and other times he told her what he'd been up to that day.

"Let's go to the rec room so we can talk," he said one night as he stood up to leave.

She bit her lip, faltered and said, "I'm not sure I can." Was she allowed to spend time with him?

"When are you off?"

"Eleven, *señor.*"

"I'll be back."

The next building over served as the recreation facility for the senior staff. A few men stood around playing pool while others played cards.

"Please have a seat," he said, when he found a spot in the back. "What can I get you to drink?"

He went over to the counter and she settled down in a chair, waiting nervously. She ran her fingers up and down the pleats of her skirt when a newspaper lying on the table next to her chair caught her eye. She flipped through it to check for obituaries but reminded herself how highly improbable that was. Her thoughts were interrupted by his voice.

"I'm sorry," she said, "it's just that..." She hesitated, feeling flustered and caught off guard.

"The hot tea is coming." He held a bowl of potato chips and a glass of scotch.

"Thank you, *señor.*"

Placing his drink on a low table close by, he said, "Please call me Mike. No more *señor*, understand?"

He smiled and she gazed at his bronzed face. He was trying to put her at ease, asking a few questions and telling her about his travels and the places he'd seen. He asked where she was from and she refrained from saying much. She couldn't tell him about the extreme set of events that had brought her to this place.

Much later that evening, unable to dodge questions about her family, Otilia slowly explained why she was working up at the camp. There was something compellingly sincere about him and she spoke freely, feeling the weight of her loss coming back in full force.

Reaching for a plastic folder in her bag, with tears falling down her cheeks, she extended a photograph. "These, don Michael, are my husband and son."

Before they said good night, he offered to drive her down to Cajamarca on her next free day. "*Gracias*," she said, her voice quivering.

Michael was sixty-three and had officially retired from working as a geologist for a multinational company that had sent him all over the world. When a position had come up as a short-term consultant in a new mine in northern Peru, he'd jumped at the opportunity. He'd lived in exciting places—in the Arctic, in Africa—and this would be his second time in Latin America. He'd never married, since being tucked away in remote places wasn't conducive to conjugal life. He'd lived in pretty rough locales, not places for a wife. He liked spending times in rugged terrain and found contentment in challenging sites around the world. He'd become sensitive to the needs of the people in underdeveloped countries and tried to help. When he was in Niger, he became close to a family who had all of their underage children working in a mine to augment the family income. When he offered the parents a bit of cash, all five kids were able to go away to a school and the family made it through a prolonged drought. Of course, he was aware he couldn't save all poor people in a country, but he could help one person at a time.

The heat in the the company jeep blew at full blast when Otilia jumped in. "I'm sorry it's so strong. Just for a few minutes, to keep the fog from forming on the inside glass," Michael said.

He asked her to buckle up before he began to drive down the mountain into the city. Otilia was silent most of the way, deep in her own thoughts. The centre of town was busy and many policemen were roaming around, patrolling the streets. They drove out of their way to find a parking spot, as soldiers on horseback, animals trained to charge on a potential oncoming mass, occupied space on the avenues. Outside police head-quarters, people were gathered at the entryway, some lining up, while Indigenous women walked back and forth selling oranges in meshed bags.

When they entered the building, and the guards at the door demanded to see their identifications. After Michael asked for directions to where they could inquire about missing persons, they were guided to the appropriate room. Money whitens, Otilia thought. Was it because she was with a gringo that they were being shown preference? Otilia didn't question it too much—she was so pleased that it was down to business at last.

"I'm trying to track down a man and a child that went missing," she said to the official at the counter.

"Where were they seen last?"

"In my village of El Milagro."

"On what date?"

The official wrote down all the information they provided him with in his notebook then stood up. After perusing a file, he lifted his head and said, "There was a Shining Path attack on that date. Are you looking for a *senderista*?"

"No, of course not!" Otilia said, becoming alarmed.

"Then why is he not here with you? Why did he flee?"

"He didn't flee, sir. He disappeared."

The officer's eyes were deep set, unreadable. "Where were you that night?" he asked. His questions made Otilia shake She fell silent. What was the use of a response? He was accusatory, wanting her to feel confused. She wouldn't let him see her distress; instead, she shot a look at Michael, who stood a few feet away.

"Is there a problem, sir?" Michael asked, coming to stand close to her side.

"You are with her?" The official said sharply, somewhat surprised.

"Yes, officer."

The officer shifted in his chair. "No, there's no problem; please have the lady fill out this form. I understand that she is claiming that her husband is gone. We'll do our best. People disappear; trails are lost. At this time we have over eight hundred complaints."

Otilia felt tears coming on.

"How much would it take to put a trace on this gentleman and his son?" Michael asked, lowering his voice. Greasing the wheels always helped.

"Please, *señor*, don't get me wrong, we are not here to sell information. We're here to serve the public and enforce the law."

They walked over to a restaurant facing the main plaza for a bite to eat and to fill out the forms to request an appointment for a hearing with a bureaucrat. Youth on the prowl lurking around the restaurant suddenly surrounded Michael, pestering him for coins. Once inside, Michael ordered the plate of the day: steak with rice and potatoes, and Otilia said she'd have the same. "That cruel little bastard behind the counter, he was only interested in getting rid of us. It's maddening to see how they want to portray victims as guerillas who deserve their fate. No wonder few people report the disappearance of a loved one; it's a dangerous claim," Michael said.

Six weeks later a notification from the police precinct arrived, giving Otilia a time and date for her to appear to make a declaration about her husband's disappearance. What if once they had her husband's name, he was placed on an insurgent's list rather than the disappeared persons list?

Michael was at his desk in his office, under a pile of papers, when Otilia knocked and he waved her in. "They've given me a date for a preliminary hearing," she said.

"Good."

"I worry that if I give them Manuel's name I might get him into trouble. What if they think he's an agitator?"

Scratching his head with his pencil, Michael thought for a moment then said, "You're smart to be on guard." He was horrified that the consequences of a civilized action could be turned against them. "What is the world coming to? I thought this country was more advanced than Africa," he grumbled. "Leave it with me, I'll think it over, talk to some friends."

So much for expecting a mild winter. Struggling against the wind, covering her face with her hands, Otilia ran from her dormitory to the kitchen. It was beginning to get bitterly cold and she realized that next time she was in town she would have to get herself a hat and gloves. She was a few minutes late and the girls were already chopping up meat and vegetables for the stew. She took her place at the counter and began to peel garlic bulbs, tuning out the girls' gossip about their romances with the miners who were courting them.

"He's full of himself, that one. His pride is easily hurt," Teresa warned Nilda, as she approached Otilia. "Enough standing. Come, let's take a break. I have to sit for a while, my back really hurts. Nilda, will you bring us coffee and some of the delicious pastry you made?"

Once they were in the small room in the back, Teresa swallowed a pill and said, "I'm stressed. I'm working so hard and it's never enough. All the weight is on me. My son's university tuition is going up again."

Teresa had described herself as a scorned wife, abandoned by her adulterous husband. He'd left her and their son to fend for themselves, while going after a much younger girl. When she saw that he had a roving eye, she'd kicked him out of the house. She'd stayed in the marriage too long.

"I don't know why the *mierda* can't help his son with his education," Teresa said.

"Hang in there, it's one more year before he graduates. He'll get a good-paying job and you'll be able to rest," Otilia said.

"That day won't come soon enough. Now I'll tell you what I heard. My ex broke up with his latest girlfriend and is accusing our son of butting in. They're the same age."

"How did you hear that?"

"*Pueblo chico, infierno grande.* I come from a small town, big hell—everybody gossips about everybody else."

Otilia looked at the clock on the wall, gulped down the last sip of her coffee and got up. "Stay, girl, you're still on your break; you have a few minutes left."

"Whatever you say, *jefa,* you're the boss."

"Tell me, how are things with you?"

"The same, no information."

"Politics has us fooled. Too bad justice doesn't exist."

The next day, after dinner, Michael had news for Otilia. "I'll tell you what I have in mind. I have to go to Lima to see some people at the Ministry of Mines. Your situation has prompted me to go a little earlier than I planned. Once I'm there, I'll talk to some people who might be able to shed some light and tell us what's really going on."

"*Válgame Dios,*" Otilia sighed. "I don't want to jeopardize you, don Michael."

"I'll find out what is happening and advise you when I get back."

"You are so good, *señor* Mike, certainly one of the least selfish people I've ever met."

Michael was worried that the Cajamarca police department was not the place Otilia should go to for help. They were too isolated, miles from the capital, and they might even be operating on their own, not following national policy. Even Michael felt somewhat removed, away from the capital, where they couldn't clearly grasp what was going on in the rest of the country. They needed more information to guide the search. Michael would get some advice from his friend John, a foreign correspondent, and obtain an objective point of view to assess how they should handle things.

8

MICHAEL ARRIVED In Lima and checked into the bed and breakfast where he usually stayed in the upscale neighbourhood of Miraflores. He was told to go on up to his room on the second floor of the old colonial mansion, where the maid was cleaning up. The windows, overlooking an inner courtyard, were wide open and the girl was plumping up the pillows, putting on a few last touches.

"I don't have clean towels yet," the girl apologized. "I'll bring them as soon as they are dry, as soon as the power is back."

The room felt familiar, with its damask bedspread and matching curtains—a few notches up from his room in the camp's prefab. He was just a block away from the ocean where he liked to take walks on the promenade. It was early spring and although the flowers were starting to bloom, the weather was still grey and damp.

Michael spent his first few days working at the Ministry of Mines where the people he talked to grumbled over hyperinflation and shortages of public services and supplies. Walking through the streets, he noticed the city was slowly falling into grinding poverty; there was increasing disrepair, and everything looked grimier than when he'd visited last. With no money for upkeep, nobody was fixing the broken sidewalks and the trash wasn't being picked up. People's discontent showed on the political messages that graffitied the buildings.

Once he was done with business, he began to focus on Otilia's case, and by the end of the week, he was ready to make his way to a nondescript office complex to meet his friend John Blythe who worked for News Twenty-One.

John was a good-looking man, considerably younger than Mike. They'd developed a friendship over time, as they kept bumping into each other at social events hosted by ex-pats from English-speaking countries around the world.

John was at his desk, ready to go for lunch, when Michael showed up. They walked a few blocks to a restaurant and were given a table by a window facing a construction site, where men without protective gear hauled buckets of cement up rickety wooden planks.

"Not the best table," Jon commented, somewhat disturbed. "It's busy, everybody's out at the same time."

After they ordered, Michael told John how he was looking for guidance to help Otilia, whose life had been suddenly torn apart.

"I wouldn't be surprised if honest people are being arrested," John said, looking at the steam rising from his bowl of soup. Before swallowing spoonfuls of broth in loud gulps, he said, "This lady's husband could easily have been picked up and accused of being a witness to a crime."

"I don't know if she understands what's happening in this country," Michael commented.

"To put it simply, from what I see, there's a lot of unrest."

"And what is the government doing about it?"

"Trying to suppress it."

"What is the position taken by the official press?" Michael asked.

"Whatever pleases them at the time. There are always two sides to a story, so they interpret actions the way it suits them."

Before the waitress came over with the main course, John explained in a low tone of voice, "It's all *cocinado*, as they say. The truth is cooked up; there's been a sharp rise in violence and the government doesn't know how to handle it, so right now they are putting the blame on the Shining Path. The economic turbulence is increasing social tension and contributing to a wave of new hostility. There's a rise of activity by the guerilla movement and it appears that the authorities are finally seeking a military solution. I've heard rumours of clandestine violent operations. However, it's difficult to get to the bottom of what is going on. For years, the government took no action and left it alone. The violence was basically confined to the province of Ayacucho. Can't understand why they weren't able to face the problem then; now it's starting to spread and it's getting out of hand. The Shining Path is gaining strength; I've heard about some pretty nasty blood baths. We have stories of how they go into the villages and force the community to join them, but when the government soldiers arrive, they accuse the community leaders of being collaborators. Then the poor chaps have no choice but to join them, for if they don't do so, they burn their homes and torture them. As I've also heard said, they are between the sword and the wall, *la espada y la pared*."

"So the population is being squeezed from both ends?" Michael asked.

"Indeed. The government is spreading the story that it's the *senderistas* that are doing the killing and terrorizing the people, in order to intimidate us all. I came across one report, from someone who would not reveal his source, which said that in one village there were few inhabitants left after an attack. The soldiers who had come to liberate the villagers were as much to blame for the heinous acts."

"Let me get this straight. As far as Otilia's husband is concerned, if Otilia were to make a declaration, would they handle it in a lawful way?"

John took a deep breath. "God knows. I hear that the government is not being upfront; they're keeping their actions hushed. One of our reporters is investigating a tip about some serious allegations of wrongdoing by members of the armed forces.

He's not written a thing yet, but has already gotten several death threats. We've sent out bodyguards to protect him."

"You're suggesting that one should proceed carefully."

John nodded. "By all means. Right now the government line seems to be that if they take a hard line, and not acknowledge their dirty work, they'll gain legitimacy."

"Both sides seem to be using the same strategy," Mike said after thinking about the comments he had just heard, "turning the tables on their accusers."

"There's a lot of confusion, a lot of ambiguity."

"Do you believe they are tracking people's movements?"

"No doubt about it; they have informers coming out of the woodwork," John said.

When lunch was over, Mike had a list of names of reporters John said would be good to talk to.

"*Buena suerte*, good luck," John said, shaking hands.

The night Michael went out to buy Otilia a small souvenir, there was another power outage. Damn it, he thought, now where to go? The streets were in darkness and all he could see were the fires of the street vendors preparing food in their stalls. All he could do was to sit on a stool and wait for the power to return. He ordered a beer and watched the men in uniform walk by. He sat in the dark for a while. He was the only customer at the stall and the vendor started to chat. He said he'd been listening to the soccer game when the power went out. "Even this little pleasure has been taken away. What do those asses think, that we will support them when they can't even let a poor little man eke out a living?" He fine-tuned the dial on his battery-powered radio. "These sanctions are taking a toll—we're being forced to alter the way we live."

"How long have you been putting up with it?" Michael asked.

"Too long, and it's getting worse. I can't make a living this way, waiting all night for clients to show up," the vendor said.

"I understand."

"Nowadays, with the cost of living skyrocketing, there're fewer people eating out."

When Michael removed a handful of *intis* from his pocket to pay for the drink the vendor said, "They're worthless. It's all a game, our currency, *el sol, el inti, el peso*, the name of the money changes, but the value gets worse."

Michael knew these people worked diligently day in and day out while holding little faith that they could improve their quality of life. All they saw was their currency steadily being devalued while they were having to constantly cut back.

By the time he finished his drink, the power had returned, so he decided to stop at a newsstand to buy some newspapers and a bunch of magazines. He observed two slim, young and pretty women in tight jeans, with purses crossed over their shoulders, flipping through some glossy magazines. They didn't seem to be affected by the current state of affairs.

Back in his room, he sank into an easy chair. The papers he'd bought were both from the left and the right, as he wanted to learn more about the positions they espoused. He read an article recounting the heroism of the soldiers fighting the enemy, claiming the government was ahead in dispersing the guerillas, while in another paper the reporter claimed the Shining Path were recruiting more women into their movement and growing in strength. The only thing all of the tabloids agreed upon was that the economy was in disastrous shape.

Michael was flying back to the camp the following morning and wondered what he would be able to tell Otilia. From all of the people he talked to, and the papers he'd read, he gathered that the state of affairs was a mess. It was clear that there were disturbances and that while in some areas the guerillas had built support across a range of groups, in others the country people were frightened of them. There was no official policy on how the government was dealing with dissenters, but it was clear they were intimidating those who questioned their actions. Michael's recommendation would be to proceed cautiously, not be prey to deceptions, as surely everyone was concealing facts. Michael had heard that in some cases, when families went to report a missing member, they were duped with information that was far from the truth. Michael didn't want to subject Otilia to unpleasant encounters; he'd need to think of some palatable way to explain to her the rude shock of what was really happening.

Hunching forward behind his desk, Michael removed his glasses to face Otila and tell her what he had learned. "I was a fool to think I could approach the appropriate authorities in Lima, report Manuel's disappearance, and expect the officers to be eager to help by opening an investigation expeditiously."

Michael shook his head, his shoulders drooping in discouragement. "After talking to John and his contacts, I realized that there were hundreds of people in your predicament, and government officials couldn't care less. I'm sorry to say that it's clear to the people I spoke to that injustices are being committed, and you should definitely not give an account to the authorities yet. Assassinations are being reported as suicides and disappearances as people leaving the country to go into exile."

"What about the Shining Path?" Otilia asked. "Will they get away with everything?"

"Reports regarding the Shining Path's alleged atrocities remain a matter of controversy," Michael said. "Some say the ones responsible for the mayhem are the government soldiers, instead. It's scary to think that desperate attempts from relatives to find information about their vanished loved ones most often amount to nothing more than a bunch of lies. I discovered that in these bleak times few can be trusted and we'll have to think of going about it some other way."

"The truth is always being disputed, but unlawful killings?" Otilia said. Her mind began racing, trying to make sense of the bits and pieces of information she'd heard right from the outset.

Michael went on to inform her that he wanted to lend her a

hand and that he understood the agony she was experiencing. If he was faced with a similar perverse situation, he told her, he'd sure hope that another person would be there for him. Otilia was touched, but felt somewhat confused—a stranger wanting to help, how so?

Michael was coming across as fiercely protective—he had even worked out a plan. "We can hire this young journalist, who comes highly recommended, to hunt down Salvador and Manuel. John gave me his name. He says this guy has an inexhaustible capacity for investigating difficult situations, and personally, I wouldn't think twice about phoning this Roberto and telling him what we have in mind. All I need is your approval to make the call."

Otilia had called her home a number of times and gotten no response. Lately she hadn't even been able to get a dial tone when she tried. She gathered the reason was that the bills hadn't been paid and the line had been cut off. She had contacted business associates and friends, but nobody had heard from Manuel. So, of course, she told Michael to please go ahead with the call.

9

"THIS TYPE OF INVESTIGATION is outside my field of expertise," were Roberto's first words when Michael explained the reasons for his call. But after Roberto listened to Michael for a while longer, he changed his mind. By the end of the conversation, he said he would think about what Michael was proposing, and call him back. "Perhaps, I can make a contribution toward combating the real looming threat the country is facing," he said, before hanging up.

When Roberto called Michael to say he was up to the challenge, he warned him that the job would take time. He faced huge obstacles getting to the facts. He had family connections that would help open doors in high places, and he'd try to get to the bottom of the story, but it wouldn't be done from one day to the next. "And remember, the summer schedule will get in the way. You know how it is, with offices only open part time. And, before I depart, I will need an advance to cover the travelling costs."

Michael said he was willing to send him a cheque right away.

Pleased that Roberto had seized the opportunity to uncover the secrecy, he went to look for Otilia at her dormitory.

"The gringo is looking for you," Berta said as she entered their room. Otilia was changing her clothes, putting on her black skirt and white blouse, getting ready for work.

"*Hermanita*, tell him I'm coming right out." Otilia, surprised that Michael had come to find her, wondered what urgent message he had.

"How are you doing?" she asked when she came out of her room to greet him.

"I got a call from Roberto. He's up for the job and he agreed to look into it."

Otilia felt her spirit lightening. The news brought her some peace of mind. "Thank you so much! You're my fairy godfather."

"*Fairy godfather*—that's a tricky term to use with a gringo. Another day I'll explain the term."

"You deserve all the credit for doing so much for me."

"Roberto said he'd be in touch in a week. He'll do his best to travel into hostile territory."

Otilia frowned. "Where is that?" She shuddered at the thought.

"I'm not sure. I told him that if he thought it necessary, he could hire an armed bodyguard. We'll wait until we hear from him and then make a plan."

Otilia began to experience bouts of insomnia once again. She'd stopped taking the sleeping pills, and tonight she lay fully awake. She was baffled by Michael's offer; it troubled her. She'd protested at first, for this was not his responsibility, she said, but he wouldn't hear her out and she'd been unable, as much she tried, to change his mind. She felt ashamed to be in a position where she was low in funds, and not able to share the cost of the search. She promised she'd pay him back as soon as conditions went back to normal.

She'd worked hard all her life and now what did she have? Not enough to save her family's life. Otilia lay on her back in her bunk and felt a tremor run down her spine. She had inherited land when her parents died, and when she married Manuel they went into the cattle trading business. They fattened the stock in pastures close to their home and sold them to butchers from the coast. They'd invested their surplus funds, buying additional animals, and one of her worries was how the stock was faring. Unless Manuel was out there tending to them, their stock would be gone as well. How would she ever pay Michael back? Right now she was left with no option but to be appreciative of the kind foreigner's act.

Thinking about what actions to take, she resolved to go into Cajamarca as soon as possible to make a concerted effort to find her brother. She couldn't suffer in isolation too much longer and needed to find a family member that would help. Though they'd lost touch, she was sure that someone would know his whereabouts.

Michael insisted he'd drive her to town on her next day off from work. So they made another trip down the mountain, this time in the spring rain. Otilia kept quiet; her eyes misted up with wistfulness as she thought about how Salvador would be managing with his father. Or was he perhaps on his own? Was he getting kisses or endearments from anyone else? He was curious and bold, a strong-minded boy, but she questioned if he could survive by himself. Had they been too indulgent with him? But he was still so young, deserving lots of parental pampering.

"Look at that clump of flowers—what beauty," Michael said, trying to be cheerful.

"There is the *cantuta*, our national flower—it's red. See the tubular-shaped ones starting to bloom on that tree?"

"It certainly brightens up the landscape."

"See the woman walking along wearing a *cantuta* flower on her hat? That is to signal she's still single."

"Very smart." Michael inserted a classical music cassette and concentrated on the stretch of dirt track ahead.

Otilia got the envelope containing Tomas's old address from her purse. Although it clearly stated he was not at this address any longer, it was the only one she had. As they got closer to town, Otilia noticed the graffiti of a hammer and sickle and the picture of Che Guevara on a wall, next to one praising the strength of the Shining Path.

"Are we close yet?" Michael asked, and Otilia began to read aloud the names of the cross streets. "We want Los Angeles."

Michael turned right, and came to a full stop in front of number five. Otilia took a deep cleansing breath and with a trembling hand gripped the handle to push open the door. She rushed out to speak to a young woman who was sweeping the sidewalk.

"I just moved in, never met him," she said, huffing disapprovingly.

Otilia walked over to see if she could talk to the neighbours on either side, but nobody was home. A fellow across the street answered the door when she called, saying that Tomas had gone to live in Lima a while back. "Times are tough; he wasn't making much of a living and said he would try his luck in the big city. I haven't heard from him since."

Otilia climbed into the car and shrank back in her seat. "He left for Lima," she said. "Left no address."

With little else for them to do in town, they drove back to the mine.

"My family has betrayed me," Otilia remarked, breaking her silence.

"I'm sure it was out of their control," Michael said. He wanted to spare her additional suffering. He reached out to squeeze her hand, which hung limp on the side of the seat.

Roberto's written report would be delayed, he said in a brief phone call he made. Roberto informed Michael that there was a worrisome event looming ahead and he wanted to obtain proper information before sharing it with them. This was just the beginning, but the information he was getting was somewhat confusing. It appeared that there was evidence that the death toll was higher than he had originally suspected.

It was disconcerting that Manuel had become invisible, and Roberto was determined to find out if anybody was aware of his fate.

When the first written account finally arrived, Michael was the first to learn that the vanishing of a journalist who'd been reporting on the disappearance of peasants, was leading Roberto to tread with great caution. Roberto provided details on how he'd combed over documents and interviewed numerous people in villages around Otilia's family residence. In his travels, he met frazzled townsfolk who'd been willing to share shocking stories of humiliation and terrorizing tactics used against them. He could confirm that people were being forced from their homes, never to be seen again, but had no information regarding Manuel.

"Here's Roberto's report," Michael said, pushing a large envelope across his desk, when Otilia came in to see him later that day. "They're pulling the wool over our eyes, saying everything is okay, when Roberto is reporting that there've been disappearances without any traces."

Otilia took the report and read some sentences out loud. "The authorities aren't investigating the violations. Complaints brought by citizens are not being properly explored."

"We must take charge," Michael said in a determined voice.

One afternoon, on the first week of November, Roberto came up to the mining camp. Otilia looked out the kitchen window and spotted a short man in jeans, climbing out of a jeep. Michael had reserved a conference room for their meeting at one o'clock. Removing her apron, she looked up at the clock and picked up the platter of sandwiches and pastries Teresa insisted she take.

Michael exchanged nods with Otilia and then introduced her to Roberto, who stubbed out his cigarette before extending his hands. "*Mucho gusto.* Good to meet you."

Michael urged both to take a seat so they could get started.

Roberto opened his briefcase and removed a file. He looked at his notes and hesitated for a moment. Otilia could see that he was having trouble deciding where to start. Otilia, trying to keep her composure, poured some water from a bottle into a glass.

Roberto began by apologizing for the delay in getting back to them. "I worked as quickly as I could, but had to be careful not to arouse suspicion. I hope my report will be helpful. I'm sorry to say I encountered unpleasant facts, as you've already heard."

Roberto was intense, gesticulating with both hands. "One would think this is a war between the government and the Shining Path," he said in a rush. "But I'm beginning to see it very differently. I don't think the origin of this wretchedness is only the *senderistas'* violence. I found out more than I bargained for," he said, leaning back on his chair. "It's been a struggle to get good information about what's really happening. It's a futile effort to try to get around the machinations of both the Shining Path and the police. The official story ... well, they're not saying much. However, they're forbidding journalists to print anything that could dent the government's image. They don't want anybody saying they're not protecting their citizens, so they're making things up as they go along."

"What do you mean?" Michael asked.

"The armed forces don't know who is a guerilla and who isn't. They haven't a clue as to how many guerillas there are or where they are. They go after anyone that appears suspicious. If they kill sixty people and three are from the Shining Path, they'll say all sixty were revolutionaries."

"You mean they are really killing innocent people?" Otilia asked.

"Definitely. I talked to one guy who was using an outhouse, hidden from the soldier's view, when he saw how they took his brothers along with his neighbours, shot them all, and then dumped their bodies into the village well."

Otilia felt a cold bolt of panic descending on her. "Were you able to get up to the village of El Milagro?" she managed to ask.

"Yes, I was there. I'm sorry to have to tell you, there wasn't much I could detect. I saw some buildings partially burned." He'd taken some photographs that he now placed on the table. "They looted anything of value and destroyed what remained. Nobody was saying much, blaming it all on the Shining Path."

"Did you talk to her neighbours?" Michael asked, as Otilia studied the pictures, not recognizing the site where her house had stood.

"They told me it all happened quickly, in the course of one night, and that all has been quiet since."

"Have people left?"

"There are people running away from every village, going to find refuge somewhere else."

"Have people been taken away?" Otilia asked, closing her eyes.

"Prisoners? There's much injustice. No one knows if they're alive or dead. One reporter claimed prisoners were taken away to deserted places. Bodies were found lying in a mass grave."

"Just like my friend John said, they've turned a blind eye to questionable practices," Michael said.

"It seems so. I speculated that Manuel could have been imprisoned, but couldn't find a shred of evidence. He's been either kidnapped or killed."

"And what about my boy?" Otilia spoke softly, sighing in a mixture of fear and pain.

"Not a word."

Otilia froze.

"But, *señora*, don't worry; I'll continue to search. I want to hear in your own words how you'd best describe him. Tell me all you know about your boy."

His question brought tears to Otilia as she began to respond. "He's slight, small for his age, and he has dark eyes and a scar on his face."

"A scar, you said?"

"A cleft lip. He was born that way. We had it repaired—it's barely noticeable. I know it's there."

Michael reached sideways to hold her hand as Roberto made notations on his pad.

"Now, my understanding is that when your husband left, he went first to hide the child. Do you think he had any reason to abandon him?"

"No!" Otilia screamed, lowering her face into her palms. "He was going to take him to Rodrigo Palma's place."

"I'm sorry, that's where I'll go next."

Otilia began to shake. Michael turned to Roberto and said, "Please continue."

"Some people have witnessed men dropped from helicopters, released like a condor," Roberto said.

"Let me get it straight," Michael said, looking appalled. "All this is going on and nobody seems to care or know?"

"Villages are requesting guards be posted to protect them from the Shining Path—"

"And?" Michael interrupted.

"*Ni hablar*, they don't. One man I talked to filed an accusation with a judge, who in turn wrote a memo to the captain of the police force, reprimanding him; that captain had his men steal everything the family had, for spite. They took radios, chickens, cows ... they're out to take advantage of the situation. Another individual told me it took him five visits after filing an accusation before anyone gave him any kind of a response. When the police finally saw him, he was told that he would have to name the attackers who kidnapped his son, before they could investigate his case. He told them he didn't know who was responsible, so their answer was, how could they possibly find his son without knowing who'd kidnapped him?"

"It doesn't make sense," Michael said.

"According to them, the law states that you have to be able

to identify your attackers before police can go after them. It's absurd, all a game."

"Correct me if I'm wrong, "Michael said. "In other words, they say that if you can't identify your attackers, the *senderistas* probably are responsible—is that what they say?"

"That's right."

"This kind of situation erodes the foundation of any democracy," Michael said.

"*Ni hablar,* of course," Roberto said.

"No wonder people are scared. Your facts support people's apprehensions," Michael said.

Roberto went on to offer greater details of how torture and rape were being used to maintain social order and eradicate subversives. "When women have wanted to know where their men have gone, they've been raped. Lives seemed to be controlled by terror," Roberto said, lowering his voice, looking at his notes.

"You mean to tell me that they are not going after the rebels and that they are covering up gang actions as if they were legitimate military tactics? Is nobody demanding answers? Accountability?"

"People are being controlled by silence and isolation," Roberto said.

The phone rang and Michael got up to answer. "I'll be ready in about another half hour," he said, and hung up.

By now Otilia had stopped listening. It didn't leave much doubt in her mind that both Manuel and Salvador were gone forever. As far as she was concerned, too much had gone wrong in a short period of time. All she could feel was contempt for mankind.

"I can't understand how there can be a total denial of reality by those in power. Don't they see how their poor judgment is destroying the future of a generation?" Michael said.

Otilia's chest rose and fell. Experiencing trouble breathing, she clutched Michael's arm and apologized, "I must go." She didn't care to hear any more revelations about how the violence was rising and people were turning fickle, changing their loyalties according to who could be most helpful to them. She didn't give a damn about the Shining Path recruiting young maids to work in the homes of the wealthy in Lima, in order to rob them blind to aid the cause of the underdog, nor for the plight of the child of a foreign volunteer who was grabbed while stopped at a red light and pulled through the window of the car. All she wanted was her husband and child.

Feeling the faint pressure at the back of her head developing into a full migraine, Otilia made her way back to the dormitory. There she found two of her young roommates quarrelling, raising their voices to a higher pitch with each sentence they spoke, and she asked them to quiet down. She lay in bed, clenching her fists. She needed to find a way to cope with the uncomfortable truths she'd learned. Kneading her temples with her fingertips, trying to rid herself of the overwhelming pain—she had to try to blank out the stories she'd heard. All night long she could feel herself trembling, drifting in and out of a light sleep. By morning, hopelessness had overtaken her core and she didn't think she could speak.

10

TOMAS DECIDED that he needed to move to Lima to make a better life. Business was slow and with the economy in the dumps people were taking fewer taxi rides. He needed a better income now that the boy had come into his life. Besides, it wasn't a good idea for him to be seen with the child. What if they got him for harbouring a rebel's child? He broke the news to his nephew one day in October when schools were shut down because of a teacher's strike. Salvador's eyes narrowed as he looked at his uncle, annoyed. "How come we have to go?"

Tomas explained his reason in a few words.

"But I like school," Salvador complained.

"I know. You'll enroll in another one in Lima and make new friends."

"Can't we wait until the end of the year before we go?"

"No. This strike's going to be a long one." The union was encouraging teachers to stay away from the classrooms until they could negotiate better salaries, although they knew the district was broke.

"I spoke to my *pata* in Lima; he wants us to stay at his house. He's a *taxista* and will show me the ropes."

Salvador was not thrilled. How could he unravel the mystery of where his parents had gone once they moved? And what if his mother showed up? "Mami said she'd come soon," he stammered.

Tomas didn't respond.

"*Yo quiero a mi mamá.*"

"I know you love your mother, but I have no alternative."

"I want to give her a hug," he said and started to cry. "I miss her."

"Stop it. I know *nada* about your parents, do you understand?"

"Why aren't you trying to find what happened to them?" Salvador yelled and ran to his room.

Pablo lived in a brick one-storey house up on a dry hill in the district of Comas, a densely populated section of the thronging city of Lima. The house stood along a rutted and dusty treeless street. When Tomas pulled up in his taxi and parked by the curb, they saw his friend standing inside the wrought-iron gate. Pablo welcomed Tomas and patted him on his back. Then he turned to Salvador and gave him a warm hug. Pablo told Tomas that we was happy his friend had finally listened to his advice and gotten out of the northern town to try his luck in the city of kings.

The house consisted of small, sparsely furnished rooms with terracotta floor tiles. Tomas apologized to his friend for imposing upon him, but Pablo laughed it off and said, "It's great to have my best *pata* in town." In the main room, a worn couch sat against a scuffed white wall. In the next room, four white plastic chairs were neatly tucked around a table covered with a vinyl cloth. Thick metal bars protected the windows facing the street. The kitchen windows were wide open and a number of flies were attacking the crumbs left on the countertops with gusto.

"You sure got security," Tomas said.

"A fortress—one of the drawbacks of living in the big city."

Pablo showed them a room in the back, containing a single bed and a cot, with a sliding door that opened onto a cement patio surrounded by several scruffy shrubs.

"Let's go get your things from the car," Pablo said, stepping back.

Pablo's mother, Norma, a full-figured woman in her seventies, brought out some *chicha morada* for Salvador and a beer for the men. "Have your drink first; then you can go and unpack," she said. In spite of a limp, Norma appeared energetic and friendly.

She sat down next to Salvador, with her own glass of sweet, cool, deep purple juice. "This is delicious," Salvador said.

"I have my own way of preparing it; it's the cloves and cinnamon I add to the water as the purple corn starts to boil."

Salvador was intrigued by her looks. She had black-penciled eyebrows and tightly permed curls. Norma informed them that she was the one who did the cooking and kept the house, and told Tomas she would be more than happy to take care of the boy while he was at work.

Salvador took an immediate liking to Norma, who showed an interest in him, and in no time they established a routine. In the mornings Norma did her housework, and when she was finished she would tell him they were free to go out. Often she prepared a *bocadillo* and took Salvador to the park to eat their sandwiches. Tomas wanted to be sure that Salvador would be ready to go into the second grade, so Norma began to tutor him in reading and math. When he wasn't doing homework, Salvador could sit looking out the window at the passing people and the aging cars. Sometimes he tried to play with Norma's cat, but the cat was fickle and only sometimes allowed Salvador to pet her.

Tomas was eager to register his taxi with the Lima municipality, so one evening, while Pablo lifted weights before supper, he pulled up a chair next to him so that they could talk about how to proceed.

"I wouldn't worry about it," Pablo said. "There are too many burdensome regulations; most cabbies don't bother with it."

"Don't passengers prefer to jump into legally registered cabs?" Tomas asked.

"Some do," Pablo responded, his breathing laboured. "Others don't care as long as the fare is right. All you need is a sign in the windshield for people to know you're willing to drive. Besides, I think that they've stopped issuing permits. The feeling is that this city has too many cabs."

Pablo put down the dumbbells, wiped his forehead, and continued. "Sporadically they'll hand out licenses to out-of-town drivers, but even if you initiate the process tomorrow and offer a kickback, it'll take you three years to obtain one. Your only recourse is to go ahead and drive an unlicensed car. But you've got to be savvy."

"What do you mean?"

Pablo picked up the weights and, standing up straight, said, "You'll have to be careful to weed out the thieves and the *choros* with gang links. You must never let your guard down. You need to study a map of the city and know your way around. Not knowing your destination might anger some customers. Disputes can turn to assaults if you make them mad."

"I have a pretty good memory. I'll memorize the routes and names of the main streets."

Lifting a heavier pair of weights, Pablo added, "And keep your windows rolled up and doors locked at all times. You don't want anybody yanking you out."

"Is this why you lift weights?" Tomas smiled.

Letting out a raspy snicker, Pablo said, "I wish I were stronger, and could scare some away with more ease." Pablo lifted his rib cage and his arms overhead. "I try not to have people sit directly behind me. I ask them to move to my right, to keep them in my line of vision and be able to see them in my rearview mirror. You don't want anybody punching you in the back. And most importantly, as you already know, if you are ever assaulted, do not resist, simply comply with the thugs." Sweat ran down Pablo's torso as he put down the weights. "I'm going to go and take a shower; I'll be right out and get you a map."

When business was bustling, Tomas drove ten to twelve hours a day through the city's neighbourhoods. He was getting better at determining distances and could now haggle with customers for an adequate fare. Pablo had made up a list of the going rates he should charge between destinations, and Tomas was able to spit out a price without hesitation. At times he didn't return to the house till late at night, having to contend with heavy traffic or be brought to a standstill by construction work. He began to make it a habit to catch naps in the early afternoon when business was slow. He'd park the car in the shade, under a tree in a park or on a side street, to evade the evening's searing heat. He was starting to feel he'd be able to give Salvador a decent education.

The only annoying problem he was having, and he'd been warned of this practice by Pablo, was encountering the police. Cruisers made a habit of looking for ways to fine cabs. The one time he was pulled over by a patrol car, the *patrullero* said he was issuing him a ticket for not yielding in a traffic circle. After engaging in some small talk, the policeman asked for "beer money," and let him go once he accepted the bribe.

In early December, Norma brought her nativity set into the main room and asked Salvador to help her remove the layers of newspaper it was wrapped in. A carved wooden stable; Mary, Joseph and the baby Jesus; plus a number of other small animals and people appeared as Salvador excitedly unwrapped the figurines. Salvador gasped when Norma placed a llama and the small figure of an Incan boy holding a sheep, on the coffee table. There was something familiar about it. Allowing his thoughts to retrieve a scene from a past Christmas, and he remembered seeing a larger version of the same boy when he and his parents had to visited an outdoor nativity scene at the church near his home. Closing his eyes, he let his memories flood him and imagined the joy he would feel when his parents showed up. Maybe on the twenty-fourth?

Norma also brought out a plastic Christmas tree and placed it in the corner of the room. They had been painting gourds in bright colours and making angels out of paper doilies and bits of yarn, which they hung on the tree. Salvador then made a glittering star out of crumpled aluminum foil for the top.

On December 24, Tomas set out to work before daybreak. It was a busy day, as people who were doing their last minute shopping waved down cabs until late.

Aromas of the roasting *pavo*, which Norma had placed in the oven early in the day, permeated the house.

"When will we eat?" Salvador asked at around nine that evening.

"We'll go to mass when your uncle and Pablo come home, then we'll have the bird. Doesn't the turkey smell good? Later we'll open gifts."

"I want to see the fireworks," he chirped.

"Those won't be on until after midnight—won't you be tired by then?"

"I want to stay up! Uncle Tomas said I could. He also said he was thinking about taking me to the bullfight tomorrow." After remaining pensive for a few moments, he looked at Norma and said, "But I'm not sure I'm up for that."

Pablo had been talking to Tomas about some top Spanish bullfighters coming to town during the holidays, but Salvador preferred watching the bulls in the fields rather than seeing the bullfights on TV.

"We're going to the Costa Verde today; go put on your bathing suit," Norma said.

Flagging down a bus a few blocks from their house, Norma ran to the bus stop in her faltering steps. Giving Salvador's behind a little push, she helped him up the steep step. She handed the driver their tickets and they went to sit by the window. The streets were filled with the clamour of buses, trucks and cars. As they made their way through a labyrinth of alleyways and backstreets, Salvador could see the black exhaust coming from most of the buses and from the old rattling trucks. It was very hot. He opened the window and was assaulted by the strong fumes as the bus continued along its route. After passing bars and pizzerias crowded with people, a sudden gush of fresh air hit his face when the driver increased his speed as they motored downhill toward the beach. His eyes widened as they passed the upscale mansions and high-rise buildings that dotted the coastline. When he heard the roaring waves pounding against the rocks, he grabbed Norma's arm and pointed excitedly to the expansive rocky seashore ahead.

"*Esquina baja*, next stop," Norma said loudly, and the driver came to a stop.

They joined a crowd of people crossing the street with umbrellas and bags in their hands. Salvador latched on to Norma, unsettled by the crowd. Vendors had lined up at the side of the road, hawking their merchandise—shoes, sunglasses, T-shirts, toys. *Cebiche* in bags and fish soup in bottles were displayed for sale on folding tables. A young girl in bright blue slacks and a pink shirt walked around holding melting ice cream cones propped up in a box. Young men in short bathing suits lay next to bikini-clad girls on bright towels spread out on the sand, their suntanned bodies sparkling with traces of lotion and beads of perspiration, while Latin American salsa music blared from their radios.

Norma removed her shoes as soon as she stepped on the sand, and looked for a spot to put their things down. While Salvador took off his shirt and ran to the water's edge, Norma remained in her place, sitting next to some ladies in their layered skirts. Salvador walked to the edge of the water and tentatively placed one foot on the last splatter of foam from the wave that just rolled in, then ran away from the next wave that splashed on shore. He did this over and over again, finally comfortable enough to walk in a little deeper and allow the waves to wash over him. He jumped up and down and waved to Norma, his face beaming. He had never had this much fun.

At the end of this special day, when they returned home, he asked Norma if she would be able to take care of him for as long as he was a kid.

Tomas learned that public schools in Lima were crowded and teachers were often on strike. He decided that since he was making enough money, he should send his nephew to a private school. He chose a school located downtown, so he could drive him early in the morning, before he started work. There was a problem, however, as the first thing they required was a copy of Salvador's birth certificate. Nobody had bothered asking him for the child's identity papers in Cajamarca, and he had not bothered obtaining one. Now he was forced to explain the boy's predicament, but in the big city, people were sticky. Rules were rules, they claimed.

"Somehow you'll have to give us proof that he's part of your family," the school secretary said.

"But he's lost everything," Tomas explained. "Even his parents. I can bring the boy to you right away." Couldn't they simply check him out, give him a test and decide which grade he belonged in? Wasn't that enough?

They weren't sure about this situation. "He could have been kidnapped," the school's secretary said.

"The boy came to me without any papers, clothes, or any other possessions. I'm his uncle, his guardian. I'm willing to take an oath," Tomas said. It wasn't enough.

"You'll have to go to the registry office and get a copy of his birth certificate," was the final word.

That evening, furious, he recounted the incident to Pablo and Norma after Salvador had gone to bed. He didn't want to make the boy anxious, not now that he seemed to be settling in so well. Ranting about the rigid regulations in a country where many other rules could so easily be broken, he knew he would have to bite his tongue, and face even worse bureaucrats at the registry office.

Armed with good will and charm, Tomas made his way to registry office. The first government employee he talked to gave him a befuddled look when Tomas told him his nephew needed a copy of his birth certificate. "But why didn't you get the papers in Cajamarca?" he asked.

"I never thought of that since nobody there asked me for them."

"Well, let me see if I can find a solution to your problem," the man said. He excused himself and went to talk to his supervisor. When he returned, he looked into Tomas's eyes and said, "Fill out this form in triplicate, go to the bank, pay the fee and bring it back. We'll see what we can do for you. Come back in a week."

It was a costly undertaking, between the fee and the time lost from work, but Tomas was determined to follow up. The next time he went to the registry office, the employee who had attended him before was nowhere to be seen. He was told to grab a number and he would be called in turn. Tomas sat in the waiting room for an hour before his number came up. Once he was at the counter, a short, balding man with a large beer belly informed him that his case hadn't been reviewed yet. Tomas explained that these trips to the registry were time consuming and costly, but the bureaucrat was unconcerned.

"So, how did it go?" Pablo asked when he got home.

Forming a circle with his pointer and thumb, Tomas said, "Zero. I was told to come back next week."

"There's no lack of idiots in the city; we'll have to think of something else," Pablo said, shaking his head.

On the next visit to the registry office they told him he

would need to go before a magistrate who would delve into his case. He would require witnesses to vouch for his and his nephew's identity.

"Is everybody here out to mess up my life?" Tomas cried irritably that evening when he and Pablo sat down to have a beer before their meal. "I'm tired of coming up with excuses. Tell me this isn't madness."

"Calm down. I spoke with my *pata* at the bar; he knows a guy who'll forge the birth certificate." Grinning from ear to ear, Pablo was pleased he could help Tomas.

11

LUCIA RAN AWAY six months after she had moved in with
Rosa. She left Rosa's home early one morning, dressed in
several layers of clothing. Her big worry was how she would
safely hold on to the money she'd stolen, for it had to last for
a while. The night before, when she saw Rosa's purse on her
dresser, she took the big bills and small change. She picked
open the lock to Rosa's drawer and helped herself to a pair of
diamond earrings and a golden ring. Now she placed her right
hand on the bundled-up handkerchief pinned to the inside of
her pants, to feel the bulge against her skin. She felt exhilarated
knowing she had control of her life. *The bitch, who did she
think she was, wanting to change me? What nerve to think I
was going to act like her—she and her girlfriends giving advice,
espousing their values, which I despise. Go to church, pray,
do your work, get some counselling, stay away from drugs ...
enough!* She'd never wanted a substitute mother.

Lucia ran until she got far away from the neighbourhood
that Rosa wanted her to call home. Walking by dilapidated
houses, she found a rubbish heap and stopped to see if there
was anything to recoup. Scavenging through a layer of litter
covered with flies, she found nothing but some squashed tomatoes on top of a soggy box.

Lucia continued walking, staying clear of the hustling kids
for fear of being accosted. When she spotted a group of teen-

agers, she turned down the lane. Vendors with vegetables and fruit piled in their wooden carts were making their way to the market. Cackling chickens penned in their cages stood at the entrance waiting to be delivered to the vendor inside. Looking to see which merchants were distracted, she noticed one woman polishing her eggplants with a cloth while talking to a customer. As Lucia walked by her stall, she helped herself to a cucumber from an open crate. At the next booth, Lucia picked up an apple from a heap and, moving onward, she snatched whatever she could lay her hands on. Suddenly she heard screams and rushed to take cover behind a pillar. She saw an armed guard beating a shoeless boy in the shins. Next to them lay the wallet he'd snatched. Lucia dashed out from behind the pillar and ran to a quiet spot in the shade to enjoy the food she had grabbed. Thinking about what she should do next, she formulated a plan in her mind. She thought she could go to Lima and get away from this place where people were always keeping an eye on street kids. She'd had enough vigilance. She'd go to work selling food at a stall—perhaps she could set one up at the side of the road, now that Rosa had taught her to cook. She could live anonymously in a tiny makeshift home, alongside hundreds of other homeless folks.

As evening approached, Lucia walked at lightning speed up the road. Beyond a gas station, past cinder block buildings with their incomplete top floors, to an area of town that housed mostly repair shops, she headed to the empty garage at the back of a tire shop, where she'd occasionally spent the night months before. When she got there, she pried open the door and discovered two girls inside.

"*Hola*," she said.

The older one ran her hands through her hair and got up from the floor where she lay. The younger one was in a fetal position on top of a woollen blanket that had been placed over several pieces of cardboard to cover the patina of oil on the cement floor. She got up and clung to her sister's pants. Lucia thought the older one looked haggard—how old could she be? Fourteen or fifteen? The younger one was no more than seven or eight. They all looked at each other not saying a word.

Lucia glanced at the wall defaced by graffiti. "This one is mine," she said, stepping up to a scrawl. "Here is my name."

"You've been here before?"

"Yep, this is my place."

Lucia noticed the lesions on the younger one's face. "I'm not saying you have to go."

"I'm Lita, and this is my sister Rita."

Lucia sat down on the floor and opened her plastic bag. "I'm tired and hungry."

"I'm really hungry," Rita said quietly.

"Shhh." Lita grabbed her outstretched hand. "Go to sleep. We'll try to get something to eat tomorrow."

"Here," Lucia said, breaking an ear of corn into small pieces, to share with both girls.

The older girl took a piece to share with her sister, but Lucia insisted they each have a piece.

"How long have you been here?" Lucia asked.

"A few days."

As they nibbled away, Lucia began to laugh. "This is fun. I've been staying at a nurse's home where I had to eat every meal very properly, with a fork and knife and a napkin in my lap." She mimicked Rosa. Lucia thought of Rosa's compulsive tidiness, and what she would say if she saw her in this wreck of a place.

That night Lucia had a fitful sleep next to the girls. She woke up with a jolt at around midnight, when the younger girl let out a high-pitched scream. Lita gently stroked her sister's back, trying to calm her down, but Rita started to cry. "Sorry," she said, holding her sister tight. "She's having a rough time; she's been having nightmares. I'll sing her a song; she'll be fine."

But Rita tossed and turned, and wet herself soon after, and the smelly puddle of urine woke Lucia up. She got up and crawled into a box she found at one end of the garage.

The girls were asleep when Lucia woke up the next day. Shielding her eyes from the glare of the sun, she made her way to the back of the lot to find the hose that was kept hidden behind the bushes. The hose was gone. She dropped to her knees, opened the faucet, cupped her hands under the tap, and waited for water to trickle out. She washed. As she dried herself in the wind, she decided she'd ask the girls if they wanted to remain together for a while. They could walk the streets, linking arms, looking out for each other.

Slowly over the weeks, the girls' friendship began to fade. Lucia was bothered by the younger girl, who needed too much attention, and by Lita who catered to her sister's every whim. Lucia couldn't feel pity. She wanted Lita to herself. Lucia began to make her own way during the day.

This morning, Lucia found a spot on a cobblestone street. She sat down on the sidewalk, in front of a bank, looking unhappy and making odd sounds, she posed. She studied the faces of people passing by, trying to guess who would be charitable and who would not. Money was what she needed to support herself. Today, jumping to grab a bill that was slipping from a lady's hand, she became alarmed when a hulking brute of a man suddenly hovered above her.

"No, *señora*, they don't need your *limosna*," he said. "Begging has been outlawed; don't waste your money on them."

Feeling her hands painfully yanked to the back, the policeman proceeded to handcuff her tightly, before she could dive out of his way.

"What the hell? Fuck face!" she yelled.

"You are loitering, time to lock you up."

"*Perdon guardia*—pardon, sir—I've done nothing wrong."

"Nothing wrong?" He laughed. "We are cracking down on vagrants." The policeman picked her up from her shoulders and gave her a shake, giving her no time to reach for the shard of glass, the weapon she carried at all times.

"That's what you say, and this?" Reaching for the piece of glass that had fallen from her pants, he commanded her to walk.

Later she realized that many of those who regularly begged for a living had stayed away. Shaken up, she was hauled to a juvenile detention centre on the outskirts of town and left locked up in a cell overnight. With nothing but a concrete bench to lie on, with no water or food, she endured numerous hours, then became wild. She hit her head against the wall, yelling frantically. Nobody came for her. She must have fallen asleep at one point, since she awoke to the sound of a bell, drenched in sweat. An officer appeared and took her to a dormitory full of girls. Lucia was given a uniform—blue shirt and blue pants, and her street clothes were taken away, to be put in storage, they claimed. She had been smart and had been able to keep her money well hidden, pinned to the inside of her underpants.

Lucia found out that most of the girls were doing time for prostitution and dealing drugs. The girls sat around talking, telling their stories and rating each other on who'd done the worst stuff. Some claimed, that as street kids, they had no alternatives to survive. They went from begging to stealing, to turning tricks—what other choices did they have? They all agreed that exposure to violence and sexual coercion were part of growing up.

When the girls came into detention they were tested to see if they carried any sexually transmitted diseases and were warned that they would have to be clean before being released. They had no lawyers to defend their cases; it was up to a judge to pass sentences. Most of them got off lightly, although if they were found to have inflicted damage to others, harsher sentences would result.

In the second week of her stay at the juvenile jail, the Matron came looking for Lucia to take her for her medical tests. Lucia was told to undress, put on a gown, and wait. When the Matron returned she checked out her clothes and found the pouch with her hidden jewels and cash. "What's this?" she asked. "Don't you know you're not supposed to be carrying your personal things? You've just committed a big violation. This will add more time to your being locked up."

The Matron inspected the earrings and ring. "You little thief," she mumbled.

"You can have them," Lucia said, as she started to tremble, trying not to show how fearful she was. "But please let me keep the money," she managed to blurt out.

The Matron continued to examine the ring and placed it on her finger. "Not bad," she said.

Standing upright, Lucia stopped breathing as she stared into the Matron's eyes. She noticed them softening as she heard an unexpected, "Deal! But you better be good, obey all the rules, and don't get out of hand."

The Matron was letting her go—Lucia couldn't believe her good luck. She bowed her head down and didn't look up; she would do whatever the Matron asked.

She tried to distance herself from the other inmates as she struggled to control her own rage at being locked up. She didn't like being caged, or being expected to act respectfully under the constant watch of the guards. One day Lucia saw one of the inmates get beaten up by a guard. The girl had refused to get in the lineup for lunch. The girl claimed she was sick of the same food every day. The girl who'd been hurt was curled up on the floor in a ball, moaning and rocking herself back and forth

"What's with her?" Lucia asked the girl by her side.

"How should I know?" came the response.

Even though Lucia's anger rose to a full boil as she watched the girl being kicked in the back, she managed to keep to herself, saying nothing, as she'd sworn to herself she'd do, so she would get out of this hellhole faster.

They got two meals a day—potatoes, lentils, and rice—no

change. They ate with spoons, since no sharp objects were allowed. On Sundays, clusters of families carrying plastic bags arrived with food for their loved ones. Some, those who got extra money from home, had food delivered from the outside. Lucia refused to spend her precious cash on some fancy cuisine; she had no friends or family nearby who could bring her stuff. Moreover, she'd need her money on the outside when she was free.

At times, a large, blonde *gringa* came with a Bible and Christian books, saying she was bringing them a human touch. One day the *gringa* came with shampoo, something Lucia hadn't used since leaving Rosa's home. Another time, she came with yarn to teach the girls how to cast. Soon Lucia was knitting and purling and making a blanket to wrap herself up with on chilly nights.

One of the inmates accused Lucia of sucking up to the *gringa* to obtain special favours. "You think you're so clever," the girl said. The moment they were alone, Lucia called her a fucking piece of shit and promised to have somebody smack her face as soon as she was set free.

Three months after she'd been forced inside the lockup, never rebelling against the harsh treatment she received, but rather showing exemplary behaviour, Lucia was told there was a place for her at a shelter. There was an opening at the House of Refuge, where she'd be protected from the street. However, she would have to abide by their rules; she'd have to obey the curfew, and attend school full-time.

12

OTILIA FELT UTTERLY forsaken. Every time she was still, her thoughts went to her husband and child. She kept her pain private and didn't bring it up when she met with Michael to discuss plans for her search. He was slow to give advice, leaving her to decide. Michael chose soothing words full of hope when talking about critical facts, which helped her regain the sense of control that, at times, she felt she was losing. She was aware of the wild accusations hovering about — that she was an accomplice, a subversive, suspected of also having dissident ideas. At the same, she felt such an acute sense of isolation that played havoc on her self-assurance and she no longer had the sharp business acumen she had possessed before. Hadn't she once been assertive and confident? It was time to get back out into the world and investigate some things for herself. Besides, she couldn't keep on borrowing money from Michael when, in the final analysis, the outcome—judging by Roberto's reports—appeared grim. When she next spoke with Michael, she told him she needed to leave for a few days.

Michael listened attentively then gave all possible reasons to discourage her from travelling unaccompanied. "They've increased the roadblocks; soldiers are checking identification at multiple intersections. They'll intimidate you."

"I have to obtain firsthand information," Otilia insisted.

"But why leave your safe haven and expose yourself? Isn't

Roberto uncovering enough information? If he wasn't doing his research, we'd be aware of just a small part of what is going on."

"*Dios Santo*, I must find where they are. I could never have imagined this. How could we have been so unprepared for these events?"

"Nobody will have answers to give you, and even if they know, they will not be truthful. You've heard over and over again that there's little or no official cooperation."

That seemed to be the case. Otilia did have some information and a few photographs of her devastated town, but what if the pictures were taken someplace else? She appreciated that both Michael and Teresa were protecting her from the perils of an exploding world, but she felt a sense of obligation and needed to verify facts herself.

She would go to see don Miguel, her trusted friend, to connect with someone in whom she had full confidence. Don Miguel, one of their customers, travelled the countryside talking to farmers and cattle ranchers. She would be able to get the whole story from him. He'd be able to tell her if indeed things were as turbulent as Michael believed them to be, if in fact villages and their people had ceased to exist. She needed to find fragments of her past life; she couldn't let her history simply evaporate.

Michael walked her to the bus stop on Saturday morning to reassure her that he would be waiting for her upon her return. "I hope things turn out all right. Just be careful, and don't let your guard down."

Otilia smiled. He was reading too much. "Don't worry."

Stepping up to board the bus taking pale-faced miners to town, she found a seat behind the driver. "*Buenos Dias*." Greetings were exchanged.

She had not made herself up. She had arranged her hair in braids, put on a skirt and a shirt, and taken along a wrap in case it was cold or she needed to cover up, to remain concealed.

In no time, the bus driver switched on the engine and they were on the steep road, going downhill. Once again she was struck by the isolation of the camp, a place she was strangely starting to call home. Thick pines appeared on the side of the road and the vegetation turned greener by the time they reached the gorge. An hour later, near the outskirts of town, the bus came to a full stop. Otilia emerged from a deep sleep, shaken up. The miners were whistling and giving the finger, and before Otilia could make out the roadblock ahead, the driver had opened the door and armed soldiers were stepping inside.

"*Documentos*," a soldier said in an arrogant tone as he walked down the aisle to glance at the passengers' identity cards, while two others stood by the door in the front.

Now fully awake, doubts about her journey began to materialize. Increasingly, it seemed, security hung on the printed name in your documents. The soldiers carried a list of last names to check against people's IDs. The inspection was carried out fast, this time without any incident, and once the soldiers descended, the nervous tension the checkup had provoked, dissipated somewhat. Once the bus was on its way, Otilia turned her attention to the men's conversations for distraction. A stocky young man sitting across the aisle, speaking in a nasal singsong, made fun of the young recruits trained to be macho. "What a faggot," he said, gesturing as he ranted about the soldiers' short-cropped hairstyles. "Did you see that tail in the back?"

A few men began bellowing with laughter after one of them told an obscene joke. When Otilia had heard enough profanities, she tuned them out. Turning her head, she leaned against the window and shut her eyes.

Once in Cajamarca, Otilia walked once around the plaza then stepped inside the church. She crossed herself and then slid into a pew. Her tortured soul needed help, and after a few minutes of prayer she felt soothed. Once outside on the street, she squeezed through a crowd of people dressed in costumes and masks, preparing their floats to parade down the street.

She'd forgotten it was February, the festive month between Ash Wednesday and Lent when everyone got ready for Carnival. She'd better leave before the party got started, for the streets would be blocked and she'd risk getting wet from the watery street battles and pranks that would soon ensue. Arming herself with courage, she moved out of the way quickly, anxious to get to the *combi* stop.

In the intense heat of mid-afternoon, the ride in the shared collective van, with its rattling windows that couldn't be opened, was rough. When the *combi* stopped at its destination, in the centre of the village dominated by an imposing church, there was not much else.

She jumped out, exhausted. The back of her blouse was wet and her skirt clung to her legs. Regaining her composure, she took a deep breath and started to walk down the street. The buildings around her, with their decaying balconies, were plastered with political slogans, and very few people were out on the streets. A young boy selling Chiclets approached her and a cloud swept over her eyes. Forcing herself to meet his gaze she smiled. He must have been Salvador's age. Crying inside, she reached for a coin in her purse to buy a pack of gum.

Don Miguel's house sat on the southern edge of town, surrounded by a dense hedge. She walked up to the house and knocked on the door. She hadn't seen him for a while, and as she waited, her anxiety surged. Otilia blinked with surprise when don Miguel came to the door. His appearance had changed. His physical deterioration was apparent; he'd lost weight, and his face was grey and tense.

"How good to see you," the middle aged man said, raising his arms and embracing her hard. The rough stubble on is face scratched her cheek.

He led her inside and gave her a seat at a table next to a window with its curtains drawn. Wasting no time, Otilia explained the reason for her unexpected call. "I have to find out what happened," Otilia said.

"I heard about the attack on El Milagro," don Miguel said. "What do you know?"

"Rumours have been circulating about who was involved. Nobody's sure."

"What are you saying?" she asked. "Nobody knows who was responsible?"

"Have you spoken to any of the folks?"

"I've not travelled that far." It seemed Don Miguel was at a loss for words.

"Have there been no complains?" she persisted.

"Communities have been silent."

"Ignoring the issues won't solve them."

"Don't kid yourself, this has become a police state. Nobody wants others putting their noses in business that doesn't concern them. It's a tragedy," he said.

Don Miguel rose from his chair and went to get two glasses and a bottle of *chicha*. He seemed uncomfortable, and gulped his liquor back.

"Please, don Miguel, I can't sleep at night. I beg you, tell me whatever you know," she said, putting her glass aside.

"We've worked hard all of our lives, in vain. Many of us have lost a great deal of our income."

"Who is behind the violence?"

"I don't know where this organized violence is coming from, or what they are after. The police are getting contradictory reports, but when they don't know which side the town folks are on, whether they're aiding or are against the guerillas, they are giving up, withdrawing, and letting neighbours work out their problems for themselves. As soon as the police vanish, groups are mobilized to guard their towns. The funny thing is that they too have arms. It's hard to know where the weapons are coming from."

"Does the military believe that some villagers sympathize with the Shining Path?"

"In effect some do."

Otilia fell into silence.

"I hear that in one town, police entered a home to rummage through, pulling out stuff from storage spaces, making a mess as they looked for proof, and when they couldn't find any evidence that the owners were members of a political group, they beat up the man and his wife."

Otilia was stunned.

"Nobody trusts anyone. Nobody's opening their mouth and you better watch out—don't go saying much. Matters remain unresolved and then they are dropped; nothing's ever solved."

Otilia was shocked. She couldn't understand what was going on. With everybody putting on blinders, silently enduring and ignoring the issues, how would she ever find her family?

"So much damage, such a waste. Some people have written letters petitioning the government to put a stop to the harassment. They've gone unheard. I've had a hard time making a living." Don Miguel's face darkened and she saw that he was unable to conceal his deep anger.

With a mournful expression on her face, Otilia just shook her head.

"It's pure chaos. Around here, we've not heard from Manuel," he said. He lowered his eyes, avoiding her gaze. "I'm ashamed. I haven't had the guts to ask any hard questions."

Don Miguel reached for a cigarette and continued to talk while it hung out of his mouth. "You must understand that the security apparatus is intimidating. They are doing their best to scare folks away. It's as if a veil has been placed in front of our eyes; we've become paralyzed, and we don't even have enough courage to track down our loved ones."

"Is everybody holding back? Is nobody willing to put their foot down and demand what's right?" Otilia asked.

"I spoke to a man whose fingers were crushed when he was arrested after he told them he had no idea what he was being accused of. They didn't believe him and said he was a security risk. They kept him locked up for months."

Suddenly, she felt an aching nostalgia for her old way of life; she wanted to cry.

"Folks disappear and nobody asks where they've gone. It's become the accepted way. We're not challenging the abuse because we've become terrified."

How could there be so much conflict, so many broken people?

Don Miguel's wife, Juana, insisted she stay the night. Otilia was exhausted but she wanted to head back. "Stay," Juana urged, "and rest. Gather your strength. You can leave tomorrow first thing—there's a bus to Cajamarca at six."

Juana offered her dinner and while don Miguel savoured his wife's cooking, Otilia barely tasted it. She was shown to a small room with a cot, and Juana placed a candle on the night table. "For the past few nights we haven't had lights."

When she lay down in the sombre stillness, Otilia felt helpless and spent. All she had left was to pray to *El Señor* for his everlasting love and his help.

"Get away, that's my best advice," don Miguel said before she departed the following day.

"What do you mean?" she asked.

"Go south, don't stay around here."

She was alarmed; perhaps, he was right. Expressing her gratitude for their kindness, she ran to catch the *combi* back.

Otilia returned to the mining camp the following evening as her roommates gathered around a long table to watch Santa read tarot cards. The small space near the entrance was just big enough for a gathering space for the women to unwind in their sparse free time. The old pieces of furniture had been brought from other locations, one at a time, when the women decided they needed a recreation space. As Otilia bent over to untie her shoelaces and remove her shoes, the room erupted in laughter. Agustina called out her name and waved her hand, motioning her to join them. Shifting her weight, but remaining precariously balanced, Otilia glanced up to give a quick smile and gingerly retreated down the hall to her room. She shied away from socializing with the girls. She was not keen on being dragged into their world, especially not on a day like today.

"Be sure to come back; I'm having my cards read," Agustina yelled.

When, moments later, Agustina walked into her room, insisting she come mingle with the others, Otilia tried to explain how tired she was. But Agustina didn't give up and, in her soft-spoken manner, talked her into sharing the company of others. Finally, Otilia hesitatingly accepted her extended arm. Otilia knew that her roommates were good women, working long hours to make the best of things and survive.

"Good God," Carla said as Otilia took a place at the table.

Santa, revealing one of the tarot cards, was concocting a story to help feed Carla's imagination about the romantic adventure she was about to have. At that moment the open-mouthed girl began to laugh and roll her eyes.

The women loved to ask Santa to read them their horoscopes and the palms of their hands. Santa, eager to demonstrate her psychic abilities, didn't have to be begged. In her phlegmy voice, she took pleasure in telling vague stories, allowing the listeners to fill in their blanks, letting them make their own connections between her soothsaying and their lives. The younger girls would screech when they heard a good omen or shed a tear when they heard something bad.

When Santa interpreted the tarot cards, she would begin by speaking cautiously and proceed in a real rush. Otilia didn't really care to have her fortune read, for she was not superstitious and did not believe in clairvoyance. But Santa insisted the cards were not something magical—they were just a guide that helped people navigate their lives. There were positive signs and also signs to help one avoid making mistakes.

The option of having her cards read filled Otilia with dread. She didn't need to rehash past events. She felt mortified to think she would be airing the events of her life to this group of girls. Perhaps she should try getting back to her room. Spotting a magazine on the table, she attempted to stand and get it, but Carla pushed her down. "Stay. Aren't you intrigued?"

"Would you like to go next?" Agustina asked.

Next thing she knew, Otilia was staring at Santa's chubby fingers shuffling the deck. "You shuffle once," Santa said. "We must transfer your energy onto the deck. Now place ten cards in a spread and concentrate on the area where you're seeking help." Otilia did as she was told and Santa studied each suit with outmost attention. "You're experiencing life-changing events," Santa said.

"How do you know?" Otilia blurted, incredulous.

"This card shows you are facing adversity. That one is telling me you are fighting opposing forces."

"You can tell all of this from looking at a bunch of foolish cards?" Otilia looked down at a picture of a tall tower pitched atop a rocky mountain where lightning struck and flames burst from windows as people tried to escape.

"It's a time of great turmoil for you. You're facing insurmountable hurdles. Out of the blue something shocking has happened and you've been left broken-hearted. I suggest you pay close attention to your own safety in your quest."

This was a startling claim. Otilia felt suffocated and couldn't utter a word.

"Right now you are shaken up by a lack of security, but not to worry," Santa went on, taking hold of Otilia's hand. "With destruction comes creation. You see this lightning bolt? It represents a glimpse of truth. Your security lies within you, you're a strong person; you'll find peace of mind. Give it time."

Otilia rose slowly and rushed back to her room. She went to get the envelope where she stored her photographs. She touched her husband's face, then her child's, and felt cleansed of her sadness for a little while. She felt a greater sense of confidence unleashing inside. An all-out force of *basta*, enough, to all of the injustices, invaded her mind. For the first time, she was willing to consider Michael's suggestion to go back with him to the United States. He'd mentioned it to her several times, but until now it seemed out of the question. She'd resisted contemplating such a move, but suddenly, somehow, it was beginning to make sense. There was nothing for her in the camp and she couldn't continue living this sorrowful life. She'd lost all that mattered; she'd best break away from this hell and start over again.

She approached Michael warily the next day, with much apprehension, but she couldn't wait any longer and blurted out, "I'm ready to think about the trip to California you've been talking about."

Michael gave her a wide smile. "Think positively. I promise we'll get to the bottom of this from abroad. It might even be advantageous."

"From far away?"

"From there we can fight with words. Here you don't have a voice. You can't act on it appropriately, you don't know if they will hear you or detain you."

Feeling the restless desire to continue searching for her husband and child, she was perplexed. She looked up at Michael and her confusion must have been written on her face. "Don't torture yourself, our congressmen will help," Michael said.

It seemed ludicrous to think that a foreign politician would take an interest in what was happening in her country, but she wouldn't argue with Michael at this time. Even though she couldn't bear to leave Peru without her family, she thought it best to give it a try—she could always come back.

"We'll set up a campaign and reach every senator and congressman in the House."

What did she know? She had no understanding about how his country worked.

13

OTILIA AND MICHAEL arrived at his sister's home on a balmy late afternoon in the middle of May. Joan greeted her brother with an affectionate hug then drew back to inspect the foreigner at his side. When Otilia stepped up to plant a kiss on Joan's cheek, Joan abruptly drew back. She seemed surprised, unsettled to have a stranger so close. Joan wrinkled her cheeks with a smile and stretched out her hand. "Did you have a good trip?" Joan's sharp aquiline nose broadened when she asked.

"Sorry it was short notice," Michael said. "The visa got approved faster than I expected and we left right away."

Otilia nodded, feeling strangely distanced from her surroundings. The six weeks that it had taken to make arrangements to leave Peru had left her with little time to reflect on the twist her life would take.

Joan leaned her back against the wall while Michael explained. Otilia stood mute at Michael's side, gazing at Joan's baggy pants then at the chipped nail polish on her toes peeking through her Birkenstocks.

"Come in," Joan said, turning sideways to let them through. Michael placed his hand on Otilia's shoulder and guided her in. As they passed an open nook, she noticed piles of boxes jammed with stuff. "Are you still going to garage sales, accumulating junk?" Michael asked.

"I'm still into my crafts—never know when some may come in handy."

At the end of the hallway stood a spacious open kitchen with an island and a hanging wooden pot rack. "This is magnificent," Otilia remarked as she automatically reached out to touch one of the copper pans.

"What in the world are you doing?" Joan demanded.

"Hush, Joan, this is all very new to her, understand?"

"You mean to tell me a Peruvian hasn't seen copper pots?"

"Only in the museums," he said.

An extended oak table cluttered with dishes was shoved against the wall. Joan cleared the dirty plates to one side, then opened the refrigerator to get a large bottle of Coke. "Anyone thirsty?" She fetched glasses.

"I would rather have a cup of coffee if that's not too much to ask," Michael said.

"Otilia will have some Coke," Michael said, once he'd asked her in Spanish what she would like.

Otilia looked at a loaf of brown bread spilling out from a plastic bag onto the counter next to an open container of margarine. She couldn't imagine having all this space and not keeping it tidy.

"*Gracias*," she muttered when Joan offered her a glass.

Michael took off his jacket and slung it over the chair before he sat down. Even though Otilia couldn't understand their conversation, she sensed tension mounting between them. She felt Joan's anger flaring up, as her shrill intonation rose up a notch with each passing sentence. Otilia watched as Joan stood with both arms on her waist, shaking her head, and saying, "A maximum of three months."

Otilia assumed the troubles were because Michael pushed through his plan without consulting his sister ahead of time. Joan probably resented that he was asking her to take care of Otilia for a period of time. For a moment, Otilia didn't know how to react. She was gripped by an irrational dread though she knew panic wasn't a good road map. She'd have to wait to see how things developed before she would decide if she should stay or not. In Michael's presence she felt safe, but she couldn't imagine how she would carry on without his help. He'd be leaving shortly, going back to Peru to finish his job.

When Joan showed her upstairs to a spare bedroom, she made no attempt to tidy it up. The bed was weighed down with pillows and clothes, and books were stacked high on the night table next to the bed. Otilia's suitcase, which Michael had carried up, lay on the floor next to a wooden armoire.

"Come," Joan said taking her by the hand down the hall to the bathroom.

Joan flushed the toilet twice and opened and closed both taps in the sink and the bathtub. Otilia took no offense but was taken aback. Did Joan think she'd never seen plumbing in her life? Otilia nodded and said, "*Gracias, entiendo.*" Then Joan left her to fend for herself.

Michael had informed Otilia that she would be welcome at Joan's in exchange for some housecleaning and meal preparation, so the following morning she got an early start. She went down to the kitchen to clean up, and when Joan walked in Otilia was bagging the trash and motioned to be shown where it should be dumped.

The days after Michael's departure were hard. Michael had been kind and given her lots of advice; he was soft-spoken, while Joan was gruff. Otilia felt unwelcome, unprotected, and she was bursting with doubt. It was especially hard since Joan made it clear that she wasn't interested in what was going on *allá*—Peru, over there, was too far removed from the realities of Joan's life. The night before Michael left, they'd had a conversation and Michael had translated his sister's sentiments diplomatically. "She has her own career and her health to worry about; it takes effort and time at her age to carry on with her active life, so she won't have much time for you."

Otilia had terrible misgivings about having accepted Michael's advice to come stay with his sister, but she had no contingency plans. She told herself she'd have to deal with her tumultuous state of mind for a while. Manuel, where was he now, her unfaltering partner, the one who gave her *consejos*, good advice? He'd always made good decisions in difficult circumstances—what had gone wrong this time? He was no slouch, her Manuel; he was bold, and when there was trouble he would cut to the core. She needed him now, to get them out of this mess they were in. But look where she was—far away and desolate. At least, if she'd remained in Peru ... at least she'd be among her own kind. In good times, people were kind and polite, willing to go out on a limb to lend a helping hand. But Joan, she sure wasn't *acogedora,* hospitable—in fact, on the contrary, she was angry at having to accommodate a stranger in her home. Otilia was sure Joan had tried to dissuade her brother from leaving her there for too long; only after Michael tried to convince her that he'd brought Otilia for her sake, to help her, for she wasn't managing too well with her health, did Joan accept her as a *muchacha*, a maid.

For the next month Otilia found herself in a constant state of exhaustion as she tried to figure out how to deal with everyday life. Alone in the house doing chores during the day, and trying to please Joan when she returned home after work, was no easy task. She struggled to do simple things, but the kinds of things that would have seemed simple back in her country were complicated here. For starters, Joan had far too many appliances and fancy utensils to figure out—more of an inconvenience than an aid. Why peel and core an apple with a gadget when a knife would do just fine? And the heavy vacuum cleaner with so many additional attachments she needed to carry up and down was killing her back. Today she had dealt with the loose knob on the washing machine and couldn't figure out if it needed to be rotated or pushed in or out. In the end she had done the laundry by hand and hung it out to dry.

She had no one to talk to all day, and even when she opened the door to step out into the streets, they were deserted, with not a soul in sight. There was a yard in the back of the house where the neighbour's lemons hung low, but she'd seen nobody come out to pick them.

Whenever she went for a walk around the neighbourhood, Otilia made mental notes of the shapes of the houses at the corner, to remind her where to turn when retracing her steps. She had asked Joan for a map, but Joan hadn't given her one yet. She practiced her English by reading the names of the cross streets—Barton, Sheldon, Nelson—but found that many had Spanish names, making them less difficult to forget. After a few weeks, the neighbourhood became more familiar, but the loneliness remained. When she heard the fast conversations people carried on at the grocery store, she resolved to learn English as quickly as possible. But it wasn't just the language barrier that kept her isolated, for even when she visited the Latino market and heard people speaking in Spanish, she was shy talking to strangers in this unknown land.

One afternoon, as she was walking back from the grocery store, feeling low, consoling herself with thoughts that triggered a torrent of longings for her past, she went by a house where a small barking terrier followed her, running along the side of the fence. He's the only one who has noticed me all day, she thought.

Once back in Joan's house, she went looking for the Bible Teresa had given her before departing the mining camp. "I hope you find comfort in these verses when you're so far away," Teresa had said. Otilia felt she needed to ask Christ to guide her along this new path; she could use nourishment for her nerves.

One evening, by the time Joan hobbled into the kitchen, pushing a walker, Otilia had set the table and was grilling a steak.

"*Que es eso*?" Otilia said.

"A walker, walk-er, to give me support." Joan spoke loudly and slowly so Otilia could comprehend.

"*Doctor dice necisito*," Joan explained, gesturing with her hands.

They both were developing somewhat of a vocabulary in each other's tongue. Every day, with the help of a bilingual dictionary, Otilia scribbled lists of words and terms she wanted to memorize. The audio books she'd checked out from the library were also helping her to communicate.

At dinner Joan balked when Otilia brought up the issue that preoccupied her. "Want speak to some about my child," Otilia said.

Joan didn't want to hear Otilia explain with gestures and simple words what she was up against. "Be patient, wait," was all she said.

As usual, Joan changed the subject and Otilia felt her anxiety heightening. She was increasingly demoralized by the day. Before Michael had returned to Peru, he had helped her get in contact with local organizations involved in human rights, but she was yet to receive any calls back.

"Michael, telephone?" Otilia asked, as she put her fork and knife to one side.

"What about?" Joan asked.

"*Disculpe*, I don't want you trouble," Otilia said and excused herself.

Bent over the sink as she washed the dishes, Otilia made an effort not to show her disappointment. How could Joan be so callous? She was sure Joan thought she'd made up a story of losing her husband and son to gain a foothold in the United States. Joan didn't seem to understand that Michael had helped her after he'd determined Otilia should flee her country to get out of harm's way. Joan didn't know that she'd been a businesswoman, buying and selling cattle, alongside her husband. Joan didn't know she carried deep scars caused by an ugly unexpected tragedy and that her present means of survival were limited by those unusual circumstances. If Joan couldn't understand the climate of fear, how without warning a violent incident had caused her husband to be ensnared, never to be seen again, so be it. She'd come to America, a disturbing unknown, in desperation, and she had the right to find out what was going on back home.

It had been Michael who had taken her to Lima to secure a passport and help her navigate the long lineups and endless paperwork. Getting her a visa in a frenzy had saved her "in the nick of time" from something worse. Michael had never once hesitated in his efforts to help her, but she'd left the country with a gnawing sensation of doubt, unconvinced that it was in her family's best interest for her not to stick around. Now, in her moments of weakness, she found herself having to fight her internal monologues, which seemed to confirm the futility of her struggle. As she dried the last pot, her mind took her to places she'd rather not go. *I have to be brave, face the irrational fears straight on. I will go down to the church on Sunday, talk to the priest and see if he can point me toward the right organization. Manuel and Salvador shall not remain in oblivion.*

On Thursday, after folding the clothes she'd removed from the dryer, Otilia began to pull together the miniature shoes Joan collected. She'd been instructed to gather them from the curio cabinet, the shelves, and from some boxes not yet unpacked. Joan wanted to know how many she had. "They have monetary and sentimental value," Joan said, "so please handle them carefully."

Otilia found dozens of tiny replicas, some in the form of vases, others used as toothpick holders, and a few salt and pepper shakers made from glass, but she didn't come across the red shoe collection, a special edition in support of heart disease prevention, that Joan had asked her about specifically. Joan wanted to take them to a function she was attending the following week. Among them was Michael's recent gift: a tiny pair of silver ankle boots with intricate filigree designs. If she were a fairy godmother, she could take her magic wand and turn every one into real shoes for the boys and girls who still went barefoot back in her homeland.

"*Buenas tardes*," Otilia called out to Joan, when she heard the front door open later that afternoon.

Joan went to sit, stretching out her legs onto the ottoman, easing her back against the couch.

"*Venga*, come see," Otilia said, running to her side before Joan made herself too comfortable and wouldn't want to stand up again.

Reaching her arm to help her up, Otilia said, "All clean."

"Wait, I'm tired, I've had a long day; what are you talking about?"

"*Sorpresa*."

"Surprise?" With great effort Joan rose. "What surprise?" she asked, shuffling her legs down the hall.

"Good Lord, look how many pairs of shoes you found! Lovely," she said, picking up Michael's gift. "No doubt about it, my brother is a kind and considerate man."

That evening, before Joan sat down to play solitaire, after the dishes were done, they had their first real conversation.

"We're very different," Joan said, comparing herself to her brother. "He's very caring, and I love him for that, but he can't save the world and he hasn't yet learned that he needs to care for himself first."

"Me, *su casa*, a mistake?" Otilia asked, wishing she could be more articulate.

"He's out to help everyone. He's done it again, one more foolish quest. I would have thought that he would have learned some lessons at his age. I won't be able to support him when he's old and bankrupt."

Joan agreed to drive Otilia to St. Augustine church on Sunday, and before Otilia got out of the car, Joan showed her where she would have to catch the bus back. There had been a phone call from Father Francisco, a member of the sanctuary movement, informing Otilia that a few people were meeting after services and she would be most welcome to join them.

The meeting was held in a room adjacent to the main sanctuary where women and men of all ages, looking sombre, waited. Nobody was engaging in conversation until the priest arrived. Father Francisco, an outgoing Latin American in his fifties, with short-cropped grey hair, offered her a warm handshake, then introduced her to the others in the room.

"The *señora* is from Peru," Father Francisco explained. "We have a little United Nations here—Mister Ramirez is from Guatemala, Sra. Venegas from Honduras, Argelio from Argentina," he explained as they each nodded. "Why don't we take a minute to go around the room to tell Otilia why you've joined the group?"

The man from Guatemala spoke first. "I work fifteen hours a day trying to raise enough money to get my wife and kids to come. I've started buying lottery tickets to get them here fast. The war has taken my brothers and I'm scared for their lives. Not a moment goes by that I don't worry, they matter so much to me…," he said. He couldn't get many more words out before he choked up with emotion. The next person, the Argentinean, became agitated when he shared that he still had no word about his sister, although it'd been months since he'd contacted America's Watch.

Father Francisco encouraged all the participants to voice their concerns, and Otilia realized that they all had experienced similar upsets. Some folks sat stone-faced, struggling with their memories, while others were more outgoing and confident as they spoke. A young man bared his soul, talking about how he was rounded up by the military in El Salvador. "I'm prepared to forgive," were his last words.

When it was Otilia's turn, all eyes were on her. She wasn't

sure how much to reveal despite the repeated reassurances that the information shared would be kept strictly confidential. Though she was guarded as she spoke, members of the group nodded when she told her story and tears came quickly to her eyes. When she was finished, she felt satisfied. Father Francisco encouraged everyone to write down a telephone number where they could be contacted, so they could be in touch. Moments later, he invited them to stay for refreshments and get acquainted with one another.

"We're all in the same boat, *señora*," Osvaldo said. "We've been forced into exile; we have lots to discuss."

Otilia was grateful to have found these folks.

14

OTILIA STARTED attending an adult English class in the fall, two evenings a week, at the high school near Joan's home. She had to drag herself to the first couple of sessions and the queasy feeling in her stomach before class made eating dinner beforehand impossible. To her relief, these feelings soon subsided thanks to her teacher, an enthusiastic young woman who had the class reading and talking in no time. With pictures and gestures, she made her students take chances communicating, repeating rhythmic intonations and staccato refrains. Ms. Albert suggested her students watch sitcoms, as the more they got used to the language, the more at ease they'd be. To enlarge her vocabulary, Otilia memorized lists of words and started listening to news.

In class, they also learned about American customs and how to fit into this new and different world. One day, during the course of a lesson, when they were talking about the stress of living in a new country, Ms. Albert said, "Most of you, I'm sure, make a great deal of adjustments, and at times feel overwhelmed by the different customs you encounter. Can anyone share some experiences you've had?"

One hand went up. "It's hard sometimes. I feel so confused by what people want."

"Tell us what puzzles you most?" Ms. Albert asked.

"People appear open, friendly, but they're not. Friendships

are not the same as in my country."

"I can't figure it out. Nobody invites us to come over, no time," another student agreed. "People too busy working all the time."

"Back home, if no room in house, we meet in the park."

"Perhaps we are too eager to connect with Americans," an older woman said.

One student complained that Americans were too direct. "They ask lots of questions and say what they think, even if they don't know you very well."

"Directness is honesty," Ms. Albert explained. "Americans don't mask their emotional responses—they are frank. This can appear rude, but they don't really mean to be disrespectful—they like to exchange points of view."

"We—how do you say?—don't rock the boat," the woman sitting next to Otilia said.

"Yes, in many cultures people try to say the right thing to please others," the teacher explained.

"I have many problems with my children," a woman sitting next to her husband said. "Once we got here, our kids, who had liked school back in Mexico, began saying they didn't have *ganas* to study."

"Really, what a relief to hear you say so. I find that with my son," a father added.

"They are caught between how we expect them to be and their own struggles adjusting," the boy's mother said.

"Are your children not having fun?" Ms. Albert asked.

"They shouldn't have fun, they should learn," a voice from the back of the room said.

"Are they learning English?" Ms. Albert asked

"Yes, it's not language, the *problema*."

"What then?"

"I'm not sure. They're called names."

"What do you mean? Are they being bullied?" Ms. Albert wanted to know.

"Miss, I think the colour of skin is for them confusion," a mom from Honduras said. "They get into fights, more than back home."

"They feel alone. Here, *uno no es nadie*, we nobody."

"Back home, there is always somebody's shoulder to cry on," a mother affirmed.

"A family here is not family. No grandmas, no aunts. At home, there's always someone."

"We had to send our teenagers back to the Philippines. We wanted them to learn manners; here they were getting out of hand. There, their grandparents will not spare the rod."

"Teenagers, bad. *Todo lo ve feo*, everything ugly to them."

"Coming to grips with discrimination is more damaging to children than adults. Children feel that they are different and they suffer for it. It is important that you make sure you maintain the strength of your family," Ms. Albert said. "You must advocate for your kids in your new country. You must talk to your sons' and daughters' teachers, develop partnerships, show them how special they are."

"Too much freedom—unsafe, dangerous," another father said, raising his eyebrows. "At night we hear shootings, sirens, helicopters over house. Criminals run through our backyard. Can't move, not yet."

"My son's school, cameras in hallways, police patrol, kids and teachers talk tough, feels like a jail not a school. I came from Iraq. I know what it's like to be observed day and night."

"In America kids are given a lot of freedom. Parents and teachers offer choices because we want young people to be creative, explore with their senses, be individuals, independent; therefore we put few restrictions," Ms. Albert explained.

"I teach important to study, don't allow much to go out, she not like that. Me no good student, not much school, I'm sorry for that," a woman from Morocco said.

"It doesn't really matter what they want; you go to your son's class, let him see you at school," a woman from Mexico ventured to say. "My mom always said, there are good, bad, but not *mediocre* people who make it. We must work hard."

Otilia found the discussion interesting. Ms. Albert believed that parents had a choice in how they approached their family's acculturation. They could be selective in deciding what elements of their culture they wished to surrender and which they wanted to incorporate. "Years back, immigrants relegated their past to history, but nowadays people want to retain their cultural identity," she said.

Otilia closed her eyes. She thought how different her life would have been had they immigrated as a family. They would be sharing experiences together. But she had done without them for so long, with time and space separating them further; it was too devastating to contemplate. She rose and got ready to leave as soon as she noticed that the other students were already tucking their books away in their bags.

The meetings Otilia attended on Sundays after church became a focal point of her week, for it was here that she met others in similar predicaments. At these meetings, she felt safe and appreciated, for everyone there understood what it felt like to go through separation and loss, experiencing a sense of emptiness. *Aquí*—here—they were all in the same boat with no *esperanza*—little hope of news from home. They'd come from different countries, but they were all Latinos and Latinas trying to figure out how to proceed with their lives. With their help, Otilia was learning to embrace the transitional state she found herself in. They missed their *familia* greatly and gave each other support, finding the strength they needed to journey forth.

"Good morning again," Father Francisco said when he walked into the room. "Today I have some good news to report. We've been asked to speak to the congregation at the Cathedral downtown. I ask that some of you come forward to share your significant stories, so others can learn what you are going through."

Father Francisco was intent on bringing every one of his parishioners' stories to light and encouraged the members to form working groups in their efforts to inform people what the South and Central American nations were up against. "Angelica, will you volunteer this time?"

"*Hay padrecito*, I can't go in front of a group of strangers—I'm too shy."

"I will," Geraldo said.

"Thank you. Just remember that *Dios nos creo a todos iguales*, God created us all equal. Nobody is entitled to take life away; we must fight for its sanctity. You must express yourselves."

Father Francisco enlisted five members of the group, including Otilia, to give a presentation. He wanted representatives from different countries, so that people in the audience could realize the scope of the violence taking place. Otilia was glad that by doing her part, she could make a small contribution.

Mist had begun to lift when the five speakers got to the city of San Francisco that afternoon. Otilia tightened her sweater around her chest then crossed her arms to protect against the blowing wind. She stepped inside the cathedral with mild trepidation, noticing how many people had gathering. The five speakers were ushered down the aisles to chairs arranged at the front facing the audience. Waiting nervously for the program to start, she assured herself she'd be all right. She looked at the paintings on the wall and a sudden image of Salvador gave her courage to speak. Why should her child have to make his way in the world without his mother at his side?

Her opening sentence was stated with strength. "My family is gone," she said, then went on to explain the dreadful things that were happening where she was from.

The following Sunday, Father Francisco informed the group that he had received positive comments from people who'd attended the talk. "Some people are offering donations; others want to get involved and volunteer for your cause. I received a moving letter that I'd like to share with you. The letter came from a lady who lost her only son while living in a town in northern Chile. She writes: *I feel the pain in your experience, since my sixteen-year-old was apprehended one morning from our home. The boy was still sleeping when soldiers pulled him out of bed. They hit him hard on the back with a rifle butt, so he lost balance and fell. He was dragged out while I pleaded with the soldiers for leniency. They say our eyes dry up from so much crying, but I'm still shedding tears every night, for I still haven't heard from him. Please allow me to join your efforts in spreading the word to the good citizens of the United States. You are doing a noteworthy job. Thank you.*

Today they would engage in a letter-writing campaign. The plan was to address hundreds of envelopes and stuff them with letters to elected officials in Washington and the fifty states, advising them how their families were being affected by violations of their human rights.

"I have a few more addresses to add to our roster," Tina said, pulling pieces of paper from her handbag. They had been given the job of collecting the addresses and names of ambassadors and heads of international organizations for a register.

Together they worked steadily. Together they felt energized. At one point in the afternoon, Otilia rose and went to get coffee for each one who was working hard. By seven o'clock nobody had noticed how late it was getting, nor did they seem ready to stop, although some had started complaining that their fingers were getting numb.

At their next meeting, as they were wrapping up, Father Francisco was somewhat disturbed. He shared that he'd received a phone call from a man identifying himself only as a vigilante. "He said he was keeping an eye on the communist dissenters the priest was out to help. He added that he didn't want people like us in his country, with our anecdotes masking the real evidence. That was the message."

"Oh my," Osvaldo said.

"Nobody will silence us; we're not afraid of extremist like him," Elena said.

"You shouldn't be intimidated," Father Francisco warned the group, "but tread carefully from now on."

The incident worried Otilia. Michael had asked Otilia to retain a lawyer to help her with her immigration papers before her visitor's visa expired, and the lawyer had recommended that she should be mindful of her activities and associations. Since she was considering applying for refugee status, she would need to show she had never been in trouble with the law.

In the twelve months that followed, as Otilia tried making a life for herself, she continued to fight off the different emotions clogging her brain. She was always on the lookout for news about her country that was in the midst of heightened difficult times. The news, however, didn't provide her with anything conclusive. At times she was utterly confused as she tried to figure out her standpoint. One thing was clear, her wound incessantly festered and there were days when she found herself fuming about the injustices she faced. She had abandoned her son. An abomination—how could she have betrayed him this way? He was her treasure, her only one. At times she resented her husband for causing their separation, especially when a certain cynicism rose from deep in her gut. She knew men liked to chase after other women. Was it possible that Manuel had run away?

But a few minutes later, she felt remorse, ashamed of herself for having such thoughts, and she put the blame solely on her government. They were at fault for not providing their people with protection and not sending a warning as danger arose. In her eyes, the Peruvian government stood accused of gross negligence. It was then that she felt a desire for revenge emerge from her heart, and she wanted to go straight to the Peruvian consulate to shoot the one in charge. Had they no mercy, those bastards—how dare they not answer her multiple requests for an investigation?

15

SALVADOR AND TOMAS moved into their own apartment in a rundown building on a noisy street, where the neighbours were impolite and behaved carelessly. While Salvador always ran up the three flights of stairs in the cigarette-butt littered open air stairwell, trying to avoid the smell of urine, Tomas climbed slowly, out of breath, and at times complaining of pain in his chest. They lived modestly, but Salvador never felt deprived of anything. They had two bedrooms and a small kitchen with a refrigerator and a hot plate. Salvador's bedroom was in the back, overlooking the wall of a taller building on the side. There wasn't much natural light and Tomas had suggested they paint the apartment walls white. The desk next to his bed was where he did his homework every night.

On the afternoon of Salvador's twelfth birthday, September 24, 1992, Tomas brought home a cake for Salvador to enjoy with two school friends. For a few moments Tomas stayed to chat with the boys, then went to his room to listen to the news. Soon he came back out, a big smile on his face. "They captured Guzman while hiding out, of all places, in a ballet studio," he practically yelled.

The leader of the Shining Path guerilla movement was wanted on charges of terror and treason. The president, Alberto Fujimori, the first son of Japanese immigrants, who had overwhelmingly won the elections two years before with promises to put an end to the violence overtaking the country, had carried it off.

"Boys, come see what has taken place. It's an incredible feat, a real accomplishment. I knew *el chino* would manage it."

The boys saw pictures on the television set of the captured rebel leader, wearing stripes, placed in a specially built cage, shouting obscenities.

"Finally someone caught the ass," Aldo said.

"Can I call my mother?" Gabriel asked, and Salvador showed him to the telephone that hung on the kitchen wall.

"When did you get a phone?" Aldo asked.

"A couple of weeks ago. You should ask your dad to get one so we can talk about our homework and the soccer games," Salvador said.

The one state-owned phone company, with its tremendously long wait times, had been privatized, and the government was allowing private companies to enter the market in droves, setting off an upturn in the economy.

That night Salvador went to bed thinking that since the insurgency was under control they would be living in less uncertain times. Their new president would make sure that he could start looking for his mom and dad very soon.

Salvador's teenage years were marked by periods of storm and stress. The country, now ruled by a *dictablanda*—a soft dictator—became even more chaotic after Alberto Fujimori enacted severe economic reforms, referred to as Fujishock. Billions of dollars were raised through the privatization of state-owned enterprises, but only a small portion would benefit the people. Most of the poor were in agony, as food, gasoline, electricity, and water prices kept rising, and still no provisions were made to investigate the hundreds of people who had vanished or were dead. When a declaration of amnesty for members of the Peruvian military and police accused or convicted of human rights abuses was set into place, Salvador became irritable. Tomas claimed the president's actions were justified to eliminate the insurgent threat, and Salvador stopped talking to him.

As Salvador thought of his parents and realized that the details of his early childhood years were quickly fading away, he became hopelessly depressed. He was constantly making great efforts to recollect the past, realizing how fragmented the memories were. Nevertheless he didn't give up, for in some dark corners of his mind he wanted to remember. Throughout this time he began to experience more of the same nightmares he'd had as a young child, of snakes climbing over his face, going for his throat. He'd wake up feeling he was suffocating, gasping for air, his body aching. It was then that he started to experience thoughts of vengeance for being abandoned, sensing that one of his duties was to uncover his parents' deaths. At times, when he felt strong, he would tell himself it was time to move on, add a new story to his life, lay aside his illusions, and work on growing up. But even though he tried to rid himself of his angst, he couldn't help feeling that his past had evaporated and he still had no recourse for getting information about his mom and dad.

Salvador continued to think that with the leader of the Shining Path behind bars, the guerilla movement was weakened, and it would be gone in no time. But every time he brought up the subject to Tomas, begging him to take him to Cajamarca, and to the town where he was born, his uncle was in agreement that security forces had unleashed an effective counterinsurgency campaign to crush the guerillas responsible for seizing control of large parts of the country, but he still wasn't convinced that leaving the capital city was smart.

Salvador wouldn't take no for an answer and when the newspapers claimed that travelling around the country was once again safe, and ads began to appear calling visitors to return to well-known tourist destinations, Salvador began to pester his uncle again, asking Tomas to consider the trip he hoped they could take. But Tomas wasn't in favour of travelling yet.

"It's too soon; if they want to come after us they will."

"They have no reason to come against us."

"Everyone is out to settle their scores."

Finally, the summer before Salvador was to go into the tenth grade, Tomas agreed to take him to El Milagro. They packed a bag and left the city of Lima early one morning in March, in the old cab. Salvador couldn't remember when he'd last ventured so far out of town. He felt disoriented yet energized, with vague memories of El Milagro turning in his mind. Getting out of the city was slow, with traffic building up. Tomas had to put on the breaks of the car at several intersections, to skirt the vendors gathering on the side of the road, and hand out a few small coins to children performing acrobatics at the red light stops. When they reached the highway that took them north along the arid coast, Tomas pressed on the gas. In Pacasmayo, Tomas climbed into the heart of the Andes Mountains and began to give Salvador a history lesson.

"Cajamarca is a city of many stories," he said. "That's where in 1532 the Spanish conquistador Francisco Pizarro captured the Inca Atahualpa, the Emperor of Peru. He was put on trial and accused of plotting against the Spanish invaders, which was a lie. He asked for his freedom in exchange for a room full of gold. He kept his side of the bargain, but nonetheless was murdered. That's how Pizarro secured the rich and fabulous Inca kingdom for the Spanish crown, and since then our people have been screwed."

In Cajamarca, Tomas took a simple room in a hostel for a few nights. It had two beds and a kitschy religious print of a Madonna and Child. The large window facing the street was protected by wrought-iron bars and the shared bathroom was situated across from a courtyard.

After depositing their bags in the room, they strolled through the streets. Becoming quiet, Salvador sensed that he'd walked those sidewalks before. They circled the plaza twice, then

headed to the market to eat at one of the stalls. He caught the
smell of goat stew and asked Tomas if he could order some.
It came on a pink plastic plate heaped over potatoes and rice.
This was the dish he'd wanted to taste so badly years back.
As he ate his delicious meal, he watched with fascination, out
of the corner of his eye, two shoeshine boys with dark tousled
hair and dirty faces, hanging around. The sight of the boys
reawakened in him disturbing emotions that had remained
dormant for a long time. On the way back to the hostel, Salvador inhaled the familiar scent of the fresh mountain air and
realized he had a headache coming on.

By the next day his *soroche*, headache, was gone as he'd
acclimatized to the altitude. After breakfast Tomas drove to
the town of El Milagro on a sharply curving road. Salvador
harboured hopes that the visit would lead him to information
and memories he could recollect, but crumbling houses and
torched barns dotted a landscape he didn't recognize. El Milagro
had changed and no sooner had they arrived than Tomas, who
had been indifferent about taking the trip anyway, was anxious
to depart. Salvador was disappointed that Tomas showed so
little interest, while he cried inside. Tomas's unresponsiveness
left him with little hope that they would have enough time in
the town to seek out any information about his parents' fate.

After parking the car on the main square they walked over to
where he thought the family home stood. The house, smaller
than Salvador recalled, was now, according to a prominent sign,
a pastor's residence, and next to it was the partially completed
New Evangelical Church.

Salvador dug his hands into his pocket to contemplate, not
sure where to head next.

"Come on," Tomas said. "Let's move on."

They went down the road to a store. "Want a drink?" Tomas asked.

Tomas bought a beer for himself and an Inca Cola for Salvador, and they went to sit on a bench in the square to quench

their thirst. They were approached by a vendor trying to sell them a lottery ticket, and Tomas shooed him away. Salvador watched a man sitting high on a saddle, trotting by. Feeling a certain pressure beginning to build in his throat, Salvador stood up and wandered off, looking closely at every person that he passed. He didn't recognize anyone in sight and nobody looked directly at his face. He had heard that people had become too *sospechosos*, distrustful of outsiders.

"Hey, buddy, time to go back," Tomas yelled, but Salvador had something else in mind. "I want to go knock at the door of the house," Salvador said, and .dragged his uncle back to his old house again.

"Do as you please, but you'll do the talking—this wasn't my idea in the first place."

Salvador's heartbeat quickened as he went up to ring the doorbell. He waited for a few minutes but nobody came. He walked over to a window and caught a glimpse of some benches and boxes full of books. The backyard was deserted, as well as the construction site next door.

"I've told you all along, there's no use chasing after imaginings," Tomas said.

Filled with surreal images of the past, he turned away, his feelings a mixture of confusion and regret. Perhaps they should go up to the cemetery next, to see if he could find his parents' names carved in a headstone. Or would their unclaimed dead bodies be lying in the common grave?

The day they headed back to Lima, Tomas took Salvador to buy some leather goods first. "I'll buy boots for myself and get you a good pair of shoes for school," he said.

In early fall, while Salvador waited to meet a friend to watch a game at the soccer stadium, he caught a glimpse of a familiar face. A good deal of time had passed since he'd last seen her. Lucia—he was sure. He stood under a store's awning, with his hands in his pockets, observing her for a while. She was sitting at an outdoor café, smoking and turning her head from side to side. He observed the bottled blond streaks in her hair and her heavy makeup. He recognized the familiar movement of her hands when she removed her dark glasses and lay them aside. Her blouse had a very deep cleavage and her short, clinging skirt moved up her legs. Salvador was deciding whether to go up to talk to her when a dark-skinned guy with a small moustache, a few years older than her, pulled up a chair to sit at her side. Salvador liked being out on his own; the sensation of freedom made him feel independent and grown up. Lucia had had a good heart, had mothered him for a while.... He wondered what she was up to now. She sat, one leg crossed over the other, moving one of her pointy boots with spike heels nervously up and down. All of a sudden Salvador saw the man stand, grab her wrist brusquely, making her wince.

Salvador's instantly ran to her side, and pushed the man away.

"*Pendejo*," she hissed as the man walked away. Then turning to Salvador, with tears in her eyes, she spat, "Bastard, what the fuck do you want?"

"I'm Salvador."

"So?"

His stomach tightened when she added, "Why don't you just piss off."

"Don't you remember me? I'm the boy in the plaza? You took care of me for a while at the cemetery." He sat down on the chair the guy had occupied.

She remained silent for a while, studied him closely, calm and shaking her head. "How you've grown. You were a good boy," she said, here smile faint. "Where did you hide?"

"I found my uncle. We looked for you, but you were gone."

She sipped her coffee and lit a cigarette. "That was ages ago. I'm not that same girl. Times have changed."

An awkward silent ensued as Lucia looked over his head at the people around them. A sneer on her lips made her look twice her age. "I've got to get going," she said, getting up.

He put his hand gently on her arm and told her he wanted to see her again.

"I mostly sleep during the day. I've got little time to waste. I'm working hard to stash money away, then call it a day before things turn to shit," she said, stubbing out her cigarette in the metal ashtray.

Her voice stirred something inside him. He suddenly wanted to be with her again, whispering soothing words in her eyes like in the past. He asked the waiter for a pen and scribbled his phone number on a paper napkin. "Call me," he said. "I need to see you again—I don't want to lose you this time."

She didn't answer, grabbed the napkin, and walked away.

That night Salvador told Tomas he had spotted Lucia at a café. "Who?" his uncle asked absentmindedly as he placed two bowls of soup on the table.

How could Tomas not remember he'd been saved from harm's way by this young girl?

"How do you know it was her?"

"There was something about her gestures, although her facial features changed. She wore big, dark glasses, had heavy makeup, and red fingernails. At first I didn't recognize her, but after observing her carefully, I was sure it was Lucia."

"She grew up."

"But there's something strange, she's different," Salvador said. "She doesn't look like a proper girl."

"What do you mean?"

"The way she was dressed, how she moved, her tight shirt exposing her breasts." "You went up to talk to her?"

"We had a chat. I noticed a bruise under her eye."

"Don't fuck around—mind your own business, my boy," Tomas advised. "She's probably dangerous, making dirty money, fooling with drugs."

His uncle was upset. "I want you to promise me you'll live

straight and clean—cut the crap, you hear what I say?" Tomas became vulgar when he was mad.

Lucia didn't call, and as Salvador couldn't get her out of his mind, he began to spend more time on the streets where he'd seen her, hoping to catch a glimpse. He walked around the neighbourhood where he'd spotted her, past coffee shops and bars, and after a while he'd give up, heading home before Tomas would get back and pester him about where he'd been. Lucia was a witness to his childhood, a link to his past, but he resented the fact that she was important to him while she didn't give a damn about him.

The afternoon he spotted her again, he was hanging out outside the music store that sold *bamba* tapes. He was about to buy a pirated cassette, when he saw her walking out of a bar, arm-in-arm with a man. She smiled at the man after he planted a kiss on her cheek. Salvador followed them until they started climbing up the stairs of a building with a sign offering rooms to rent.

"Wait," he called, but his voice was inaudible. Under his shirt the dampness of a cool perspiration was building up. He left the scene in a hurry, accelerating his steps, to catch his bus home, as heavy sweat covered his face.

That night at bedtime, he felt ashamed of himself; he vowed to stay away from Lucia and concentrate on his schoolwork.

One day at school, he stumbled upon a notice on a bulletin board, announcing that a meeting for admission into the police academy was coming up. He had already been thinking about becoming a policeman so that he could look for his parents from the inside. He thought that once he was in the police academy he would have access to classified files, and would get more insight.

He made a note of the date and place of the meeting, then made his intentions known to his friends. But his friends laughed at him; all they felt for cops was contempt.

"In cops we trust; all others are suspect, right?" Marcos said, giving him a hard time.

"You might want to be a cop if you find humour in other people's stupidity," Pepo taunted.

"You'll be rich in no time," Nico teased.

Salvador knew that not all cops were the same. It was common practice to grease a few hands, and with salaries low, policemen willingly accepted bribes, but he would be different.

"You insignificant bastard, you think you'll make a difference?" Marcos asked.

"He'll comply with high standards," Nico said. "Face it, they're unethical and that's ingrained; you'll end up becoming a shameless *tramposo* yourself."

"I'll show you guys I won't turn rotten," Salvador said before saying goodbye and heading home.

Even though Salvador was the butt of his friend's jokes, painful memories of his parents compelled him to attend the information session. He'd been deprived from living a family life and that made him angry, and he vowed that a similar tragedy would not befall others during his lifetime. His math teacher let him skip class to attend. He wore a clean white shirt and grey pants, the only ones he had, and since Salvador had begun to shave, this morning after he stepped from the shower, he applied cologne to his smooth face.

The session was led by a tall, corpulent man wearing a dark suit and tie. Only a pin on his lapel identified him as a member of the police force. He was persuasive, talking about how the police were trained to rush to people's aid. His delivery was stimulating, his manner intense. "This is a great, stable job for those of you who like to take risks, who are adrenalin junkies at heart," he said. "This is a new era; your job will bring you prestige and respectability. You'll protect the public and have the power to arrest, incarcerate and shoot. Remember that without law enforcement, no one would be safe."

All eyes were on the man who kept his young audience mesmerized. "New young recruits are needed to turn things around and restore public confidence. Recruits today are a different breed, trained to maintain transparency. The new police corps wants to shape young men and women with different values from the past. Honesty is what we are looking for."

Not only would the few lucky students admitted to the academy be ensured jobs, but on the way they would get rigorous physical training and academic skills. The recruiter closed the session by assuring his audience that they would have good futures, and make decent salaries while protecting the citizenry.

The day Salvador went for his interview, he brought along a letter of recommendation from his math teacher and a copy of his last report card. The recruiter was extremely polite, offering him a seat and telling him to relax. "If you are interested in becoming a policeman, we'll keep the red tape to a minimum," he said, after examining Salvador's grades. "Tell me, why do you want to join the force?" he asked.

Salvador was frank and explained that he had lost his parents in the dirty war and wanted to find out what had happened to them.

After listening to Salvador's response the interviewer admonished him. "Don't get caught in your personal story, young man, when you're called up for your next interview. There could be potential problems, and it might be perceived as a conflict of interest, and that you are holding a grudge. Do you understand?

"Not quite," Salvador said, rubbing his hands along his trousers.

"If your reason for joining the force is revenge, well, that would be considered unacceptable. The higher-ups will definitely turn you down."

"Thanks, *señor,* for pointing that out; I think I understand."

There were a few more questions, until the recruiter said,

"You'll be hearing from us shortly. In the meantime keep up those good grades."

Salvador nodded, realizing he would have to be more discreet and that honesty didn't necessarily prevail despite the new ideals of the current regime. He decided he'd play the game, and take the necessary steps to gain entrance into the academy that would eventually help him do what he needed to do.

16

ONE SATURDAY MORNING Otilia stood at the gate, waiting for the church janitor to arrive, when Osvaldo showed up with the news that the government of Peru had captured the leader of the Shining Path. "Look at this article," he said as he opened the newspaper and read. "Today the people throughout the hemisphere are relieved Guzman is behind bars."

"Will this bring to a stop their militant activities?" Otilia questioned. "Will the guerrillas be finally defeated? I frankly don't think troubles will end with his detention. There's been a shoddy misuse of government powers for a very long time," Otilia added.

Once the janitor unlocked the gate, they went in to prepare for the meeting Father Francisco had arranged. As Deborah had asked Otilia to set up lunch, she headed straight to the kitchen to get organized. "We'll talk later," Otilia said, waving Osvaldo goodbye.

Otilia was up on the stepladder, pinning the tapestries up on the dining hall wall when Father Francisco came over to lend her a hand. The colourful patchwork images of the *Arpilleras* had been delivered last night by Mr. Medina, today's guest speaker. They were designs made with scraps of fabric on burlap. Born of a dark past, they told stories of what women in Chile experienced when martial law was declared and dissenters were rounded up. Some of the pieces were created by imprisoned women to convey messages to their families on the outside. *Enchainment*, the piece she was hanging, depicted protestors chained to the gates of Congress, demanding information about those that had not come home. *Waiting* showed a woman at a window, looking out at the ocean. In the background, stood a table with the photo of a man in a frame, with the words, *Where is he now?*

Otilia stepped down from the ladder, taking hold of Father Francisco's hand. "Upsetting," she said.

"Weren't these women smart? Desperate to be heard, they embroidered stories of their lives," Father Francisco said.

The lobby was full of people when Otilia went to stand at the door of the conference room to usher them in. She noticed a timid young woman with a slender build walking up; she was missing her two front teeth. Brushing a loose strand of hair from her face, she turned to Otilia and said "*Hermanita,* am I in the right place?"

"For *señor* Medina's talk? Yes, you are." Otilia recognized the familiar accent. "Welcome," she added with a smile.

The woman muttered *gracias* in a low tone of voice. "Come," Otilia said, showing her to a seat in the front row. "I'm also Peruvian—we'll talk afterwards."

When Osvaldo came to sit next to Otilia she noticed that, as usual, he was wearing his wire mesh bracelet on his wrist. This identified him as a survivor of torture now living in exile. He had lost his wife and his passport had been stamped with an L, making him a persona non grata, unable to return to Chile, his country of birth.

"I need to hear what my *compatriota* has to say and find out how to legitimize my case," he said.

Over the years that Otilia had been coming to the meetings led by Father Francisco, attendance had grown. They usually gathered around a table to have conversations about how to address the problems they faced, but today was a special occasion. They'd spread the word that there would be a guest speaker, a Chilean who'd gone through a terrible ordeal after the coup in his country. He'd been a lawyer back home and had come to the U.S. in the last months of the Carter administration, after the U.S. Congress passed the *Refugee Act,* increasing the eligibility for those seeking political asylum. Mr. Medina would share how he'd managed to flee from Chile and his struggles to find legal recourse to remain in the U.S.

When Mr. Medina stepped up onto the platform, the room quieted down. Jammed with tortured souls who'd come to glimpse this real version of history, he connected with his audience right away. "I'm here *damas y caballeros*, ladies and gentlemen, to implore to you to keep on with your fight. We, as family members of victims who have disappeared, need to demand the truth from our governments. Slowly and with the help of international organizations, we are getting to the bottom of what is going on in our countries, but we'll only be capable of getting all of the information we're after if we keep the pressure on. We need to cast light on what is happening to citizens in Argentina, Uruguay, Colombia, Chile, Peru, Guatemala, and El Salvador—to name only Latin American countries—where societies have forgotten the meaning of human rights. We must speak out, inform our fellow citizens, and make people aware of the many secret operations carrying out injustices. We cannot condone the covert actions of criminals. We cannot allow governments to continue subjecting its citizens to excesses, tortures, and abductions. We must denounce them and demand that they give us the facts."

Loud applause followed and the audience rose.

"We must unify and fight for our rights, keep up the pressure, and keep questioning, because those scoundrels are out only to protect themselves. We must find out *la verdad,* the truth about what happened to our loved ones. Truth isn't 'We don't know what's happening.' This goes for all of them, from the judiciary to the church. They must be made accountable. They claim they've done nothing out of the ordinary, that they are only protecting their country from far-left regimes. By arresting, torturing, and killing human beings, I ask?

"The year 1980 marked the first time we heard from the Organization of American States when they reported on thousands of disappeared people in Latin America. It's been years and violations continue to occur. We now know what is going on; we have reports from your countries' citizens, testimonies from survivors, and tensions continue to rise."

Otilia felt a weight squeezing her heart. Had Manuel been abducted, subjected to torture, and what about her child? When her attention returned to the speaker, he was telling the audience his personal story. "There was a round-up and they came looking for me. I was one of many on their list. It appeared that a friend under torture had spilled out my name. We weren't people who posed a tremendous threat. We were mostly young students and professionals, wanting to live in a democratic country. We were social activists who all of a sudden found ourselves identified as the enemy. The use of torture for extracting information was standard practice and no one who was arrested escaped it."

Stopping to get a sip of water, he went on.

"The torturers used assumed names so nobody would find out who they were. When they interrogated us, we were blindfolded, but trust me, I remember the sounds of their voices. They didn't wear uniforms, so we, the prisoners, couldn't identify their ranks. This of course was done with the intention that if one day, in the event they were called to justice, they wouldn't have to give a response."

Otilia felt queasy; his story was uncomfortably personal. The same mechanisms were no doubt in place in Peru.

"I've found out that my Chilean government was in cahoots with the Argentinean government. The *New York Times* uncovered a story about bodies of Chilean citizens that had been found near Buenos Aires. They were unrecognizable as the bodies had been burned. When families in Chile reported their disappearance, the government claimed they had left the country to join an extreme left-wing Argentinean group and got the punishment they deserved."

A hand went up from a woman in the audience. "What do you know about the men and women in Argentina who've been thrown from aircrafts?"

"Alive." Somebody pitched in.

"Yes, that is correct. At this time the government is of course denying those claims, but there is evidence. Bodies have been found. Prisoners were drugged, knocked out with an injection, then dropped off planes."

"Virgin Maria, are they admitting to this disgrace?"

"Not yet."

"And I've heard that some babies, delivered by women who died during torture, were given up for adoption to military families, is that so?"

"Whenever atrocities are committed, the ones in power withhold information. They're denying all of their mayhem, blaming the opposition for spreading vicious propaganda."

Otilia's body stiffened and sweat appeared on her brow. Suddenly she had a nightmarish thought. What if Salvador had been found, turned in to a social service agency, and put up for adoption? What if he'd been sent abroad? Europeans were looking for children, but wasn't he a bit old?

Otilia tiptoed out of the room, edging around the group, to arrange the tables and heat up the food for the potluck lunch.

A quick glance at the room and it looked fine; the tables were covered with white tablecloths and there was a stack of paper plates and cutlery at a centre table. She tossed the green salads and placed the casserole dishes in the microwave one at a time, but she was still shaken from the stories she'd just heard. She took a deep breath, waiting for her fear to dissipate before going to get the *pupusas* and the platter of plantains. Uncorking a few bottles of wine, she gripped them hard, hoping they wouldn't end up on the ground. When Elena entered the room, Otilia opened her mouth to speak, but all she could do was gasp, still horrified by the stories she had just heard.

"*Mami*, it's hard," Elena said, as she embraced her.

Someone placed a cassette on a ghetto blaster and the song *Si vas para Chile*, "If you go to Chile the country folk will come and greet you," began to play. Just then, Mr. Medina walked in with the priest.

"*Vamos a revolver los sabores*," Father Francisco announced as he took his place. "Nothing better than to give thanks to the Lord that we can be together and taste some great Latin American delicacies."

Otilia tried to be sociable as she offered guests wine and water at their tables.

"The harsh reality is that survival for those who were uprooted lies in the ease in which we can adapt to a new life," she heard Mr. Medina comment to Osvaldo, his compatriot.

"For some, it's a simpler task than for others. Thank you, everything is delicious," Osvaldo said, turning to face her.

"Intimidation," "amnesty," "arrangements made through a distant acquaintance to save his life," "struggle," "important to focus on what is happening now," people were venting, using these words in their conversations. Otilia grew weary; it seemed that the whole continent was going mad. Forcing herself to look cheerful, she put on a smile.

Otilia took her place at a table next to Violeta, the young Peruvian girl she had met at the door. During their chat, Otilia noticed Violeta had not let down her guard. She'd arrived only a few weeks ago and she was still somewhat bewildered. "We were living in Mexico, as both my brother and I got humanitarian visas, but he didn't see any opportunities there—he couldn't find a job and was anxious to come to the United States."

"And your parents?" Otilia asked. Violeta was still young.

"My parents..." she stammered, as tears rushed to her eyes.

"I'm sorry," Otilia said, touching the girl's hand.

"Arrested, accused of providing medical help to the guerillas—a lie."

A dense cloud fogged Otilia's brain.

17

THE TIME CAME when the Peruvian president, the son of a hard-working cotton fieldworker who had saved enough money to start a tire-repair business, ran out of luck. When his government began to unravel, he called for a *cambio de rumbo*, a change of course. With the support of the military he carried out an auto-coup to ensure his re-election as president for a second term. By 1995, his opponents had nicknamed him *Chinochet*, referring to his authoritarian neighbour to the south, the Chilean dictator, General Augusto Pinochet. In 1999, even though technically he had been in office for two terms, he announced he'd run again. The media, weary of his lust for power, started to dig deeper into his leadership, uncovering a number of criminal allegations: bribery, money laundering, arms trafficking, and abuses of human rights. When a television station broadcasted footage of the Chief of Fujimori's National Intelligence Service bribing an opposition Congressman, the scandal erupted in full force. Caught in a tightening noose of political scandals, Alberto Fujimori succumbed. Loosening his grip on the helm of his nation, he resigned from his presidency while in a conference in Asia, making his announcement to the nation from Japan.

Salvador had been promoted to the rank of police officer when, early on November 20, 2000, he received a call from his precinct advising him to report immediately to work. A large number of demonstrators were expected on the streets and they needed all of the law enforcement officers they could get. Rushing to fix something to eat, Salvador woke up Tomas, to give him the news, shouting, "At last, the bastard is gone."

The president's supporters were shocked that Fujimori had chosen to make this important announcement from abroad, and Salvador had no doubt that his opponents would seize the opportunity to rejoice on the streets.

"Maybe things will open up," Salvador said, buckling up his boots.

"What did you say?" Tomas appeared in his robe.

"Watch, he'll be indicted one day."

"With Fuji gone, the country will go to hell; who do you think restored us to the global economy that gave us this long-term financial upturn?"

"At a very high social cost."

"Think of the days we were living with hyperinflation—that was no fun."

As far as Salvador was concerned, things had to change. He kept his thoughts to himself. Injustices had been committed, innocent people had been harmed; even his own attempts to report disappearances had proven futile. God only knew he'd tried, but had been disregarded time after time, even met with hostility. He was sure that his case had been postponed, along with hundreds of other complaints. Over the years, the Inter-American Commission on human rights had received numerous grievances accusing the Fujimori government of violations; these had gone mostly ignored, and instead of responding to the families of the victims, Fuji had enacted a shameful blanket amnesty for those who were linked to the armed forces and involved in the crimes. At last it was time for a democratically elected government to revoke the cloak of impunity that protected the perpetrators, and to help those whose families had been torn apart. "They've been covering up crimes and I will demand to know what happened to my mom and dad," Salvador yelled before shutting the door behind him.

"Dream on," he heard Tomas yell back.

Salvador reported for duty and was given his assignment: he was to join the police in riot gear to direct traffic on the streets.

Sweating profusely under his clothing, and despite the discomfort, he was elated to see men, both in suits and in overalls, waving flags in favour of the fall of the old regime. Peaceful demonstrators, mothers and children, teenagers, and office workers chanted together "*el pueblo unido jamas sera vencido*—a people united will never be defeated." They were gathering more support as the day went on. It was an inspiring moment for Salvador, endorsing his own views, and fuelling his commitment to seeking justice for all those who had been harmed.

With Fujimori gone, in April of 2001, Salvador voted in the national elections for the first time. That evening, glued to the television, both he and Tomas watched the returns, and Salvador was happy to learn that Alejandro Toledo was ahead in the presidential race.

"When a man turns tyrant, it's his own freedom he destroys," Salvador said, thinking about the bastard president who had ruled for ten years and successfully blocked efforts to expose the bad apples he'd surrounded himself with.

Tomas laughed. "Where did you hear that? Since when are you turning so philosophical?"

"Maybe things will open up."

"What do you want?"

"A different attitude—transparency for one thing." The thought stirred him up. He was thinking specifically of a criticism he'd heard from a member of the Inter-American Commission on Human Rights. The committee received hundreds of complaints accusing the Fujimori government of violations, but as yet no attempts to look into them had been made. He even remembered his exact words: "Appeals by relatives of the victims prove fruitless. The same people who bring about disappearances hide the evidence and play a key role in the investigations. Most of the time cases are shelved."

"Oh, grow up," Tomas said. "In Peru things will never change."

On July 30, 2001, Salvador sat in front of the television to watch Alejandro Toledo's symbolic inauguration in the citadel of Machu Picchu. Toledo, a poor shoeshine boy from the countryside, one of sixteen children, had risen above his socio-economic condition by getting an education with the help of Peace Corps volunteers who had come to his neighbourhood, including a PhD from Stanford University. He was the first Indigenous person of Quechua heritage to be elected chief of state, and he had come to this spot to give thanks for the force and the courage placed on him by Mother Earth. He was at the Inca sanctuary, perched high in the mountains, to herald a new dawn for his country. Salvador gazed at people in traditional Andean costumes, playing the panpipes as two barefoot priests wearing red ponchos carried out the ceremony. Mr. Toledo was given a golden axe and presented with a golden necklace bearing the Inca cross. Salvador's chest swelled with pride as he took in the scene. He checked his watch and realized that he had to get ready to report to his job, and reluctantly he turned the TV off.

These days, Salvador was assigned a beat on the street to protect the citizens, for street crimes were rampant and bank robberies on the rise. He watched out for sly kidnappers who forced people to empty their wallets and their bank accounts. But the "lifting" of businessmen was emerging as a common crime. Kidnapping a member of a wealthy family and extorting money for their release had become profitable for the gangs. The problem seemed without solution until a few months ago when it was discovered that some law enforcement officers were providing the kidnappers with logistical support in exchange for half of the proceeds from the payoffs. When the officers in question were arrested, the trouble quieted down.

The day the workers called a general strike, Salvador was assigned to control the planned protest. A month ago, farmers had blocked the highways, and seven police officers had been injured, jumped by the mob when the protest got out of hand. The police had learned their lesson, and in order to minimize the damage, they assigned more police to handle the crowd. Salvador was disappointed to learn he'd been assigned to watch the home of a high-ranking member of parliament that lived nearby. The property he was to guard stood a few blocks from the spot where thousands of workers were expected to congregate. Its high fence was crowned with electrified wire and a couple of German shepherds roamed restlessly inside the yard. Across the road, the stores had been shuttered and the streets were absolutely quiet except for a few barking mutts.

Salvador walked the perimeter of the land several times and when, sometime later, he was joined by a colleague, they determined there was little to be concerned about, they decided to sit on two wooden stools next to a small table by the gate, to play chess. After spending close to twenty minutes on their first game, they heard the sound of helicopters hovering above. "Time's up," Salvador said, as he rose, and Sergeant Mora pointed to a cloud of yellowish-grey smog hovering some distance away.

A couple of cars raced away, while some panicked protestors ran past them, yelling. Salvador and Mora stood at attention while a few slow-walking, shocked stragglers stopped to help a man who'd collapsed on the sidewalk. After helping him to his feet, they dragged him away, grabbing him by his arms and his legs. A grief-stricken group walked by, coughing and crouching, while one young man's vomit projected toward them.

"Bastard," Mora said. "He did it on purpose."

When a few men started calling them names, it inflamed his nerves, but Salvador refused to let the insults rattle him.

"Pigs!" someone yelled. "You put on a badge and you think you are above everybody else."

"Just shut up, for Christ's sake," Salvador wanted to say, as he noticed his pulse quickening, but he remained steadfast. The bastards wouldn't be taunting for long—his buddies would make sure of that.

Cheers reverberated from the rally several blocks away, while cars zipped by, honking their horns. Young boys had climbed up onto the flat roof of a half-built brick house across the way, grabbing onto the steel rebar. Salvador approached them demanding they descend, when a pop can came flying his way. Mora placed his hand on his gun and Salvador did the same, forcing the kids to go on their way.

A crowd was approaching and there were only the two of them. At the police academy they'd been taught how to ward off rocks and Molotov cocktails, but this was a minor scuffle, not yet requiring the use of arms. Salvador became concerned that things were starting to escalate. He was trained to resort to force when a pack grew disruptive, but he figured these sleaze balls were unpredictable; anything could be expected when they became frustrated. Salvador hoped he could keep them appeased so they would disperse soon. His duty was to ensure that the protestors wouldn't damage common property, therefore he needed to remain alert, yet show he was cool and willing to cooperate. The hooligans were not out in high numbers in the area, but if more drifted to the site, they might go crazy. If and when they got out of hand, he knew how to carry out arrests and restraints, and how to increase the margin of safety for himself. Police were always a target, and he would need to protect himself.

18

SALVADOR COULD NOT WAIT. The Truth and Reconciliation Committee had been ratified in September 2001 to give Peruvians the opportunity to promote democracy in the troubled land. Twelve commissioners were appointed, amongst them academics, clerics, human rights experts, a former congresswoman, and a retired army man. Their mission was to look into complaints of human rights violations by accumulating information through testimonies of those who suffered abuses during the past administration. Up to now, there had been rumours and speculations based on sensationalist articles in the smutty press. There'd been contradictory stories and exaggerated conjectures of what had occurred. Finally, some light would be shed on the grim facts that had taken place. Tragic stories of countless instances of cruelties would unfold and Salvador was sure he would learn if the violence had been caused by the *terrucos*, the terrorists, or the state force.

Stories unfolded slowly even though people were reassured they were to be kept in strict confidence. Those testifying were told they should feel safe, for everyone was protected from reprisals by the state. With the help of the press, who were starting to expose the patterns of ensnarement people had been caught in for years, newspapers exploded with accounts, bringing the issues to the forefront. When Salvador cut out a photograph from the paper showing bodies exhumed from a pit near the village of El Milagro, to put in his scrapbook, it hit a nerve. Now was his moment to come forth. The new government was beginning to do some good work and he would go seek information about what the committee was prepared to do for him.

The day Salvador returned home from picking up an application from the Truth and Reconciliation Committee's office, he was overjoyed. It was a promising start. The only thing that mattered to him was how soon they would be able to start an inquiry into the disappearance of his parents.

"You were up early." Tomas sat at the kitchen table, eating his breakfast.

"I wanted to be the first in line."

"How did it go?"

"It was fast. There were only a few people in line. I have to fill out this application, lots of questions," Salvador said, holding the form in his hand.

Tomas remained silent as he turned his attention to the food on his plate.

"I think there's a chance that I will be able to learn the facts. For years, Fujimori has kept a lid on damning information; he fed us *calumnias*, just lies, *Tío*. Murders, disappearances, tortures, rapes—all committed by agents of the state and they've gone uninvestigated."

"Calm down. What's the use? It's too late to bring people back from the dead. If you ask me, I'd say wait a while before you put yourself out there. Don't be the first to testify; wait until people start opening up. It could all be a set up," Tomas said, taking hold of his coffee cup.

"*Por Dios*, *Tío*, have some trust. You can't be paranoid all the time. We need to find out what happened."

"Why don't you let this go? You need to date. Find a girl, for heaven's sake."

Salvador was furious. It was no use trying to talk to his uncle. The older he got, the more stubborn and set in his ways he became.

Salvador's day off was Monday and he set off to deliver his completed application as soon as the office opened at nine. He stood in line for a short while and, when his turn came, he went up to the counter where a friendly receptionist greeted him with a smile. She was soft-spoken and helpful; after taking a quick look at the form, she said, "Thank you, please come back in a week and we'll let you know if your case is admissible."

When he returned the following week, the same young woman took care of him. She gave him a bunch of new forms and said, "Your request for a review of the case was accepted; you may proceed to the next level. You'll see here that we ask for more detailed information."

"I hope the red tape won't delay the process," he said.

"Not to worry, every account is important to us."

Salvador began a routine of going to the commission's office once a week to see how the paperwork was moving along. He would make sure his case wouldn't go by the wayside and be left in another pile of forgotten files. Every Monday the clerks sat at their desks typing away on their typewriters, while the same beautiful woman sat at the receptionist desk. One Monday, when there was no one waiting in line, the young woman engaged him with a few words. "I'm Carmen," she said.

"*Mucho gusto*, pleased to meet you."

"Salvador, right?"

"You are the receptionist?"

"I'm one of the psychologists, but I come here one day a week to help at the front desk. Many people experience difficulty filling out the forms. Some are a bit bashful about going through the process. Not like you; you're quite keen, I'd say."

"I've waited for this moment for a long time," he sighed.

"You're courageous. I'm glad you've decided to consent and are allowing us to proceed with a full investigation."

"Doesn't everyone?"

"You'd be surprised; folks are on guard."

Was he a fool to open up to yet another government agency?

"So many people have been left rudderless, trying to navigate the pain of loss. You're doing the right thing," Carmen said. "We want to reach all the survivors and focus on their health and improve their quality of life. You have no idea how much damage was caused and we've had only a small portion reporting abuses, requesting help."

"My parents vanished; everything changed and the pain will never dissipate."

"Our task is to acknowledge what happened. My job is to help return people's sense of dignity and peace of mind. Hopefully, with time, you'll get some answers. We're working hard to lift the lid of silence and denial of events that took place."

Salvador took in her words and nodded.

"We want to know why it happened and who's to blame. A country which forgets its past is condemned to repeat it," Carmen said.

"If only it were that easy."

"We've established ten regional offices and hired 340 employees to do the work."

"A big project," he said.

Carmen rose to her feet when she saw an older couple approaching her desk. "Thank you for your help," Salvador said, extending his hand to shake hers before he departed.

The following month, Carmen asked Salvador if he would like to attend a hearing that would be transmitted on closed-circuit television from a town in the highlands. She gave him the address of the auditorium where it would take place, and told him the function would be on Wednesday at eight.

When he walked in, just a small group of people sat in the amphitheater, facing the large screen. He noticed Carmen sitting alone in the back and went to sit by her side.

"These are some brave citizens who've agreed to come forward to unburden their hearts," Carmen said. "So many people I've encountered have been uncomfortable about giving oral testimony. The majority of them are skeptical at first, but after some convincing, they realize its importance."

"Have you met any of them?"

"Not the ones testifying tonight. I've been working in the city, mostly with women who were able to escape their homes. I've been helping these wives, mothers, and sisters process their pain. It's not easy work; they're very suspicious and fear the stigma of working with a psychologist. They have the notion that only very sick people seek counselling. Some would rather talk to a priest."

The hearing began promptly with a few opening words from an official representing the commission in the province. One by one, men and women of all different ages came forward, taking the microphone to tell how they had been witnesses to disappearances and death. Some were shedding tears, while others were composed; they told difficult stories about turbulent days. They said that many in their village had not come back after a conflict in 1992.

"It's important to listen to each one. Each story has value," Carmen whispered when there was a short break. "We want each man and woman to know that people in our country, and in foreign countries, are watching. It's a matter of principle— their accounts are important, we need to collect systematic data to rewrite our historical events."

That night Salvador left the auditorium feeling spent. Guilt was the predominant emotion he felt. Should he have insisted on staying with his mother? Could he have forced his father to remain at their side? But he was so young at the time—and powerless. And he knew there was little he could have done as a small child. But he was more determined than ever to do what he could now.

Salvador was getting tired of having to deal with Tomas's ways; his *tío* was definitely getting on his nerves. He'd had enough of Tomas's verbal abuse and decided that since he was making a decent living, he needed to look for his own living space.

When Salvador returned to their apartment, Tomas was sitting on the couch, drinking beer and watching a boxing match. Salvador would have preferred to avoid him, to go straight to his room and relax, but Tomas wanted to chat.

"What did you find out?" Tomas asked.

"It's all very upsetting."

"What do you mean?"

"People's testimony. Horrible."

"They're inventing the ... so-called ... facts; it's a setup to show the people this government has their best interests in mind," Tomas said, slurring his words.

"What? Have you lost your freakin' mind?"

"Surely, it's just a scam. If people were apprehended or disappeared, there was a reason. *Por algo sera*," Tomas said, folding his arms.

"Nonsense. People provided testimony about families splitting up. Some were forced to flee, leaving everything behind. Their stories revealed how they'd have to put up with incursions from both guerillas and soldiers."

"They're looking for reparations."

"You crazy old man, you've certainly gone out of your mind."

"I'm convinced they're telling their stories because they want rewards," Tomas said.

"Oh, come on," Salvador said, shaking his head in frustration. He rose and headed to bed.

The next morning Tomas was waiting for him at breakfast. "About our conversation last night..." he said.

"What about it?" Salvador asked.

"I thought policemen were smart, but you ain't."

Salvador remained silent. He'd awakened feeling distressed. The stories he'd heard had an impact, leaving him sadder than he'd ever felt. He had no urge to engage in an argument with his uncle.

"It's arranged, nephew, believe me. People's accounts will always change, depending on whose version it is. How can you trust them? This charade is meant to collect an account of the past that suits the present political landscape. Why can't you get it through your head that the military thought the repression was necessary? There were areas of the country where there was too much going on—they had to regain control."

"And kill anyone they deemed suspicious on the spot? What crap!" Salvador was becoming increasingly irritated.

"Stop exaggerating. At times you need tyranny to stop the insanity happening all around."

"And discredit the sovereign state?"

"What are you talking about, sovereign state? When have we had one of those?"

Salvador was alarmed. It was time to squelch the discussion.

"You'd better watch out—next thing you know they'll be scheming against us."

Salvador was enraged; he'd heard theories about how much was at stake for the one who cooperates, but these were different times and now they could bust the rhetorical crap. "One is morally required to reveal what one knows when serious wrongdoings take place," he said grimly and stormed out.

A week later, he was on his way to pick up Carmen after work. He had a strong desire to be with her. Not only was she beautiful, but she was deep, and understood the pain of his loss. Knowing that in a few minutes he'd be at her side having dinner, discussing matters dear to his heart, made him smile.

Carmen had long black curly hair and white, even teeth. She wore large golden hoops on her ears that framed her face exotically. She walked with elegant ease and this evening she'd wrapped herself in a shawl to keep the chill from creeping into her skin. She was waiting for him in front of the building where she worked, and in no time they found a quiet hole-in-the-wall specializing in *pollo a la brasa,* where they'd have a bite. They ordered half a rotisserie chicken each, accompanied by *salsa verde* and fries.

"I don't drink," Carmen said, when Salvador asked if she wanted beer or wine. "Not after my father died of liver disease."

During dinner he asked her questions about her family and she shared that she was the youngest of four. "I was the mistake, my mother claimed. I'm seven years younger than my little brother."

Carmen lived with her mother, a widow, in a house in Miraflores where they rented out rooms to students to make ends meet. Carmen's father, a businessman, had made some money, but when illness struck him at fifty, his partner bought his share of the company and her mother invested the funds in the property.

They talked as they ate and laughed as they licked the grease from their fingers at the end of the meal. After Salvador paid the bill, Carmen said, "I must go now. I have an early meeting to attend tomorrow morning."

"Can I take you home?" he asked, his smile wide.

"Sure," she said, sliding out of the booth. He linked his arm with hers, and they walked a few blocks to the bus stop. When they reached her house, he gently kissed her on the lips, then, placing an arm around her, he pulled her toward him. They kissed again and afterward she pressed her face to his chest and gently stroked the back of his neck. He couldn't remember ever being caressed by a woman with such tenderness.

On his next trip to the committee's office, he was surprised and pleased that Carmen had brought some books for him. He loved to read, but since graduating from school he hadn't had much of a chance; with no access to a lending library, and short of cash, he couldn't afford to pay the steep prices to purchase them.

Checking her watch, Carmen said, "I only have a half hour of work left. Why don't you have a look at these and wait?

He sat in the corner of the waiting room and opened one of the books, placing it close to his face, trying to hide from the security guard who liked to chat. Next thing he knew, he became immersed in the psychology text. The index indicated there was information on sadness, anger, anxiety, and confusion; he turned to the chapter on posttraumatic stress.

When Carmen came up behind him and wrapped her arms around his chest, he was startled. "I'm done for today," she said with a giggle.

"This is serious stuff," he said, closing the book. "I've been reading about abandonment, a core fear in all humans." He rose to give her a tight hug and they walked out of the office with the books under their arms.

Carmen telephoned Salvador to ask if he wanted to accompany her to a gathering of friends who met once every two months to share the stories they collected during their travels to the countryside. "They're nice people volunteering for the committee, collecting testimonies from victims who've suffered distress."

"Yes, I will definitely come along," he replied eagerly. "Let's meet by the water fountain in front of the main building of the university grounds," Carmen said.

Salvador was already waiting when he caught a glimpse of Carmen in the distance. His heart quickened when he saw her approaching, waving her hand with a flirtatious smile. She wore a short black jacket and boots over her tight jeans. When they exchanged greetings and kisses, he caught the scent of her perfume, which was becoming familiar. He held her close and noticed how quickly she kindled his cravings for more.

They entered the old colonial building and made their way to a classroom down the corridor. "We gather once a month for conversations; really the purpose is to get the horror stories off our chests. It's part of our work, and very therapeutic for all of us. I hope you'll be okay," Carmen said.

The group was seated in wooden chairs that had been placed in a circle in the middle of the room. Salvador took a seat next to Carmen, who immediately started to chat with the girl at her side. After a few minutes, one of the fellows brought the meeting to order saying, "*Patas*, we need to be out of here by nine."

They all knew each other and Carmen introduced Salvador as her guest. Then the men and women took turns revealing stories they'd heard from citizens they'd encountered on their last trip. Salvador marvelled at how well-spoken they were, polite in their conversations with each other, and respectful to those who had suffered great losses and humiliations. One of the female volunteers cried as she talked. She apologized and explained she'd been haunted by the story she'd heard. "When they went searching for their missing relatives, they became victims of sexual violence. She was a young mother, holding a newborn in her arms. This was the tool the bastards used to degrade and intimidate women, hoping they'd remain in their places for fear of being more severely penalized," she added.

The next volunteer shared facts coldly. He described his conversation with a woman whose spouse had undergone a traumatic death. Another volunteer tried to insert humour as he described the circumstances that had placed some people in their unfortunate situation. Each one had their own way of keeping up their morale while working through the troublesome narratives they heard. They hoped to gain an understanding of what people had gone through by charting new territory, listening to their stories. They wanted to bring the challenges the country faced out in the open by acknowledging the harm and betrayal perpetrated on the population.

Feeling anxiety rising in his chest, Salvador pushed his chair closer to Carmen's. He was finding this a harrowing meeting and needed to feel safe.

"How are you managing?" Carmen whispered. "I hate to see you upset."

"How can you do this work?" Salvador asked.

"We are learning to live with a hole in our heart. That's why we need to support each other."

"Where are the widows, anxious to pour out their stories?" one frustrated young woman said. "I spent a week in this village and not one was willing to talk. They're still resisting."

"They're very suspicious. Rumours are spreading that they'll be in trouble if their stories come out," another woman added.

"Yeah, they think that the commission intends to do them in."

"Have you heard the public service broadcasts explaining our purpose?" one of the volunteers asked. "I'm afraid it makes us sound like father confessors."

"Are we not convincing the people that they'll be fine, that we understand that some of them were tricked into joining the insurgents, and that their names will be cleared once their stories are heard?"

"Our questions are eliciting anxiety and suspicion," another volunteer called out.

"People have crept around afraid of their own shadows for too long. They're holding their secrets close to their hearts and are scared to speak out, scared they'll be ostracized."

"One man told me that our questions were hatched far away, here in Lima, where nobody understands what happened to them."

"They're concerned about the legal implications of talking, of what consequences their talking will have. A middle-aged man lamented that no amount of words would bring his son back," a young woman explained.

"They're also worried that we don't understand their positions—how they were caught in a catch-22 situation, how their passive resistance to the guerilla movement eventually led them to a place which was exploited by the armed forces. They feel tricked and betrayed by the rebels and the state, and are uncomfortable testifying to members of the government."

"I heard one woman explain that we must understand there was a high level of deceit; the insurgents would classify some villagers as 'red,' meaning they were for the guerillas, and others were seen to be supporting the state. This commission will do the same. This lady said that at one time both the state forces and the Shining Path relied on undercover agents, and she wondered whether we were the new spies. During the conflict they would have female soldiers dressed in brightly embroidered wool skirts, passing as one of them or have guerillas wearing military uniforms, infiltrating to determine which camp the village was in. Both sides lied about their intentions and now these people don't trust a soul."

"Posters are up offering explanations of the medical and therapeutic benefits of coming out to testify, but we might be going about it the wrong way. They don't see the need for confessional talk—their *susto,* their fright, is healed only by the *curanderos*, not psychologists like us," Carmen said.

"Yes, I agree, I heard a lot of talk about how conversation is not their idea of healing. Only the medicine man can remove their distress."

"Besides, they're looking to restore a sense of community, of cohesion and solidarity; they don't want to start pointing fingers, or see the expulsion or imprisonment of fellow villagers."

It was incomprehensible, Salvador thought; nothing made sense. The social makeup of the villages was deeply disturbed. He could only shake his head and think of the thousands of people and their unendurable pain. He opened his mouth to say something to Carmen, but closed it again. He thought of

El Milagro, where he no longer had any roots ... perhaps, finally, some bleak facts would come to light.

In horror, Salvador continued to listen to the comments. His body had stiffened and he remained frozen in place until Carmen placed her hand on his lap. "I never realized the numbers involved," he said.

Her eyes showed concern, but she had only a few words to console him. "I'm sorry, I should have realized this would be really hard. I thought it might help you to understand you're not alone in your grief."

19

THREE YEARS LATER, Salvador and Carmen, with their witnesses at their side, stood in front of a priest and exchanged wedding vows. She looked radiant in a simple white gown cinched in at the waist, sporting a tiara of flowers on her head. Surrounded by family members and a small group of friends, they chose to fuse the civil and religious ceremonies into one. Once the *padrinos*, their witnesses, had signed the documents, the waiters came around with Pisco Sours and Carmen's brother proposed a *brindis*, a toast to the bride.

In an intimate venue with an outdoor space, large umbrellas shaded elongated tables draped in white linens and satin overlays. When an assortment of platters—including *cebiche*, roast turkey; *ají de gallina*, a rich velvety stew of chicken; and *anticuchos*, skewers of beef heart—were laid out, the guests were asked to take their place. Musicians played some music during the meal and once dinner was over, when it was time for the dancing to start, they struck up a Peruvian waltz. Friends and family started to clap as Salvador and Carmen stood up to dance. Halfway through the next song, Carmen's brother and wife approached the bridal couple, and partners were exchanged. Little by little, other guests came up to salsa with the bride and the groom. The music became more energetic throughout the night, as dancers swivelled their hips, and showed off some intricate steps. Later, during a conga line, singles were asked to join. Forming a circle, then gathering steam, the guests livened up the party another notch.

A three-tier wedding cake was carried in by two waiters and placed on a small separate table at one side. Under the stacked layers of butter cream, a series of white ribbons streamed down the side. All the single women were called to assemble around the newlywed couple and were instructed to hold onto a ribbon while the first slice was cut. After they tugged their ribbons, the young women examined its attached charm. All of a sudden, one of the young woman in the crowd screeched, "I'm next in line!" She was holding the ribbon that had a ring attached to it.

Salvador fed Carmen the first bite of cake as the guests clapped, demanding a *beso*—a kiss—to display their love.

Carmen's mother gave a heartfelt speech. She hesitated before confessing that initially she hadn't been pleased with her daughter's choice of boyfriend, but once she'd gotten to know him, she began to feel very differently. She knew how much they cared for each other and she cherished the fact that the young couple seemed happy together and were ready to make a life for themselves.

Carmen's mother had expected her to choose a banker or a lawyer, a husband who would provide. Her spinster aunt, who lived with them, took her mother's side. With a lowly policeman's salary, they said, Carmen would have to work outside the home and make sacrifices in order to afford a comfortable life. But no matter how much they both protested, Carmen, a strong and self-assured woman, always responded in no uncertain terms that she was the one who knew best who suited her as a mate. By the time Salvador approached Carmen's mother to *pedir la mano*, ask for her approval in their marriage, Carmen's mother felt she had no choice but to consent. By then she'd become fond of Salvador who came to court her daughter with small gifts for his beloved and flowers for herself.

Carmen made Salvador's life joyful and she steadied his nerves. At work he was content enough, and even though his last performance review had been strong, and he had an understanding boss, he often felt his stomach churn before reporting to his precinct. In his line of work there was no such thing as a standard day. Often. he had dinner at midnight, having had to work back-to-back overtime shifts. The clerical work was easy, but patrolling particular neighbourhoods produced great strain. There were days when he came home to Carmen with stories to tell, and others when he had just gone about quietly with his work and didn't have much to say. Tonight he would share a story that had just been revealed: a fellow policeman had been discovered working for a drug cartel.

Dinner was waiting for him, warming in the oven. He was a few hours late, and Carmen was sitting in front of the television tuned to breaking news, trying to determine if there was a reason for his delay. "Thought I might learn why you're so late," she said, getting up to place her hands on his face. "Are you all right?" she asked tenderly.

"Fine," he said.

"What held you up?"

He told her how he'd been called to investigate a fellow officer's house. "We found machine guns and ammunition hidden away in his garage and uncovered thousands of dollars in cash."

"Was anyone hurt?"

"No, he didn't resist; he gave up without a fight."

"It concerns me to think of the danger you face."

"Nothing to worry about," he said pulling her close, and embracing her tightly.

"How did they find out?"

"A tip off—a guy in custody snitched."

"How many years will he get for protecting drug dealers?"

"Who knows, depends on the judge."

"How was your day?" Salvador asked.

"I had a day off, and spent it with my friend Julia who is shopping for wedding gowns."

It had been a month since the day Salvador noticed a billboard announcing a new television show—a reality show featuring people who'd been separated from their families and were trying desperately to find them. Today, he entered his apartment in a flurry; there were five minutes to go. He turned the television on and waited for the announcement that the new program was about to start. He had been working the streets in a faraway neighbourhood, and with the traffic congestion, he was lucky he had gotten home in time.

The show started with the stylish host shaking hands with the people selected to participate. It appeared the producers had chosen people in extreme situations and they'd packaged their stories for a scintillating show. He'd been sucked in by the advertising, which claimed that Peruvians would be appearing. Standing in rapt attention to catch a first glimpse of the participants, Salvador let out a whistle when he heard that the woman in front of the camera was a native of his land of birth. Although his heart beat with hope, deep inside he knew that this would not be the way he'd find his mom. Still, he felt compelled to watch. He stepped up to the screen and crouched down to examine the faces of each of the participants. It was an international cast, people from a number of different countries where turbulence had disrupted their daily lives.

The camera scanned the faces, zooming in from one to the next. It had been a long time since he'd last seen his mother. Did any of these women resemble him? One woman in particular drew his attention. Sitting cross-legged in front of the TV screen, he stroked her cheek, wanting to capture the details of her face, and hoping to find a trace of familiarity before the camera went to focus on someone else. Stepping back, he removed his shirt as drops of perspiration formed on his forehead. He collapsed on the sofa when the announcer came on and said, "And this evening, ladies and gentlemen, directly from our studios in the beautiful city of Miami, we have mothers who decades ago had to abandon their own families, and their native countries to save themselves. These are our heroines tonight, living right in our midst. They've come from harsh places and now seek to reunite with their loved ones whom they left behind. This segment of *Heroes in Our Midst* will ignite your heart and help you alter the way you think about some fundamental human rights issues. Yes, ladies and gentleman, there still is violence, trauma, and genocide in the world, and these women are a powerful testament to human tenacity, the indomitable spirit which allows us to take great risks and survive when faced with terrible odds." The camera followed the host stepping up to a podium set to one side, as Michael Jackson's "Heal the World" came on with a bang.

His heart beating rapidly, Salvador wondered if the show was real or a setup. "Unfathomable," he sighed. What was the likelihood that his mother would be on the show? So many years after the all-encompassing horror of Peruvian life, could she really still be alive?

Listening to the words of one of the mothers brought chills down his spine. "I kept the promise," she said in a low, husky voice. Her thin face was deeply wrinkled, and she had black circles under her eyes; she was haggard, looking much older than his mom would be today. Her face had been made up for the cameras and her grey hair done up in a bun. Would his mother's untold story also unfold?

"She always does small things with great love," was the phrase that popped up in Salvador's head. It was one thing he remembered his father often saying. He couldn't remember much else. He wanted to recall other instances so badly, but the memories few and far between. He clung for a few minutes to his newly found one.

During the first commercial, he pulled the sliding door to the balcony wide open to allow the cool night air to freshen the room. He went to kitchen to get a beer from the fridge. The voice he was hearing in the background didn't stir any sensations. There was nothing even faintly familiar about it. Then he heard the woman say, "We were living in a village near Ayacucho when the troops arrived...." That's all he heard—it was the wrong location. The program then went to another commercial.

Back in the living room, he turned his attention to the screen. The same woman was sobbing, her hand on her mouth, apologizing and explaining that she had lost everything that was precious in her life. "When I couldn't find my husband, I walked for days through the forest hoping to find him," she said.

Salvador wanted to hear his mother's story, hoping that it would help him to understand his own. He was thirsty for facts, even if they would prove painful; but this woman wasn't his mother—she came from somewhere else. "Damn it," Salvador muttered, feeling something collapsing inside. Had he deceived himself, thinking he would be able to find her through this program?

As the show unfolded and Salvador continued to watch the host grilling the guests, with questions—"Were you actually there? What did you see? How did you feel in that moment?"—Salvador noticed that some were avoiding the questions outright. It was then that the cameras spotlighted the live audience, who had been watching in silence, but were now given the opportunity to participate. With their hands raised in approval, they cheered, shrieking, "We love you. You're brave." The cameras moved on to the host, soaking up the applause with a self-satisfied smirk on his face.

Salvador was disgusted and angry. What a hypocrite the host was, asking provoking questions, using overblown words. And with his bogus smile, looking so pleased with himself. When one of the women described being raped, Salvador became indignant and screamed, "Fuck you!" stomping his foot hard on the floor when the host asked her to describe the scene.

When Carmen walked in, she was alarmed to see her husband so agitated. "What's going on?" she asked, slipping her arm around his neck as she leaned over to give him a kiss.

"This show is disgusting," he scoffed. "Pandering to people's curiosity, exploiting folks who've lost so much. Scripted, unbalanced, tragedies belittled—it's appalling. Is there no dignity left? The producers have come up with this idea not out of any kindness, but are motivated by profit, to benefit themselves."

When he looked at the television again, the host, facing his guests, was saying, "This situation begs the question—" Salvador had had enough. He switched the television off and sighed loudly. "I get so discouraged. Why is it so difficult to track someone down?"

"Your parents disappeared into the landscape years back."

"My only encouragement is that little by little more information is being made available here," Salvador responded, closing his eyes and holding his face in his hands.

He would continue on his own path, relying on his own common sense while trying to connect the dots. Never again would he think that some voyeuristic exposé with no depth would lead him to a consequential end. He was confident that no matter how many years it took to find his parent, he wouldn't lose faith. He'd leave no stone unturned investigating the violation of their sovereign rights. "No one is going to stop me," he said, coming to sit close to his wife. "And I *will* find them."

20

"I'VE GOT *LA TRACKA* ready; will you give me a hand?" Laura said, and Otilia followed her ample body to pick up the last few shopping bags to be placed in the truck. Laura was taking her sister, nieces, and nephews to Mexico to share Christmas with their relatives, who would welcome them with open arms. Laura had wanted to buy airline tickets, but when they discovered how high the fares would be, she decided to put their two thousand dollars toward the purchase of the Pathfinder, which was parked in the garage. Laura had mentioned to Otilia that they were expected to be all decked out when they arrived in Mexico. "It's about making a good impression—supposed to be *a la moda*, with matching purses and shoes." So, for the past few nights she'd gone shopping. "They expect us to be rich, living in *El Norte*, even though we may be having a rough time."

"Drive carefully," Otilia said, extending a hug.

"Hope it won't go kaput on Interstate 35 or on the Ruta Nacional. I'll ask St. Christopher in his infinite mercy to protect us," Laura said, making a sign of the cross as she climbed in, and reaching out to touch the plaster saint on the dashboard. "Take care of yourself and make sure to look after Neron," she laughed.

Neron, Laura's boxer, started to bark when he heard the tires backing out of the gravel driveway. He was a handful—hyper, boisterous, and playful—but would offer Otilia protection while she remained alone in the house.

A few months after leaving Joan's place, Otilia began working as a live-in nanny, helping to raise two baby girls while their parents were at work. When her last job ended, Otilia moved in with Laura. The couple she had worked for were good people, and she had developed a bond with them. During the five years that she lived with the family, they had encouraged her to continue her education and had paid her tuition for business school. And before she left them, they had helped her obtain a job as a bookkeeper. Otilia was still with the firm and she had recently been promoted to the position of senior bookkeeper. She shook her head at how things had changed in her life since she'd left Peru more than a decade and a half earlier.

She had met Laura at the park where she used to take the family's two girls. They quickly became friends, as they always found plenty to talk about. Laura, in her early forties, had been raised in a small town in the province of Jalisco, close to Guadalajara, and came from a family of ten. After high school, she'd taken a sewing class and gone to work for one of the *maquiladoras*. She'd come to the United States after marrying a former neighbour who'd gone to work in construction in the East Bay. When after two years he left her for another woman, Laura remained in California; by then, a few of her siblings had immigrated as well. She hadn't re-married, but she had a host of nephews and nieces with whom she was close.

One day Laura announced that she was leaving her nanny job to find different work and that she was planning to rent a house of her own, where she in turn could rent out the spare rooms. So it was that when Otilia needed to find a place to stay, she called on her friend. Laura offered her a small room of her own on the lower floor of the house.

Otilia worked hard, and she always agreed to work overtime for she tried to save as much money as she possibly could. She knew intuitively that one day she would need funds for an urgent cause. She didn't have much time to spare during the week, but she made it a point to see Michael regularly. She rarely ate out, and never frequented Starbucks; instead she brought her own food and coffee to work. When both she and Laura were home on weekends, they cooked, and they always prepared extra to freeze so they could help themselves during the week. Otilia never let dirty dishes stack up in the sink, but she didn't let Laura know she wasn't doing her part since Laura had been so generous by providing her a nice home. Sometimes, at night, she followed the news on television, but she often feel asleep on the couch watching the Latino soap opera that followed.

Laura had rented another room to two sisters who'd made their way to California from El Salvador. They had paid a large sum to a coyote, one of many such shady people who were getting rich by smuggling immigrants into America. The girls were in their mid-twenties, and one had left her preschool daughter with their mother back home. They'd come from Tijuana where they had been working at a factory on the assembly line, and when it closed they decided to come north. They were quiet, shy women who kept to themselves. Otilia heard them walking in the early mornings and late afternoons, for her bedroom was directly below theirs. There had been a few Sundays when they all had breakfast together and chatted, but Otilia knew very little about their lives. The sweatshop where they had worked nine hours a day, six days a week, to send a share of their paycheck back to their family, had no doubt shaped them. Not allowed to talk to others while at work, they learned how to remain silent most of the time. A few days before Thanksgiving, when Otilia came home from work, Laura was crying while placing the sisters' meagre belongings into plastic bags.

"What's going on?" Otilia asked.

"*La migra* picked up Lucy and Ana. Lucy just called. They're being detained and deported. I called Leonora to find out what happened and she told me all of her girls were arrested while they were cleaning a house in Montclair. She's washed her hands of them and is not taking any responsibility, saying she'd made it clear that the minute someone got into trouble, they were on their own. Can you believe it? She was totally unperturbed, saying she needed to find others to replace them, because she has lots of work."

"So where exactly are you going?"

Giving a little shrug, Laura said, "I'm going to see them, to take them these few things that belong to them."

"Where are they?"

"In Richmond. I need to check on visitation times."

"How come the *migra* got hold of them?"

"Leonora thinks the boyfriend of one of the others squealed. He was upset and wanted to spite his girlfriend, take revenge."

"The bastard."

"Lucy and Ana were at the wrong place at the wrong time. I called Justo to get some legal advice; he said that if they have money, they can arrange to post bail and be set free until a court date is set."

Picking up a pair of tennis shoes from the entryway, Laura turned to face Otilia, looking vexed. "I really can't help them; I can't post bail for them. I've only known them for a short time. Justo asked if I knew whether they had already signed a declaration confessing to being here illegally. If they did, they'll be dispatched to the border immediately."

"Did you ask?" Otilia said.

"I didn't think to do so."

The sister's didn't return, and in the New Year Laura was expecting a new occupant, a woman from Poland who'd come to America to go to graduate school.

As Otilia began to accept the misery that had been inflicted on her life, she noticed that, with time, her despair was dissipating. All along there'd been people who'd helped her move on and she slowly learned to embrace life as it was, and she avoiding becoming a hostage to the ghosts of her past. But she wasn't fully there yet. Every now and then, she still found herself having to make a great effort to carry on, and it was then that she'd put on a mask, turning on her charm to hide the enduring pain she felt. And when thoughts of loneliness and longings for her family emerged with great force, she'd catch herself making plans to return to Peru. It was during those times, when thoughts rumbled in her head, that she would call Michael for advice. With tears running down her face, she'd ask for the hundredth time, "What would you do if your wife had gone missing?" Michael would always offer words of comfort and tell her to be patient, to wait before returning. He felt that things were still too chaotic, and she had no way of anticipating the outcome. His latest advice was, "Hold off until the new government is safely in place."

Even though so much time had passed, Otilia knew that the political climate was still precarious. Until a new president was elected in Peru, and the formation of the Truth and Reconciliation Commission to investigate the violence committed in the previous twenty years had been completed, there was no point for Otilia to return home. Why spend the great amount of money necessary to make the trip when she knew that the government continued to wash its hands of the violence inflicted by the military and the guerillas? She would not be able to obtain viable information. However, once the Commission finished its investigations and President Toledo was willing to take responsibility for the events that took place, then Otilia's would have a better chance to find the answers she was looking for.

With little rest time on her hands, Otilia had been able put fears aside, hurtling onwards, making her way in her new world. She now felt at home, helped by a sense of belonging in her church's activist group. It was with them that she recharged and renewed her commitment to the search. In the beginning, the gatherings had been a way of joining others facing shared injuries, supporting one another in their pain, but once the group determined that they must find ways of getting their voices heard, they became strong advocates for themselves, and others. They put a lot of effort into writing letters to reveal their stories and to ask for help. Over the course of several years, they collected statements, dozens and dozens of them, from people whose lives had been haunted by similar events. There were times when Otilia had stood in front of the Xerox machine making copies for hours, then hauling them in wicker baskets back to her room where she would stuff them into envelopes, ready to be dropped into the mail.

Recruitment of new volunteers and constant attention to detail kept them moving forward and, bit by bit, word of their work began to spread. Persistently putting pressure on individuals and organizations that could press their cases, the church group held public forums, documented situations, and ensured that local newspaper articles were written about their cause. They enlisted the help of those with a knack for writing editorials to voice their points of view, until they were able to take their campaign beyond California, inspiring family members of victimized people everywhere to join in their search for redress.

What frustrated her most were the thwarted attempts to obtain information from the Peruvian government, itself. In the 1990s, relations between the U.S. and Peru had become strained, and with amnesty laws shielding the police and military agents from prosecution for human rights violations, it was impossible to dig up the truth. But even now, in this new era of more openness, it seemed that there were still no means of extracting the facts.

All along, Michael, who in his retirement was living nearby, remained Otilia's staunch supporter, encouraging her on every step of her tumultuous trek. In the early days, he transformed her worries into hope by helping her file a refugee claim, proving she was a desperate civilian caught in the midst of a dirty crusade. He'd help her decipher official letters mired in legalese, and suppressed her desire to back away when the going got tough, until she became a lawful permanent resident. He'd stood by her side some years later, as her witness, attending her naturalization ceremony where she took the Oath of Allegiance to become a citizen.

By the time Otilia was ready to join Michael at his home for Christmas dinner, a heavy rain had started to fall. She drove to the holiday gathering, straining to see the road. Otilia found parking, opened her umbrella, and walked up to the building where she found Joan being wheeled from the handicapped taxi that was dropping her off. Joan had aged poorly and was no longer capable of living independently in her own home. Crippled by arthritis, she had difficulty walking and had moved to a seniors' residence. Otilia bent down to kiss Joan hello, and told the driver she could wheel her the rest of the way.

"Eight o'clock then," Joan said to the driver, as Otilia pushed her up the ramp.

"What do you know, my two favourite ladies arriving at the same time," Michael said, as he opened the door of his apartment and stepped out to the hall.

Michael took the wheelchair and pushed Joan inside, placing her close to an armchair. Lifting the footrest as Joan unbuckled her seat belt, he extended his arms to help her get up, and then sit back down into the comfortable armchair.

Michael's home contained a bewildering assortment of things he'd brought from his overseas trips: Indigenous crafts, colourful carpets and animal skins from a time long ago, before they became illegal.

"How can I help?" Otilia asked.

"I placed some *empanadas* in the oven; will you please take a look and see if they are warm enough."

Otilia walked into the kitchen where a salad was ready on the counter and a whole grilled chicken was covered in foil.

"Michael, why didn't you let me help?" Otilia said, when he walked in. "I'm pretty good in the kitchen these days." He was wearing a red turtleneck sweater and over it a festive Christmas apron. He looked very chipper.

The dining room table was set for five with a floral arrangement of white and red flowers as a centrepiece. The bell rang and Michael went to open the door to welcome his friends, Richard and Hugh. They had brought along several bottles of wine, which Michael placed on the bookshelf.

Otilia shook hands then returned to the kitchen to check on the cocktail-size pastries turning golden brown.

"Now for drinks," Michael remarked. "I have scotch, gin, beer... What can I offer you?"

"Do you have any decent wine?" Joan asked.

"Pinot Noir?"

"Did you make these delicious things?" Richard asked, turning to Otilia as she offered the *empanadas*.

"No, they're Michael's hard work," she said.

"I must confess I got them at the *pupuseria* down the street."

Joan placed an *empanada* in her mouth and withdrew it immediately. "Ouch, it burned my tongue." She was as disagreeable as ever, Otilia thought.

As Michael went into the kitchen, Otilia followed him to help assemble the salad while he carved the bird. A few moments later Michael announced that dinner was about to be served.

"*Buen provecho*," Otilia said when she sat down.

"Bon appétit," Hugh responded, looking at Otilia with a smile as he picked up his napkin and placed it in his lap.

"Merry Christmas," Michael said, raising his glass.

"How is it going?" Hugh asked Otilia, sitting beside him. "Anything new?"

"I'm planning to go back. I think that finally the time is right."

"Really?" Hugh said, sounding surprised.

"I was ready to go last year, but when that car bomb exploded outside the U.S. embassy, I chickened out."

"When was that?" Richard asked.

"March 2002—just as President Bush was about to visit. It seems that now things have quieted down again."

"Did Bush change his plans?" Joan asked.

"He wasn't intimidated," Michael responded.

"They say it was the Shining Path's response to Bush's declarations that he would fight against terrorism around the world," Richard said.

"Weren't the guerilla movements defeated?" Joan asked.

"They did take responsibility for that incident," Michael replied.

"They've had a presence, but only in remote areas," Otilia added.

"Well, the good news is that now the government is acknowledging past wrongdoings and is beginning to bring some perpetrators to justice. Fujimori's years in office were like reading a political thriller. I just found out that the Peruvian Truth and Reconciliation commission has requested President Bush's assistance to expedite the declassification of American documents on violations that are stored in the archives of our agencies," Michael said.

"I guess truth committees are the new tools for scrutinizing past events—South Africa and Rwanda, for instance," Joan said.

"Guatemala, Argentina," her brother tagged on.

"It's a good thing when the voices of the victims are heard," Richard said.

"Do you really think those investigations will lead to healing and change?" Joan asked. "In the land of *mañana*, excuses will abound and the truth will never be revealed."

"It's about getting *testimonios*, to examine abuses. There've been years of negating the atrocities committed; it's about time people speak up. Perpetrators need to be investigated, brought to justice. There's been such a slow follow-up of the people who've been accused," Otilia said.

"You just hope that courageous folk will come forward to confirm the facts. A toast to Otilia for her commitment and bravery. We wish you a safe trip," Hugh said.

21

IN NOVEMBER 2003, the Peruvian president, Alejandro Toledo, apologized on behalf of the state to all those who suffered during the years of unrest. He asked for forgiveness from all of the victims of violence and terrorism—the dead, the disappeared, the thousands who had been displaced, who were tortured, or left undocumented.

In January of the following year, Otilia boarded a plane from San Francisco for her twelve-hour flight south. Once she was settled in her seat, she fingered the letter she'd received from Nora, taking a closer look at the photograph she'd sent, to make sure she would be able to identify her at the gate. There was an elegance to the woman, with her striking features and her straight stance. She'd be waiting outside the airport building wearing a pink scarf, as people who were not travelling were not permitted inside. Otilia had begun a correspondence with Nora when someone had passed on her name. Nora Bedoya was the president of a woman's organization of family members of those who had disappeared or been detained, and for years they'd remained in touch. They kept each other informed of their work, and when Otilia wrote that she was contemplating a visit to Lima, Nora insisted she stay in her home.

When Otilia landed in Lima, she got off the plane and followed the crowd down the corridor to the immigration lineup. She carried the two forms she was given on board, one for immigration, and the other for customs. When she presented the officer with her American passport, he questioned the reason for her visit.

"Tourism," she said, while the officer studied her passport.

"You're Peruvian by birth."

"That's correct."

"Do you have the *papelito* they issued you when you left?"

"Which paper are you referring to?" Otilia asked.

"This exit form."

"No, I'm sorry, that was so many years back, I'm afraid I didn't keep it."

"Well, all right, but make sure you keep this one with you until you depart," he said, stapling the form to a passport page.

She couldn't believe the stupidity; after all the turmoil the country had gone through, and the bugger wanted an ancient form? She walked over to the foreign exchange counter to obtain local currency; she'd been advised to be careful where she exchanged her dollars, for the country was flooded with counterfeit cash. When Otilia exited the building, Nora took her into her arms and told her how happy she was that she'd come, as these were auspicious times; there was a political will to investigate and closely scrutinize wrongful actions of the past.

Nora lived in a spacious house where Otilia was shown to a sunny room on the second floor, facing the yard. "I've planned your three-week holiday," Nora said and laughed. "I'm warning you, they call me bossy for a reason, so do stop me if you think I'm driving you too hard."

For Otilia this wouldn't be a vacation; she was in town to work, anticipating she'd be able to obtain information and move ahead.

"I've made an appointment with a lawyer, and another for you to meet with a Truth and Reconciliation officer. We must go to the vital statistics office and I want you to meet with don Lorenzo, a community leader who is compiling information from people who've come down from the north."

Otilia was pleased that these appointments had been set up, but she also had different plans in mind. First, she would start where she last saw Manuel and Salvador.

The bus trip from the capital city felt long. She tried to sleep for a while, but with each bend on the road, her head bumped against the window and she awoke. As the bus started to climb the winding road, she noticed the familiar sites along the green countryside, seemingly unchanged by time. The landscape ahead brought her a measure of comfort and she perked up to be on the lookout for a cluster of huts. A truck going by raised a cloud of dust but she still was able to catch sight of women with their portable looms, sitting on the ground, busy at their tasks. This was the corner turnoff she'd often taken when going to see the livestock dealer they did business with. Suddenly her mind went to the times they attended the many *fiestas* celebrating animal brandings at don Miguel's, when cows, bulls, and sheep of reproductive age were "baptized," to mark their ownership, their ears festooned with colourful yarn. As the bus passed the spot where she'd hailed down the truck that had taken her on the long and perilous road to the austere setting of the Cerro Obscuro mine, she thought she ought to visit don Miguel on her way back. How fate had made her world change at the blink of an eye!

By the time she spotted the red tile roofs of the small homes huddled together up on the hill, she was drowning in melancholy with thoughts of Salvador as an infant, and their beautiful family home, now gone. Moments later the bus made a sharp turn and stopped abruptly in the station's covered yard. She stepped off the bus and walked out of the station in a rush. Her body trembling, Otilia lingered on the sidewalk in the sun. Looking around, she intuitively found her way to her house. A feeling of dread coursed through her as she walked up the street. The village seemed familiar, yet so dissimilar, and much frayed. There was an eerie silence. On impulse, she turned left and walked toward the stone bridge at the far edge of town. At least the bridge is still here, she thought, taking a deep breath. Wanting to catch the mood of the spot she knew well, Otilia leaned over the railing to listen to and contemplate the running water. She felt transported to old times when she would sit on the rocks by the side of the creek to heal her nerves. This is where she came after returning from the hospital when her mother's cancer got worse, and following the news that her father had passed away from a heart attack.

On her way back to the centre of town, she saw a group of fragile, older men sitting on a bench outside the post office, chatting away. She approached them, ready to engage to talk them, but when they looked up and nodded, then turned back to their conversations in the Quechua language, she excused herself and continued on her way. Poking around the village, she passed by some newly built one- and two-storey houses. There were some vacant lots, too, ones she didn't remember from before. Colour had been added to a few of the dwellings, recently painted in washes of green and blue. Dogs from behind fences barked as she passed and she took note that there were no vagrant dogs wandering the streets any more. Realizing she was avoiding going to the place where she had lived, and banishing the haunting thoughts that had started creeping into her head, she took a deep breath and resolved to head over there and see what remained.

Feeling a little wobbly, she stood in front of her lot. She wasn't quite sure if she still felt a connection with the place at all. Her house had been replaced by a structure that looked like a church. She was baffled and wallowed in an unnerving reflection on "what if?" things could have turned out differently. It was inexplicable—meant to be permanent, gone in a flash. She had repeatedly imagined living there all this time and rapidly became overwhelmed by an overpowering sense of loneliness.

She knocked on the door and a woman with a baby in her arms opened tentatively. She called to a man who came to her rescue and Otilia introduced herself, explaining she'd been the former resident. He appeared surprised, but didn't seem to care much. He was sorry he said, he didn't know what had happened since he'd only been living in the house for a few months. "God has sent us to transform lives. We're sharing the gospel," he explained. "I heard a few shocking stories about what took place, but as you realize, that was a long time ago. We're here to help people start anew."

"This is where my house stood," Otilia mumbled to herself, turning away. There was no use asking him questions—he was a newcomer. She nervously remained silent, unable to find the words to express herself.

An old man with concave cheeks, huddled on a chair on the front porch of the house next door, waved. Otilia walked up to greet him with a mixture of curiosity and fear, for she wondered if this was Mr. Olivares, who had pulled through. If it indeed it was he, there was a chance to obtain information about her property. He motioned her to come up close, and she quickly realized that he was deeply hard of hearing and couldn't make out her barking words. He had aged, and she feared he'd become demented as well.

Revisiting streets she knew well, she was on the verge of bursting into tears when she noticed Alba's property lined with roses in bloom. Alba's son had been a guerrilla; what had become of them? She walked toward the house and was dismayed to see it was crumbling from neglect. It was a very different place from the dwelling she once knew. Two front casements were boarded with rough-looking wood and the drapes on the side windows were closed. There was no sign of life. Otilia decided to knock on the door and she tapped it several times. Alba opened the door, and though momentarily startled, she threw her arms around Otilia in a warm embrace.

While fumbling in the pocket of her skirt to retrieve her handkerchief, Alba said, "I've often thought of you, *comadre,* come in please."

Alba had aged; her hair had turned completely grey, and she had a noticeable curvature in her spine. "My knees feel loose," she said, as she held onto her cane, urging Otilia to take a seat.

Why hadn't she responded to her mail? Otilia wanted to know, but hesitated to ask right away. Over the years Otilia had mailed Alba many letters, but never received a response.

"I was scared," Alba confessed, after they had been talking for a while. She hadn't sent letters abroad for fear of being exposed.

Alba offered Otilia coffee and they sat at a table where they shared news about about distant friends and common acquaintances, about how some had left, while others had died. Alba revealed what she'd had to endure in her personal life. "We worried when our son became a revolutionary, but he came into this world with ideas of his own, destined to do unusual things. I can't tell you the details of how he became involved; he told me he didn't owe anyone explanations, but that when the revolution succeeded, everyone's life would improve. When I objected, and told him to be vigilant, he said he had his reasons for doing what he needed to do, and as far as my ideas were concerned, they were out of touch, forged by propaganda and lies."

Clasping and unclasping her hands, Alba said, "Due to his actions, my life changed. After he was arrested, every time I heard the phone ring, or some footsteps outside, or a knock on the door, I thought it was my boy."

Otilia felt her heart ache as Alba explained how she had been shunned. She couldn't understand why people were so indifferent to her now. Her life had taken a turn for the worse and nobody helped. "Faulty memories," she claimed. "We are the fallen victims of hatred and shame."

"What do you mean? Otilia asked.

"We were all members of the community once. I don't comprehend what has made people become so detached. I don't
have any sympathetic neighbours left. But, my friend, I'm sorry
to be burdening you with my problems. *A cada dia su pesar
y tal vez su esperanza.* Each day brings its own regrets and
sometimes hope, and today you've come."

Otilia placed her hand on Alba's arm, noting how fragile and
vulnerable her friend Alba had become. "Please do go on."

"There are those who feel betrayed and won't talk to me.
I'm resigned to the fact that I'm here on my own. Where else
can I go?"

"Why not go stay with your daughter?" Otilia asked.

"She won't forgive me. She says that since I protected her
brother from the law, her life was destroyed. She stays away.
You know how it is—people talk, there's gossip, and there's
nothing to stop it; who knows what she thinks I did?"

For a time both women were silent.

"Times have changed. There are no bonds left after years
of torment; even relatives don't communicate. The war pitted
neighbour against neighbour. Why remember, some ask? Turn
the page; forget, they say. Nobody wants to listen; even fewer
are ready to make amends. As for me, I don't trust anyone.
I'm better off taking care of myself."

After years of fighting the government from a hidden guerilla base, Alba's son, one of many suspected radicals under
surveillance, had been caught. He served his sentence, then
was shot. On the wall, in a family photo, the son responsible
for the family's demise, smiled. "They took him away; then
they came for Rogerio as well."

All along Otilia stammered apologies, allowing Alba to
speak. She felt a strong affinity to this woman who, with her
son and husband gone, was all alone in her sufferings. Her loss
of family had left an irreparable void that Otilia knew well.

"The town's not the same. So many people left and didn't
return. The young don't understand what went on, but that's

another story. *Comadre*, it's getting late; what about something to eat, and you'll spend the night here with me, won't you?"

Otilia hesitated a little before saying, "You're so kind."

Alba stood and went to gather cutlery and plates. "I don't have much, only the basics; the rest I've had to sell." She laid out some bread, corn, and potatoes while explaining how she had downsized and was living only in one part of the house. "I was left with no source of income, so I partitioned the house off, blocking out the rest to lease," she said, pointing to a wall.

"My Rogerio always said you were a good cook; he especially liked your *sancochado*. Do you still cook so well?" Alba said.

"Not much these days."

"I prepared your stew once, but Rogerio fed it to the animals, he said it was inedible." They both had a laugh.

Otilia didn't sleep well. The bed sagged and the coils of the mattress pressed against her ribs. Before she departed the following day, Otilia heard another cruel detail of those troubling days. She thought she would faint.

"There's one matter I didn't bring up. Forgive me if I upset you. Are you aware that Manuel returned after you left? They found the burned-out shell of a car; they said one of the bodies was charred, and that perhaps it was Manuel's."

Otilia studied Alba's face and felt paralyzed. She lost all the colour in her face.

"You should see Jose Matanzas, he might have more information. Do you remember him? He's got his hands in a few things. When you see him, bring him a gift."

Otilia was mystified. He'd been a notary public, a man with greasy hair, a corrupt, scathing liar. What would he know?

Had Manuel really been caught in a clash? Was that the cause of his death? But wouldn't there have been information about the accident? She was impatient to leave. Beleaguered by staggering thoughts, she pushed herself out the door to catch the bus on time, thanking Alba as she ran out the door. Perhaps don Miguel would be of help.

When she saw don Miguel on her way back to Lima, it was the tone of his voice that disturbed her. Tackling her questions with caution, he drew back at first and then he confirmed that there had been a great deal of violence. People had abandoned their homes, then the looting commenced. Furniture, clothing, cows, and farm equipment were taken from people's properties, and those who remained became suspicious of those who left. The information he had obtained in those days had been full of contradictions.

Otilia's trip back to Lima was tough. She was tired and aching from sitting in one position for most of the ride. How would she navigate through the information? She had to calm down. Was Alba's unspeakable revelation true? And Salvador? Nobody knew where he was. Could Manuel not have averted an approaching disaster? Was foul play involved? Could she possibly find any sense of meaning in her own life after this horrible news?

She arrived back in Lima at sunset when the city streets were abuzz with vendors of all kinds. Walking by a man frying up *chicharrones* in a cast-iron pot, she choked on the smell of smoking oil. Coughing, she slowed down her pace, and came upon a mother and a stalled child; the boy was bending over to pick up one of the pork cracklings that had fallen to the ground. "*Mal criado*," the woman yelled, "you want this, you want that, now look what you've done." Once she got ahead of them, Otilia thought of her son, wishing she'd had a chance to indulge him in his whims. Hurrying by to catch the rickety bus that would inch its way through traffic, she hopped on to get back to Nora's home.

That evening, she remained in her room contemplating the grim and heavy burden inside her, not wanting to talk to anyone. She worried that if her husband had indeed been killed, she would probably soon discover that her son was dead as well. Guerillas and government forces battling for control had created a chaotic world, causing a jumble of accidents. How could a young boy manage all on his own? There were so many misconceptions, and now she was more confused than before about what had taken place. How would she ever make sense of what had occurred? She'd have to find out; she carried much shame for not having been able to protect her young son.

"I'm in trouble," Otilia said to Nora at breakfast the next day. She told her about meeting Alba and the stories she heard. "I don't know what's in store further ahead."

"We'll continue our search for proof of the events. We've got to uncover the facts, do our homework, and not rely on anybody's word. Lying is a routine event in this country. There're too many people willing to deceive others," she said, shrugging her shoulders. Nora obviously wasn't convinced Alba was telling the truth.

"But why would she do that? Don Miguel confirmed there had been similar incidents."

Nora didn't mince words. "Who knows why people lie— ulterior motives perhaps? People make up stuff. You've come from abroad; outsiders are considered fair game for fibs. Some folks have enriched themselves at other's expense."

"Would she be twisting the facts?"

"Oh *mija*, you've been away for too long. She could have altered them. We'll see if they check out. Come now, we better get going to the vital records office; hearsay isn't evidence. You need a certificate, proof of death."

Otilia took a deep breath. She didn't want to think about the government offices with crowds of people waiting in corridors speaking in loud agitated voices, complaining about not being served, about having to put up with so much delay. She'd have to fill tedious *formularios*, an endless number of forms, and go through the daunting bureaucratic paperwork. On one of the forms, she'd been asked to describe the clothes Manuel wore when she saw him last. What the heck?

"Proof of death is key," Nora said, interrupting her thoughts. "That's the only way you'll be able to claim your land."

She picked up her purse and followed Nora out to the car. Claims were not what she had in mind. She first had to paste together the shattered pieces of information she'd obtained about the last days of Manuel's life. How could Otilia keep all of her emotions at bay? She'd been warned by people in the United States that her trip would be tough, and she had to be mindful not to let herself fall to the pits of the earth. Now she understood why, but she wasn't up for any evil games; she would let no one waste her time.

22

ONE EVENING during Otilia's stay in Lima, Nora took her to a weekly vigil held at a downtown square. They decided to take public transit since at rush hour it would be difficult to find parking nearby. Over eighty people were gathered, holding candles, and wearing wooden crosses around their necks, bearing the names and dates of birth of their disappeared loved ones. They stood side by side, speaking with hushed voices, conveying the stillness the meeting called for, until someone in the crowd yelled, "We'll never forget," and the group responded, "They can't shut us up. We're present, listen up, you can't make us step back ever again."

"Disappearances?" another one called. "Never again," the chorus answered back.

Otilia was dazed, thinking about how public the losses had become. Once kept so secret, relatives now demanded to know the fates of those who had vanished mysteriously. She gazed at a giant poster some people had propped up. It depicted a meadow filled with decaying bones in an open grave; standing next to the corpses was President Fujimori's picture with the word genocide scribbled across his chest. Flyers were posted on lampposts, inviting the public to show up every Wednesday night.

These brave attendees had started a national debate by bringing attention to the grossly unfair treatment shown to the families of victims plucked out from their communities far from the capital, and forced to flee. Many were women who had known Nora for years. Nora, now in her sixties, had always been a community organizer, and was trained to raise women's awareness and improve community life. In her twenties, she'd started her career by volunteering at one of the *comedores populares* in the *pueblos jovenes*, the slums. In the tradition of mutual help practised by the ancient cultures, collective action had dictated that four or five women prepare meals to overcome daily hunger. They would serve over one hundred residents in communal dining areas close to their homes, to help reduce poor families' household expenses and to free women's time. In the early 1990s, Nora learned that one of her friends who sat on the board of a popular dining room had been targeted and killed when Shining Path guerillas attacked during a communal lunch. After this incident, many communal dining halls went underground, and some even temporarily shut down; but Nora, determined not to withdraw her support, continued on. It was a time when there was an increasing influx of migrants coming to settle in Lima, escaping the lack of security in their provincial hometowns.

When Nora became aware that there were many more women and children fleeing than men, she wondered why and made a point of spending time talking to the people newly arrived. Nora found out that most of the women felt alienated and were desperate for psychological support, for they had lost so much. Nora started small, inviting a few of the women to join her at the community centre to play cards and share some sweets, while letting their voices be heard. Nearly all of the uprooted women had a traumatic story to tell, holding secrets that they'd desperately tried to conceal from the world. Slowly, over the course of weeks, many started to talk, telling each other about their sleeping difficulties, their *nervios*, their emotional pain, and their sense of hopelessness. And once they got to know each other, they began to generate a sense of solidarity and trust. It was after hearing so many sad stories that Nora decided she wouldn't let the perpetrators get away with their crimes and, with the women's consent, she began to record their experiences. A natural born organizer, Nora took on a leadership role, moving the group forward, strengthening their means to take collective action to advocate for justice for themselves, and others.

Later this group would become a women's organization to help those who'd been displaced, enabling the women to stand up for their civil liberties, demanding their right to be heard. She achieved this at a time when the government was still bullying the refugees into believing that the fracture of their communities had been brought on by their own men. Nora believed in following protocol, and over the years, although circumstances had been slow and frustrating as the rift between the government and the people grew wider apart, she coaxed women to file legal cases and stood by their sides. When the new government came into place and expressed a willingness to listen to people's claims, Nora and her women were ready to lay the blame.

"The turnout is small, but as people feel an increasing sense of confidence in the new government, so we hope attendance will increase," Nora said.

A priest came forward, taking hold of the microphone as sunlight was fading. Eager to extend his support, he gave a short explanation as to why they gathered together every week: "We grieve in unison to find a little bit of closure in our hearts."

Nora offered to light Otilia's candle, and as it illuminated, Otilia closed her eyes. She needed to feel solidarity with others in her same predicament. Otilia sensed Nora's great kindheartedness when the older woman linked her arm with Otilia's. Then she heard Nora say, "I can't believe those *zánganos* are still coming out to protest."

Otilia opened her eyes to see a group gathered behind red pylons on the opposite side of the street. Orange-clad Fujimori supporters stood tall, holding signs objecting to the memorial gathering.

"Stop the persecution of our good men," Otilia read on one of their posters and thought, How dare they chew out ordinary folk?

"I hear that some of them are paid to attend. They come and stand there for money, not sacrificing their own time. Their leaders will do anything for attention from the press, but nowadays they're not getting any write-ups." Nora said, raising her eyebrows.

"Could they be agents watching the people who are gathered among us?" Otilia asked.

"So what? They have no power under this present government."

Nora introduced Otilia to a woman who came to stand by her side and asked if Nora could spare a few minutes of her time.

"I've made the rounds of the offices, responding to variations of the same questions, only to be shoved from one office to the next," the woman complained. She had experienced a great sense of indifference and unwelcome advice from unconcerned bureaucrats. "The Ministry of Defense was not willing to release any information, and they lacked the goodwill to even consider my case. They said I wasn't convincing enough. *Ay, señora,* I came across many insincere and verbose people out to control my fate." Red-faced and teary, weighed down by her frustration, she placed her head on Nora's shoulder.

"I understand. You must stay strong; justice moves slow," Nora said, lifting her head and looking into her eyes.

When a few heavily armed police officers, quick to crush the demonstration, started to walk about, the crowd on both sides of the street rapidly dispersed.

The following day, Nora took Otilia to see an attorney, a single practitioner with an office on the second floor of a shabby colonial building in the historical downtown. "He doesn't charge much and has brought lots of hope to relatives who've been waiting for answers for a long time. I think he'll be a good go-between while you're away, navigating between police, government offices, and yourself. Cases tied to administrative processes need close attention, otherwise they get bogged down along the way."

They took a small elevator to the fourth floor and walked down the creaky, dim corridor. Nora introduced Otilia to the lawyer, then stepped aside to allow Otilia to give him a complete rundown of her situation. Otilia read the white marble nameplate that stood in front of a pile of files: Ernesto Malfi, *Abogado*, while the lawyer put on his glasses and struggled to find a notepad from under the piles of paperwork on the desk.

Mr. Malfi was soft-spoken and mild-mannered. He explained what he had done to help many families in similar circumstances. "As a matter of fact, all of these," he said, placing the palm of his hand on his files, "contain information of people trying to locate their unaccounted-for loved ones."

Otilia hoped she had given him enough facts so that he could begin hunting down relevant documents to build a case. He'd listened hard, seeming to pick up on her sense of urgency, and Otilia trusted that Nora would also follow up.

Days passed and though Otilia pursued every possible avenue for a glimmer of information that might help untangle the confusing events that led to Salvador's and Manuel's disappearances, she came up with more questions than answers. Had Manuel really died in a car accident? Was there nobody around at the time of the crash? Why had they not identified the victims? Could it be possible there were still no clues? She had no doubt that the daunting process to discover the truth would be slow, but she questioned whether there was a will to pursue the facts. Otilia worried she'd have to go home with nothing to show for her efforts, although Nora reassured her that, even without her around, everything would continue as planned. Out of a sense of desperation, Ottilia thought of turning to a shaman for answers. Perhaps a shaman would give her some peace of mind.

Otilia asked around for the name of a *curandero*, keeping the information to herself. She knew that if Nora ever found out what she was up to, she'd tell her it was wizardry and she'd laugh. Nevertheless, she made an appointment with don Esquivel Roa, a descendent of generations of respected healers, and then went to see him at his home on the outskirts of town.

The short, Indigenous middle-aged man with a full head of hair and bright red cheeks, gave a big smile of welcome. He showed her to a poorly lit room in the back of his modest cinder block house. Images of saints and small, homemade, cloth dolls were pinned to the walls. Candles were propped up in bottles, and straw baskets, overflowing with sparkling ribbons, lay on the floor. A healing altar was arranged with a few shells, quartz crystals, and a bowl containing herbs. Otilia sat on the alpaca rug on the floor to tell him about how her existence had been ruined by political events, while all the time she concentrated on the amulet of a glittering animal tooth that hung on his neck.

He murmured a short prayer in the Quechua and Spanish languages while selecting some dried mushrooms and aromatic plants. "I'm choosing the herbs that will dispose of your of bad thoughts; we need to make sure we clear your road, divest you of any bad people blocking your way." Shaking his hands in the air, he started to chant as he whirled around, entreating the gods to show him the way to her sorrows. He ingested the potion he prepared, then offered her some. "It'll cleanse the impurities in your mind and clear your path, helping you keep the faith."

Otilia wavered between calmness and fear that she was wasting her money and precious time.

"Everything has a meaning," Roa said, as he sat down next

to her and took her hands in his. He looked at her with great concern. Was he a charlatan? Yes, this was *brujeria*, witchcraft, Otilia reminded herself, but perhaps he would find a remedy that would help calm her. He suggested she try the power of prayer to find answers as well, so they could draw inspiration from the lessons they will have learned before they met again in a few days. "We must be good listeners before we can accept help; listen to your inner self."

The clock was ticking; the countdown was on and, after roaming the halls of a few more government offices and meeting with hollow, mechanized, complacent officials not fully invested in their jobs, Otilia felt weary and had second thoughts about catching her plane back to the States. Much to her consternation, she still couldn't believe she would have to head back without even a small piece of information that would help her figure out what had happened to her family. How was this possible? She'd met a number of scoundrels, people adept at dodging the rules, thinking themselves smart, promising they would come up with the answers she was looking for. She'd heard from others who at the outset would not commit to combing through information until they'd assessed how they could benefit. How many times had she heard, "I told you this wouldn't happen today," even though they had promised details by that date. She felt disappointed, let down by the many unethical people she had met. The only good news was that Nora and the lawyer hadn't abandoned her. In vain, she tried not to worry and to feel grateful. She prayed and took the herbs Mr. Roa prescribed. With only a few days left before she had to return, only a stroke of luck could provide her with evidence while she still was in Peru.

How would she ever repay Nora for her guidance and tremendous help? Otilia decided she would leave a donation to Nora's women's organization to show her gratitude and help others move on.

Otilia had come to terms with the fact that in Peru nothing moved along fast. Peruvians had a different sense of time. "*Eso es Peru*," people said. That was how it was. She would simply have to continue being patient.

23

AFTER RUMMAGING through the bedroom closet for an old pair of jeans, Salvador got ready to paint the walls of their living room. Carmen had left early for work with his assurance that the job would be done by the time she returned. He was puzzled at how adamant she was about improving the look of their apartment, determined to capture a certain style. They had settled on teal with one contrasting wall in coral, to complement the upholstery of the furniture in the room. It was all about mood, she claimed, for they needed both tranquility and vitality when they came back home from work. She'd created a board where she pinned pictures from interior design magazines and small textile swatches she'd picked up over the course of a few months, to build up an idea of what she would like. Salvador knew he didn't possess his wife's flair for decorating and didn't have much to say, but wanting to please her, he offered to paint. Carmen had grown up in a well cared for home, enhanced with many comforts, while most of the places he'd lived in had been dismal and sparse.

As pigeons cooed on the patio, he laid down newspaper to cover the floorboards and got furniture out of the way. He sanded the walls, patched up some holes, and was about to open the can of paint, when he remembered the onion Carmen had said he should cut in half and place on a dish to absorb the heavy smell. He worked until he was close to finishing up.

At that point he began to regret being stuck in the apartment all day. He would have much preferred to be outside, playing soccer with friends. He relaxed when he was playing *futbol*. He looked at his watch and figured that by now his *patas* would be heading off to a bar for some beers and camaraderie. He laughed when he thought about their routine. One of his friends always order only one bottle of beer and a single glass. He would fill it up, drink it all at once and, after a few burps, pass the bottle and glass to the next guy.

When Salvador finished painting, he collapsed on the sofa waiting for Carmen to return from work. A few minutes later, she strode through the door as the early evening sun brightened the room and cried, "*Bacán,* cool—it looks great." She rushed to hug him, "It's perfect," she said, hanging onto his neck.

She was anxious to get the apartment back in order, but Salvador said they should wait until the paint had dried and cured. Carmen had bought a grilled chicken with fries and they decided to eat outside on the balcony. They moved a pile of knickknacks to one side of the small table that was already out there to make room for cutlery and plates. But after Carmen had pulled up a rattan chair to sit on, she dropped her head into the palm of her hands and sighed loudly. Salvador knew that despite her excitement about the apartment, she was truly upset.

When the Truth and Reconciliation committee was formed in 2001, to determine the numbers and the whereabouts of the victims of the twenty-year Peruvian conflict, its first report, published in 2003, gave an account of the magnitude of the violence. It was higher than anticipated—69,000 civilian lives lost and 600,000 people displaced from their homes. The report provided a gruesome image of the aggression that took place, drawing attention to crimes committed; it also provided a glimmer of hope for justice to come. Violence had created social and psychological problems, with so many people suffering significant trauma caused by unanticipated shock, and there was a need to help those who'd experienced armed clashes, loss of family members, and economic difficulties. As the report findings became known around the world, foreign funding began to arrive to help the disenfranchised. Sweden, Japan, Italy, Germany, and the United States contributed toward reparations and many non-governmental organizations (NGOs) sprung up. Carmen got hired by one NGO to look into the needs of women whose exposure to cruelty had caused traumatic stress. There'd been a recent appreciation of gender differences in war-torn countries with the realization that women reacted to conflict differently than men.

"You had a bad day?" Salvador asked, when his wife's sudden silence piqued his curiosity.

She took a few shallow breaths and made a gesture as if to dismiss her problem. "Let's eat, I'm starved. Was it a hard slog?" she asked, turning her head to look at the newly painted walls inside before walking back to the kitchen to get their food.

"Not bad."

She returned carrying a tray in her arms, and placed the food on the table. They chatted a bit as they ate, but Salvador noticed she was distracted. "What's going on?" It was not like her to so despondent.

As if trying to shake the uncomfortable thoughts that roamed in her mind, Carmen started to tell Salvador some of the things she'd heard from the women who had given depositions that day at work. Steadying her voice, she told him about a group of women who had been coerced into participating in a massive sterilization campaign. The campaign was a result of official state policy; women had been advised that a law had been passed that made having more than five children a crime.

"Was it not a family-planning campaign?" Salvador asked.

"They called it family planning, driven by the Ministry of Health, but it seems they were conducting sterilizations without consent."

"When did it start?"

"Around 1995. I feel so ashamed and embarrassed to live in a country where women were treated with so little respect."

"Reducing population growth was a big issue then. Would you like a beer?" he asked.

"It was all about doing away with poverty; however, the way they decided to go about it was abusive."

"Family planning meant birth control, am I wrong?"

"It meant sterilization. These women were not given a choice; they had to submit to some unorthodox practices. They received no advice about contraception; they were told that having a large family was unhealthy, and that if they underwent tubal ligation it would save their lives, and prevent infant deaths."

"Was there no negative attention from the press?"

"I don't know. I think a few women came forward some years back, but as usual, when it comes from the poor, it falls on deaf ears. Nobody readily listened to them. Now there's a huge basis for grievances. They are being advised to file formal complaints, as these women were duped, told that if they didn't comply they could face fines, even do jail time."

He noticed she was holding a French fry in her hand, but was not eating anything.

"Yes, it was abusive, considering that most of them were poor and some illiterate. Many of them said they weren't willing to cooperate, but when health workers came to their villages, they told them family planning would give them reproductive rights and control over their own bodies. They would get *buen trato,* be well cared for, and could take a rest from their responsibilities for a couple of days, so some changed their minds. But it is clear that the government didn't have the women in mind—it was a scheme to reduce birth rates. Fujimori thought the average number of children born to poor families with no education was too high."

"Have some chicken, my love, you need to eat."

"There were no good intentions. It was all a scheme. Women were sterilized for free, but if they suffered complications from the surgery and needed follow-up medical attention, they were charged. Most of them couldn't afford the fee. Some of the ladies today even talked about their relatives that died."

"These folks have been exploited time after time."

"Imagine, they trapped them, herded them off like cattle to precarious makeshift sites."

"What are you saying?"

Carmen went on to tell Salvador how women had been bribed, then misinformed about what to expect. In one village they had a sterilization festival to inform families about the benefits of family planning. "A festivity they called it, so the men put on nice white clean shirts to attend a party with their extended families; the next thing they knew, as alcohol flowed free of charge, some of the men got drunk, and the women were kidnapped, while their husbands were to inebriated to notice and to rescue them."

"Kidnapped?" Salvador asked.

"The women were captured—rounded up into groups, forced into a trolley, and tied up."

"Were there doctors involved?"

"After they arrived, they were each given a shot to knock them out on the spot. Without their consent, their tubes were tied."

"That's outrageous," Salvador said, clenching his fists.

"Others were told they could have a free checkup if they went to a clinic, and when they arrived, the doors were locked behind them. The sad thing is that they weren't informed about other alternatives, which wouldn't have been permanent and irreversible."

Carmen's appetite suddenly disappeared and she pushed her plate aside.

Salvador started to nibble on the food from her plate. "Those folks are hard workers and for them there's always been room for one more child—what was the government thinking?" he asked.

"Some of them told us they went through surgery because they were promised food incentives for their families. Others said they would never accept bribes, that with their few chickens, pigs, and the occasional cow, they could take their crops to market, and have plenty to eat. I'm sure they didn't have much, but they figured that was their lot in life. They'd seen troubled times, knowing that some years were good, while others were not so good, and when they went through a poor harvest and a lost income, they shared whatever they had with their neighbours. One woman said that before the campaign the women would get together to share their happiness; sometimes they laughed until they cried, but now all they have is sorrow. They have to bear the medical consequences of the procedures—some are lethargic, others complain that they feel dizzy. Some said they have trouble walking, and one said she is nauseous all the time and can't work the fields."

Salvador shook his head. "Can I get you a cold drink?"

"I heard other shocking stories," Carmen said, her distress palpable. "Among those testifying was a health worker who told us the doctors were forced to comply with a minimum quota of sterilizations per month. The clinics got so-called incentives—money for each surgery they performed."

"But, didn't they need the women's consent?"

"It seems that they did; however procedures were not in place. Once they were inside these clinics, the women were asked to sign permission forms before the doctors could go ahead. And if the woman was illiterate, they would apply her digital prints on a form she couldn't comprehend. Even those that refused, once they woke up, found their prints on the document."

"Nobody listened to them."

"Apparently not."

"It was insanity," Carmen said fretfully. "The last report revealed that around 300,000 women were sterilized to diminish the number of births. These women are broken."

Salvador knew how much Carmen struggled with the issues

she had to deal with at work, and that her empathy for the women that she worked with was all-encompassing. "These women are lucky that they have you to help them understand what happened to them," he said. "You are an advocate for them, and I am certain that they are grateful for your support."

"Salvador, you know as well as I do that a lot of what I do is all theoretical. Liberation psychology—big words—but from where will the money come to make these women feel adequate again? It makes me ill to realize that all I can do is to listen, and can do little else to really help make them feel whole again. It makes me ill. They have lost their dignity as a result of the injustices committed against them."

"Darling, maybe it's time you do something else, something to take care of yourself."

"You've got a nerve!" Carmen said, raising her voice.

"We all need some respite at times. You take in more than you should."

"I'm sorry. I shouldn't be voicing my frustrations at you. I'll try and keep it together," she said, bringing her tone down a notch. "I shouldn't be burdening you with this." Carmen stretched her arm across the table to slip her hand into his.

"Don't say you're sorry," Salvador said, lifting her palm and kissing it tenderly. "I love you and your passion for social justice. I just cannot bear to see you in pain, and I want you to know how much good you are doing in the world, for these women and for others to come."

"I'm fine," she said softly, her voice hardly audible, as she slumped back into her chair.

Salvador knew well how hard it was to seek restorative justice and he worried that Carmen might be pushed to the edge.

"Stories like theirs must be told," she said, smiling weakly.

Sensing she didn't want to talk any longer, Salvador followed her cue and they both rose together. As he carried the tray of dishes back to the kitchen, he said, "Give me a few minutes to do the dishes then we can put the furniture back in its place."

24

ONE EVENING Salvador came home after a long day at work in the foulest of moods. Thinking it unfair to bring Carmen his problems, he decided to go for a walk around the block. The brisk walk calmed his mind, so that by the time he placed the key in his front door, he'd regained his composure. Tucking his shirt into his pants he rushed to take Carmen into his arms, and tell her how deeply he cared for her.

He found Carmen chatty, delighted to gossip about one of her co-workers who'd fallen for a man half her age. Bursting with curiosity to find out what Salvador thought about such a relationship, she questioned him relentlessy. He pretended to be interested in her conversation, but she noticed he wasn't really paying attention. "So, you're preoccupied?" she said.

Salvador shrugged and walked to the bedroom to change his clothes. He wanted to get out of his uniform, as he always did. In their bedroom, he took pleasure in feeling the comforts of married life. He appreciated the clean lines on their bed, the white bedcover stretched tightly over the mattress, adorned with decorative pillows in shades of orange and grey. Books were stacked high on the night table by Carmen's side and Salvador smiled, thinking how she encouraged him to read before falling asleep at night and how, most of the time, he was so exhausted that before he could take a book in his hands, he was asleep in her arms.

Carmen came into the room and sat at the foot of the bed. Leaning forward, she asked, "What's troubling you?"

"I couldn't protect her," he muttered.

"I'm sorry, I don't understand."

"They left her to rot in her cell—she committed suicide."

"*Hombre*, who are you talking about?" Carmen snapped.

"Lucia. I failed her," he said, sitting next to Carmen, taking her hand.

"*Dios Santo*, that's awful, but quite frankly I hadn't given her much thought lately," she said. "What on earth happened?"

"When I patrolled the area of town where she used to hang out, I kept an eye on her comings and goings. I could never convince her she had other alternatives in life. She never listened—constantly sitting at bars, waiting to turn the next trick, in and out of *hotelucho*s, cheap hotels, with unsavoury guys. She didn't want to give up the kind of money she made."

"You'd seen recently her?"

"This morning, I noticed her name on a document. She had been arrested and was left in a cell last night; when they went to see her in the morning, she was dead. I asked to be let into the cell, but it was too late. It had been cleaned, and her body taken away. Late this afternoon, the coroner's report confirmed she'd hanged herself."

"I am so sorry, Salvador. When did you last talk to her?"

"Not sure—a couple of months ago. Let's face it, she was an addict and needed rescuing," he sighed. "Maybe this was bound to happen sooner or later."

He put on his jeans and a T-shirt and followed Carmen out of the room. Placing his hands heavily on the dining room table, he waited for Carmen to bring out his soup. He thought about the time when he was in desperate need of shelter and Lucia came to his rescue. He felt an anxious flash go by; he owed her tremendous gratitude for teaching him how to survive on the streets. It would be hard to forget her, for she was the one he had to thank for being alive today. She'd always been on his mind and he'd wanted to help to her—damn—when he found her, it was too late. She'd been living a rough life and she had not been willing to rehabilitate. Once, when he approached her in his uniform, Lucia ran away, thinking he was going to harass her. When he caught up to her, she hadn't flinched, just pushed him away, then lunged to punch him in the face, calling him names.

"She'll go straight to hell," he said.

Carmen placed a generous portion of *caldo de gallina* for him on the table and said, "Try to forget her."

"She was so neglected, and in such a bad situation. She was unable to turn her life around. Now she's dead."

"She couldn't help it," Carmen said, coming to sit by his side.

"Jesus Christ, did it have to end this way—why couldn't she have cleaned up her act?"

Salvador had often talked to Carmen about Lucia, but he knew she'd heard the same story too many times and he also knew perfectly well that she maybe didn't want to hear any more about Lucia.

"I believed her when she said she would change, get clean, but she lied. I only deceived myself," Salvador said, slurping his soup.

"There's little you could've done. She'd suffered too much in her childhood, and needed to cover her deep pain."

"I feel I was the only person looking out for her. Life squeezed her hard," Salvador said. He was starting to sweat. Removing the napkin from his lap, he wiped his forehead and the back of his neck.

"Salvador, please keep in mind that you knew her when she was a child; you never knew the adult she became. You barely spoke to her."

Carmen was right. Lucia had disappeared from his life once he went to live with his uncle. "I find it hard to believe that she wouldn't have chosen something better for herself. She was smart. How could she have let herself be dragged through the gutter? At the end, she must only have felt loneliness and rage."

"You have no obligations to her. An addict grows old fast," Carmen said.

The truth barrelling out of Carmen's lips upset Salvador. "I should have attempted to persuade her to seek medical help," he said, in a defiant tone.

"You wouldn't have been able to make her do anything that she didn't want to do; she was headstrong," Carmen said, removing his bowl from the table and leaving the room.

Salvador woke up early the next morning feeling troubled. During the night, it had struck him that in order to alleviate his burden, he would have to do the right thing. He would claim Lucia's body and give her a proper burial, take her back to the cemetery in Cajamarca where they'd spent time. He had no other alternative, for otherwise her remains would end up in a pauper's grave.

When he hesitantly mentioned his thoughts to Carmen over breakfast, she shrugged her shoulders and, without much expression in her voice or her face, said, "If you must do this, go ahead."

Salvador was watching a soccer match with Carmen on their television when the phone rang. He turned down the volume as the voice on the line informed him to report to work without delay. They were experiencing disturbances at the stadium, and with the situation getting out of hand, they were urgently in need of backups.

"I've got to go; they need to intensify the surveillance on the streets," Salvador said.

"But it's Sunday, and you're not on duty," Carmen complained.

Salvador felt bad. Not a good day to take off without warning; this was his day at home with his wife, but today the *barras* were acting up. Backed up by criminal gangs, these fans were out to cause havoc and he'd have to face a thankless task.

There'd been warnings that trouble could brew between rival team fans after the match. Now they had surfaced early, before the game came to an end, and the hoodlums were already out to make trouble.

Salvador put on his uniform and got ready to leave. "There's no cause for alarm," he said when he saw the look of concern in Carmen's eyes.

"Stay safe, I'll be waiting when you come back," Carmen smiled, reaching over to press her lips against his.

Cursing inwardly, Salvador closed the door behind him and headed down the street to catch a bus.

Young men with cigarettes clamped between their teeth, faces painted with the colours of their team, waved banners in the wind. Some of the troublemakers were known to the authorities as violent fans, and it was precisely these young adolescents whom the police worried about. Concerned authorities had met with the coaches beforehand, demanding that they control their fans, but the clubs stated they couldn't assume the responsibility. The talk in Salvador's precinct was that the sports clubs didn't want to share in the cost of policing.

In the human sea in front of his eyes, Salvador spotted boys wielding bats and others getting into fist fights. He knew there were criminals among them taking advantage of the crowds to pick people's pockets, while others grabbed and threw rocks to vent their frustrations on the faceless crowd. Throngs of bystanders were caught in middle of a crowd that was getting out of hand. When Salvador came upon a group surrounding a car, shouting their team's cheers while trying to overturn the vehicle, he seized two boys at once. Others ran off as they dodged the broken glass flying from the car, ready to join another swarm. In a laneway, Salvador saw a group burning trash and black smoke was rising into the sky. Regular fans, sporting their team's shirts and hats, stood frozen in fright. They were simply trying to make their way home. A few of his colleagues carrying clubs knocked troublemakers to the ground before applying handcuffs. Men covered in blood, kicking and spitting, struggled to get loose from their restraints, as the cops became more forceful in their conduct.

"Take them away," a couple of breathless women wailed. "They're just out to make trouble."

Salvador was given orders to divert the crowd and to guide a police armoured van that was approaching to help a handcuffed boy who had convulsed and was now sitting on the curb,.

"Please, I've done nothing wrong," Salvador heard another man moan as he was shoved inside.

When Salvador saw the glare of additional police cruiser lights approaching, he felt a sense of relief; one thing was clear, tonight the police were outnumbered by the mob. Trying his best to keep his cool, he noticed ordinary citizens' faces growing pale as thugs intercepted them on their way home. Some tried to flee, but some couldn't run, for the hoodlums had spread gasoline on the road and a fire was starting to catch. A thankless job, Salvador thought, as a simmering anger spread through him. One hooligan grabbed the *muleta* of a handicapped child and, hollering loudly, lashing out to the left and the right, used the crutch to clear a path for himself. Feeling revulsion tinged with rage, Salvador cursed under his breath and ran to rescue the child. Instinctively the father lifted the boy to his arms as Salvador arrived at his side.

The tension escalated further and the violence worsened. It was an impenetrable jungle of young men pumped with drugs, acting like madmen, loudly rooting for their teams as they roamed the streets, mocking and confronting police. One young fan approached him, pointing a piece of broken bottle at his face, and Salvador went for his gun. He realized the fan was a boy, not even sixteen, who was now running away fast. Salvador had no doubt there'd be many stab wounds and a few deaths tonight, and he would have to be mindful not to endanger himself.

When the water cannons converged, his orders were to retreat from the scene right away. His cheek had been grazed and he was taken to see a paramedic who applied first aid. This disorder had surpassed any others he'd seen. Although hundreds would be arrested for inflicting serious damage, Salvador was sure there wouldn't be much of an investigation, and only a few would go in front of a judge. Most of them would be out on the streets before the next game came up.

He didn't get home until late; he was tired and every muscle in his body ached. He stood in the hallway before stepping into their bedroom, afraid to let Carmen see the shape he was in. Carmen lay still, breathing heavily in her sleep. Tomorrow she would insist he see a physician and be attended to properly to avert an infection, but he had other plans in mind.

25

SALVADOR KNEW that the morgue would only hold Lucia's body for a few days, and if nobody claimed her she would be interred in a common, unmarked grave. He would have to make arrangements to transport her body and have her cremated today. He reported to his precinct and as soon as he determined that he'd been scheduled to do paperwork, he asked his superior for permission to report to the coroner's office, to collect a prisoner's body whose death— seventy-two hours before—had been caused by asphyxia by hanging.

At the coroner's office, Salvador explained that he and the prisoner had been childhood friends and he was sure there would be no relatives coming to claim her, for during the war she'd lost contact with them. "I'm here to collect her body," he said, full of confidence. He was asked a few questions to establish the legitimacy of their relationship, then asked to return the next day. When on Tuesday he got confirmation that they would release the body, rather than having to dispose of it themselves at government expense, Salvador proceeded to make arrangements to have it cremated the following day.

How could he explain his need to give Lucia a proper burial? And why did he want the presence of others at her funeral besides just himself? The question arose as to who else he could ask to attend. He would have to hold back asking Carmen to come to Cajamarca with him, since she didn't care much for

211

Lucia—not enough to miss work. No matter how often he mentioned how unjust Lucia's hellish life had been, Carmen couldn't understand why he was obsessed with her funeral. Whenever he brought up her name, Carmen didn't hesitate to repeat, in a rather condescending way, "*dime con quien andas y te dire quien eres*—tell me who you associate with and I'll tell you who you are." Carmen insisted he was free to deal with Lucia as he wished, but she wouldn't be part of it. Thinking about Carmen's disapproval made him wince. Feeling a twinge of regret as he contemplated how lonely Lucia's life must have been, he struggled to think who else he could get in touch with. He knew so little about Lucia and even less about the company she'd kept.

All of a sudden a thought crossed his muddled brain. Lucia had talked about a nurse with whom she'd lived for a short time after she was raped. It had been an unsettling transition from the street to a home, and Lucia had run away because the nurse had been very strict. But perhaps the nurse wasn't as bad as Lucia had made her out to be. Wouldn't she have had a kind heart to take Lucia in? Had she been crushed when Lucia left her? Maybe the nurse would be open to hearing from him, and would help him make peace with his past. He tried hard to think of her name, but it wouldn't come to his mind. Nevertheless, he felt a certain sense of relief as he made the decision to go looking for her as soon as he got to Cajamarca.

Salvador took a week's leave from his job to go on this trip. He felt restless during the ride through the vast terrain and, after a while, became upset with the smell of eau de cologne reeking from the passenger sitting beside him. He grabbed a newspaper and glanced at some of the stories, but he was incapable of focusing, and in the end he realized he hadn't concentrated enough to remember any of the articles he'd supposedly read. He nodded off for a while and, when he awoke, was relieved to hear the belching of motorcycles moving alongside the bus on Cajamarca's main boulevard. When he stood to retrieve his backpack from the overhead bin, he saw the street vendors manning their sidewalk stalls near the bus depot.

He descended as a loudspeaker announced the arrival of their bus at gate twenty-nine. A saucy boy walked by, swinging a polishing kit in his hand; he asked Salvador if he wanted his shoes buffed, while another asked if he could help him carry his load. Reaching his right arm back, he patted the bulge in his pack. Soon he'd be able to leave Lucia to rest in a place she was worthy of.

He made some inquiries and started to walk in the direction of the women's clinic. He wondered if anyone there would know about a young woman in bad shape, who'd been rushed in for attention early one morning after being raped, during the time the country was in utter turmoil. Would anyone recall that after convalescing for a few days she'd been taken in by a nurse? Would anybody have noticed? Would Lucia have mattered to anyone else? Rosa? Was that her name? He had no last name to go along with it, but yes, that was it—Rosa. He was sure. In his excitement he increased his pace.

Salvador went up to the clinic's receptionist, a middle-aged woman with a round face who sat behind the counter rifling through mounds of paperwork. For a moment he was speechless; how could he explain his strange request? He inhaled quietly and began to tell her his story, about this girl he had met at the town square when he got separated from his parents, of how she'd taken him to live at the cemetery and showed him how to survive on his own. How, when he eventually found his uncle, he'd left her without saying good-bye, and by the time they went looking for her, she'd moved on. He tried to give a few details about discovering her some years later in Lima, where they'd had a few conversations. Then a few days ago he'd found out that she'd been arrested and had killed herself in jail. Now he was here to give her a proper funeral.

"She told me a kind nurse at the clinic had offered her shelter," he said. He found his voice cracking as he looked into the receptionist's eyes, while she patiently waited for him come to the end of his tale. Dropping his voice and his eyes, he said, "I've come to bury her in the cemetery where we lived."

It was strange but he felt relieved telling this stranger the motive for his trip. The woman looked up with suspicion and Salvador noticed the line that had formed between her eyes. Did she think he was out of his mind? She told him to wait and walked to a door in the back, which she shut behind her with a loud bang. Salvador felt foolish for having such vague information, and began to feel a degree of pressure mounting in his chest. He, too, would be skeptical if someone came up to him with a similarly half-baked story. He tried to regain his composure and went to sit in the waiting area next to a group of women, trying to appear nonchalant. When the receptionist returned, she waved him back to the counter and said, "You'll have to wait, but someone will be with you shortly."

It was nearing the end of the day, and after a lengthy wait, Salvador was becoming edgy. He slumped in the chair and tapped his foot nervously on the floor to get the receptionist to notice him. She lifted her face, looking up in annoyance, as if he were an impertinent child. Why should it matter if she liked him or not? he thought. Thinking it best to stay on her good side, he stopped fidgeting. He lowered his gaze to stare at the floor, pretending to be wrapped up in his own thoughts, but inside he was a bundle of nerves.

A woman dressed in white pants and shirt, with a stethoscope around her neck, finally came out from the back and walked toward him. "You have some inquiries to make?" she asked. Salvador leaped to his feet.

"I'm Dr. Cisneros," she said, stretching out her hand. "Please follow me this way."

After their meeting, Salvador was elated; he couldn't believe his good luck for he now had a telephone number and a full name. Once he arrived at the inn he had booked, he reached into his pants pocket for the coins to make a phone call.

"I won't waste your time," Salvador said, explaining the reason for his call.

"Why don't you come see me tomorrow after work," the woman on the line said.

Putting down the receiver, he remained standing. Impulsively, he started dialing Carmen, then stopped. He ached to tell her about his day, but this time, although he hated to admit it, he'd have to handle his emotions himself.

A procession of black limousines, with headlights burning dully in the glaring sunshine, followed the hearse that arrived at the cemetery as Salvador walked up to see if he could make arrangements for Lucia's funeral. He moved to one side to let the vehicles pass as they drove through the wrought-iron gates. He stared at the people getting out just ahead. They walked solemnly down a path to congregate at the side of an empty grave. People dressed in black appeared to be in deep mourning, shedding tears of grief. A woman opened her arms to embrace a fragile elderly gentleman, then buried her face in his neck and remained still in his embrace. When a priest in a flowing white robe showed up, people started lining up to shake his hand. From his hiding place, Salvador heard the cleric repeat "*Que Dios lo Bendiga,*" God be with you. Peering intently from his place behind a tree, Salvador was frankly curious. Unaware of how much time had passed, he suddenly spotted six stern men clad in tuxedos and white gloves. They were standing proudly next to the casket, getting ready to lower it into the freshly dug earth. Salvador began walking away as he heard the priest asking God to accept the soul of the deceased into the gates of paradise.

Salvador cut a deal with the funeral director to have a burial for Lucia by the end of the week. He'd been forced to grease the director's hand to get a site on such short notice. He didn't even think about the cost of the bribe, as he had a limited time to deal with the enervating arrangements.

Slowly, he made his way to Rosa's apartment, stopping to watch little children trip and tumble playing ball in a nearby field, then walking through the local food market, his old stomping grounds. His head was filled with thoughts of his time living alone, struggling to survive. Fighting off a flash of fear as he observed dead chickens hanging in a row from the hooks at the butcher's stall, he was grateful those days were long gone. Staying alive had been scary, but he had been made stronger by the experience.

Salvador listened attentively as Rosa shared with him how Lucia had broken her heart. "But mind you, she was a hand-ful—so many rough times. When I met her, all she had was a cool gaze and an ill-fitting dress. She talked very little about her past. Frankly, I was not able to get to know her well. Not to say I hadn't felt a strong desire to protect her. I saw how destitute she was and took pity; I liked her spunkiness. I can't say I ever got to the stage of loving her—she never allowed me to get that close." Rosa seemed mortified to admit this.

Before long, Rosa brought out a few pictures and told him about the endearing young girl Lucia could sometimes be. "At times I felt I was ready to adopt her—she could be so sweet."

Salvador scrutinized the photos and told Rosa about the months he had lived at the cemetery with Lucia. "Nothing scared her—she wasn't one to let fear get in her way. She saved me during the first cold days I was by myself. I couldn't have survived without her," he said, choking up. "I followed her with a sense of wonder as she navigated the streets, fending for the two of us. When I saw her again, I wanted to help her. I wanted to give back and get her away from the punishing life she was leading in Lima. I wanted to get her into a detox program, away from the world that fed her addiction, but she refused, time and again." Salvador asked if he could take a few of the pictures to get copies made. "Of course you may."

A wisp of a smile came over Rosa's face. "She was a strange one; she wanted to find out what life would be like for her in this part of town, but made no attempts to show gratitude. Perhaps I drove her out of the house. I couldn't figure out how to help her extricate herself from her past," Rosa continued. "She staked out her territory in my home, then thought it cool to withdraw into a world of her own. What was she thinking? I was always unsure of where I stood with her. I wanted to guide her and offered to take her under my wing; I wanted her to settle down into a steady routine. She conveyed such innocence, but was she ever shrewd.... Of course, she would have none of it. She confined herself to her room, amassing whatever she could, rather than sharing my life. What was I thinking?" She laughed.

"She was stubborn,' Salvador agreed. "That's the way she was during her whole short life."

Salvador continued to look at the photos, drawn to Lucia's dark, intense eyes.

"When she left, I was enraged," Rosa said. "She took some money and some jewellery. By then I was exhausted. I knew nothing good would ever come of her."

As the anecdotes tumbled out of Rosa's mouth, a picture of Lucia's life with Rosa emerged. The information filled some of the gaps and Salvador got a better sense of the life of his unpredictable friend. When Rosa had finished, Salvador asked, "I've come to ask for your help. I feel terribly sad having to bury her alone—would you consider attending a simple funeral?"

"I must confess that when I took her in, I wanted a child. Her departure was hard, but I had to accept the truth—we'd never find common ground. At times, a feeling of guilt still weighs on me. I should have done better; she was only a child. Yes, I will join you, and I will pay her my last respects."

26

O N THE BUS going home, reflecting on how many hours it would take to finish her work, Carmen glanced at the file she'd put inside her purse. The deadline for the grant application was due at the end of the week, and with one of the members of her team taken ill, she had agreed to complete what was left to be done. Getting off the bus at her stop, she began walking down the street, tucking her purse securely under her arm when she sensed that somebody was following close. Feeling uncertain, lightheaded with fear, she hastened her pace. When he started calling out endearing names she relaxed, for she knew that if she paid him no mind, his attention would fade. "*Amorcito, cosita rica,*" he said. Typical male behaviour, she thought; but once the words turned lewd, she increased her speed, practically running toward her apartment building. Once inside, she took the stairs two at a time.

Salvador was out playing cards with friends and Carmen decided to first do her usual twenty minutes of aerobic exercise. She needed to move, having sat at her desk all day. Then she'd get to work, and if later she still had time, she wanted to hang some of the family photographs she'd put in frames. She wanted a wall with pictures that would tell their family history and create a memory trail. Last February, on the anniversary of the day Salvador's parents went missing, Carmen gave him an empty frame and asked him to place in it a drawing of his parents and himself. Salvador had expressed no interest in her project, saying he wasn't ready to capture his unsettling past; his family life had commenced once they had gotten engaged and they had plenty of photographs capturing their current fortunate life. Although Salvador had been forced to become responsible at a young age, making something out of himself out of the sheer need to survive, abandonment was still a raw emotion in his heart.

"You don't have to do a perfect portrait. You're a good artist, why not try? We have no formal records of your family as it existed; we should try to recreate your past," she maintained.

But he wasn't ready. "Some events are not meant to be recorded," he claimed.

Realizing that the memory of separation was still too painful, Carmen left it alone until the next time he tried to bring forth memories that were blurred in his mind. Then she begged him again. One day the opportunity came up again when she talked to him about how art was currently being considered as a therapeutic tool, and they were going to start making use of it at her work. "The ultimate goal is to use art to help those who went through traumatic experiences to improve their emotional well-being," she said.

It took months before Salvador yielded to Carmen's request. As he pondered and overcame his indecision, he started to sketch. "I can recall a few things from my childhood, but my parent's looks, forget it—they're long gone. Perhaps I could make up a family tree with some stick figures and names, but I can't do more," he said.

They laughed at a draft depicting a family gathering where relatives resembled caricatures of themselves. "That was Pepo; he had a chin as long and narrow as a pin, he was so wrinkled. He passed away shortly after." Since Salvador's early years were a mystery, he'd done his best to recall a few of his family member's salient traits.

She arranged the frames on the dining room table and looked at them. She reached for the silver heirloom frame they had received as a wedding gift that featured a photograph of her *abuelos,* her grandma and grandpa. They sat dressed in their Sunday finest, posing stiffly, and gazing raptly at the camera lens. Next, she picked up the light wooden frame holding Salvador's work.

She was up on the stepladder, hammering skillfully, when Salvador walked in. "What a nice surprise, you're not too late," she said.

"The guys wanted to go out to a bar, but we were warned that the *peperas* are out actively targeting men. Last night, young women were found to have spiked a cop's drink and the drugs caused a pulmonary edema. He's dead."

"Glad you came home."

"My work of art," Salvador said, going to stand to contemplate his composition on the wall. Can I give you a hand?"

"Wait, I'm coming down."

Salvador stretch out his arm to take hold of the hammer she held in her hand. Smiling, she nuzzled his neck, kissed him, and then placed her fists on the small of her back.

"We have to talk," she said, dragging him to the couch, then sitting upright to face him. "I thought you'd be interested in this notice." She reached for a piece of paper that she had tucked into the pocket of her jeans. "There's a need to train members for additional forensic teams. Work is moving ahead fast, as they've been uncovering many more burial grounds. There is a real shortage of people to do the job. They're estimating that there might be more than four thousand sites scattered throughout the country, and they need to lay out a national plan to recover and identify remains. I thought of you , Salvador."

Salvador looked at her silently. "I don't know if I could handle that line of work. Am I cut out to dig for corpses? It'd be unnerving; I'm not sure I can summon the strength. It's too close to my heart."

"I can understand."

"I'll have to think about it, sort it out in my mind."

Always the practical one, Carmen could not hold her tongue and said, "It would be a great break for your career, definitely a step up. Why not give it a try?"

Salvador shook his head.

"Take your time," Carmen said, stroking his arm. "Don't rush into negative thoughts. Think of it as a helping hand for people to gain some peace of mind."

"What about us? It would be hellish. We'd be involved with even more gory details of the past."

"We'd make a pact. We'd have to set those conversations aside, play more chess, go for long walks in nature, or, tune into soap operas at night."

"Yeah, and get another glimpse of imaginary turmoil," Salvador laughed.

"Listen, Salvador, as a cop on the beat, your life's at risk every day; if you switch jobs you will at least be safer."

"And perhaps I'll finally learn how my parents were finished off."

Salvador was accepted into the crime investigator's training program the following September. He attended classes for six months then job-shadowed a couple of forensic officers before qualifying for a post. He soon discovered that trying to recover victims of armed conflict was no easy task. "The bones tell the story," one of the instructors had informed the class, and so it was.

Digging graves for remains required a strong stomach and a resilient mind. On one of his first field trips, he was sent along with a team to a remote site, a considerable distance from the nearest road, across a brook and up a hill where, in a clandestine grave, over two hundred bodies were said to lie. The foul odor of decomposition was a struggle to tolerate at first. Disgust and fascination guided his days as they excavated bodies, digging with shovels, refining with trowels, unearthing small bones, uncovering skulls. Salvador had a constant lump in his throat as he collected and documents pieces of clothing.

At times, they were joined by people from the villages nearby who'd heard that they would be looking for the dead. People clustered near the grave in bewilderment, some silently cursing, making signs of the cross, some observing fearfully, others annoyed or agitated. On one occasion, as the team began lifting buckets of earth in a gentle, respectful manner, a few older widows, holding pictures of their missing husbands, began to pray.

The team conducted exhumations in the most professional way, according to international standards, to determine cause of death. They wanted to establish proper identification, but at times this proved complicated. A body that had been buried and exhumed would carry with it the telltale signs of the burial place, but it was like working a puzzle, piecing together the unknown. The team would screen the dirt for bits of artifacts to determine the cause of death. Had there been injuries? Could they verify an individual's gender, age, race, height, and weight? Was it possible to obtain fingerprints? Had there been executions? Had they been planned? Had the victims struggled? Did the remains bear signs of execution style killings? Was there a trace of physical violence, a single gunshot wound to the head? Would they be able to obtain eyewitness accounts?

In one case, after great deal of painstaking work, only a few fragile bones were unearthed. They were put aside to attempt to establish identity at a later date. Each body was mapped to its location in the grave and then placed in a body bag for further examination. Meticulously scrutinizing a body was part of the task.

By the end of the day, covered in grime, after they had documented exactly what, where, and which items they had unearthed, Salvador would be more exhausted than he had ever been in his previous job. He didn't complain—the wealth of information obtained was of utmost importance for telling the victims' final stories and would provide their families with closure. Carmen had been right; he was doing his bit to help bring about a new sense of hope and to get the guilty to own up to their crimes.

At night, after they covered the pits where they'd worked with tarps, they carried their shovels and picks back to their trucks that were parked close to their makeshift camps. Local women provided them with hot meals and the local men with security around the work site. Before collapsing into bed, they scrubbed away the dirt and the smell of earth in the icy brook running through the area.

The first time he came home after several weeks in the field, Salvador felt dismal. Chairs, lamps, pillows, plants—everything was neatly in its place. The curtains were drawn and not even a pallid light seeped into the living room. Feeling as dark as the room itself, he was in need of silence, wondering how he, one of the many survivors, would ever heal from his ordeal.

He'd made sure he was back at the apartment before Carmen came home, as he had no words to explain what he'd seen and how he felt. Over the years, he'd heard many gruesome stories, but experiencing the grave sites was something altogether different. Getting a close glimpse of what had gone on was not like reading a book—it rankled the brain. After all these years, he'd expected his work as a policeman to have hardened him, but this wasn't the case. He felt tense and needed time on his own to recover from the harsh weeks. As the minutes passed and he started to feel less disturbed, he rose from the sofa to get a beer from the fridge. Recalling that he had drunk the last one before he had left for the field, he felt disappointed. It was just what he needed to calm his nerves. But when he pulled open the door to see what else he could have, he noticed the fridge was well stocked; Carmen had bought beer for him. He smiled. This was the kind of attention he appreciated from his wife.

He sat listening for sounds, and when the front door unlocked, he jumped up, and pulled his wife into his arms.

"You look exhausted," she said, after pulling back from a long kiss. "Was it a difficult trip?"

Staring fixedly into her face, he related the details of the past weeks of work.

"You've got to be strong," she said. "This is important work."

The muscles of his neck tensed as he said, "What if one of the bones I unearthed belonged to my mom?"

It would take time before he could go about his work with dispassion. "The sheer magnitude—I'm in shock. I can't help but feel both pity and rage."

"But think about it, you are collecting tons of evidence and will be able to pursue further federal aid."

"As we dig, townspeople come over to look. I wonder how they keep it together. They come to get a glimpse of the bodies. While standing around they pray, for the dead and the living, I guess. What do they think? How they've lost everything and can't forge ahead to make better lives for themselves? Or are they thinking about their dead son's marital infidelities, the illegitimate children he left? Or maybe about their dead husband's gambling problem and his debts?"

"Please, Salvador, cut it out," Carmen said.

"And the dead, what secrets did they carry with them to their graves?"

His hair had grown since he departed, and he swept back a strand from his forehead. "Several dozen shrines had sprouted by the time we left. They expect us back."

"Graves are the homes of their loved ones' spirits; they've come to honour them. I'm glad they came to pay homage—it's good to know they feel safe enough to do so."

27

SALVADOR NOTICED the envelope with his name lying on the kitchen counter. Turning it over, he recognized the return address. A few months had elapsed since he'd appeared in Cajamarca at Rosa's door, and when he departed, they'd promised to keep in touch. Salvador tore open the envelope, unfolded the paper, and read it twice. His heart started to beat fast, for no one would have imagined he'd get the news he just did. Rosa was inquiring if perhaps there could be a link between him and a woman she'd met up at the Cerro Obscuro Mine in the 1990s. She was sure she'd kept her name and address, and had found it last week when she'd had the time to dig for it up in her attic. She remembered the lady had a somewhat unusual name, and when she heard him say his mother's name was Otilia, something clicked. The woman had left her an address before she departed with an American gentleman to the United States, saying that if anybody wanted to find her, that was where she'd be.

Otilia Campos de Perez, he read and started to shake. Could this be his mother? But Perez? Was that his real family name? Was Perez the name Tomas had done away with when he acquired the new birth certificate for him? Salvador was too young to remember when Tomas first told him he would be changing his surname. It had to be done, he had said, so he could get into a good school in Lima and have a chance at a life. He vaguely remembered going along to visit one of Tomas' friends, but had no recollection of what had been discussed. Once he obtained a birth certificate with a different name, Salvador got explicit instructions not to tell anyone. The one time he slipped, Tomas had gotten upset. They'd been visiting neighbours and the conversation had stopped abruptly; Tomas corrected him, explaining Salvador's mistake. "An adoption," Tomas had said.

All along he'd heard from his uncle that his parent's name was tainted and he warned Salvador to be careful or, "They'll come after you, next time."

As the years went by, the young Salvador didn't give the matter much thought and he continued his life as Salvador Rosas. But as a teenager, not wanting to tarnish the memories of his past, he asked Tomas questions about his mom and dad and the reasons for his change of name. All his uncle would say was, "It was easier on both of us." At the time Salvador hadn't complained, but now he wondered why he hadn't put up a fight. He was horrified and annoyed at himself for becoming hard to trace.

Looking once more at the letter he held in his hands, Salvador couldn't believe that this was how the information he laboured for years to obtain had at last shown up. With sweat running under his arms, he went to dial Rosa. "I got your letter," he said, in an almost curt tone. Realizing his lack of manners, he paused, then took a deep breath. "Rosa, this is Salvador, thank you so much for your note." Still in shock, and hardly able to fully absorb the whole story, he asked, "How did you meet her? What was she like?"

"Salvador, I'm sorry. I don't recall exactly who she was. Just a vague recollection of a woman who appeared anxious and sad, and had an unusual name—but there were so many others. It was a long time ago, my boy, and I don't have a clear memory of the incident."

"Where did you say this was?"

"I worked as a nurse a few times a month up at the mine. What was unusual was that she had run away and had arrived at the mine by herself, scared the armed forces would come after her."

"Are you sure she was alone?"

"Yes, I remember her telling me she lost her husband and child."

"What did she look like?" Salvador asked, his stomach tightening.

"I can't answer that. I suddenly had a flashback a few days after I met you, recalling that Otilia had given me an address and said that if ever someone came looking for a mother who lost her husband and child, this was where she went."

Was she still at that location? he wondered. In the United States? His heart hammered and, gripping the phone, he called the overseas operator to ask for the state of California, so he could obtain the phone number for his mom. "S-w-e-e-n-e-y," he spelled, and a few minutes later, a recording was telling him that the phone number was no longer in service.. He hung up. His English was not very good. He'd wait until Carmen got home to ask her to speak to an American operator and see if she could understand what was said.

When Carmen came back to the apartment, Salvador was distressed and tense. Without saying a word, he handed her the letter he was trying to decode. Carmen scanned it carefully and then looked at her husband, a flash of hesitation in her eyes.

"I've been trying to call and a voice tells me the number is no longer in service, or at least, that's what I think it is saying."

"I can't believe this—maybe this is the miracle we've been waiting for," Carmen said, as she sat down next to him, and put her arm around his shoulder.

"Or maybe it's a hoax. Can you please try to get information?" he said, handing her the phone.

They didn't get far in their search for leads; the phone had been disconnected and there were no other numbers to dial.

"I'll write a letter, but I need to pick your brain first," Salvador said, inspecting the address Rosa had sent.

"We'll discuss it over dinner. Is that all right?" Carmen said, walking away. "There's no point in saying too much," Carmen called out from the kitchen as she washed her hands.

"I agree, just the basics. Why would she have gone to a mining camp?"

"She was running away. We must find out what happened that day. But why would she have left the country?" Carmen asked.

Carmen was impressed at how rapidly Salvador came up with ideas for actions he could take to find this Otilia. The doors to his past had been locked and now that he'd found a rare opening, he was acting fast, scared he'd lose the trail.

"I'll call the mine and talk to the human resources department," he said. With paper and pencil in his hand, he looked up at Carmen and asked, "What should I say?"

With a heavy hand, he started to write and didn't look up until he'd composed a draft: *The family separated ... disappeared without a trace ... haven't been able to track down my mother ... asking to please pass on this information....*

Carmen stood behind his chair, looking over his shoulder to offer suggestions as he read her the sentences he had composed. "I'm worried that your deep wounds will be torn open again," she whispered when he was through.

"Please understand that I must follow this lead," he said, turning around to embrace her. Placing his hands on her back, he pulled her tightly to him.

"Tomorrow we'll have the letter translated and mailed," she said.

"Let's see where this city is located," Salvador said, walking over to the bookshelf to pick up the world atlas. Turning the pages, his mind froze for a second. "Close to San Francisco. This is where the conference was being held," Salvador said, running his hands over his face. "I'll be there in a few months," he added.

Carmen looked at him, perplexed. Salvador hadn't told Carmen that his boss had recently shown him a flyer announcing an Interpol training workshop to take place in San Francisco. He frankly hadn't given it much thought, but all of a sudden this trip was imminent and he shared the details with his wife. He jumped up. He had to let his work know right away that he was ready to go. In anticipation, he couldn't think about anything else. His mind was full of possible outcomes.

"Excellent!" Carmen exclaimed. "If we don't have an answer about Otilia by then, you can get your colleagues at the conference to help find her," she joked.

28

O TILIA RECEIVED a call from Michael to say that he had a
letter for her from Lima in his hands. "It came to Joan's
old address—can you come pick it up after work?"

Otilia was taken aback. "Who is it from?" she asked.

"There's a street and number, no name: Does General Bulnes
235 mean anything?"

"Not a thing. I'll be there a little after five."

When Otilia got out of the elevator, Michael was standing
at the door waiting for her. He was starting to look rather
frail and today he looked considerably worn out. There were
holes in the elbows of his sweater, and he had on thick horn-
rimmed glasses. Even though his frame was lean, he was slow
in his actions; he was hunched over and he shuffled his legs.
He did not venture far from his home these days, claiming he
became easily fatigued. He had not seemed old until recently.
He was lucky, though, that his mind was still sharp and he
could still discuss the ins and outs of any issue, at any time.
Otilia continued to appreciate his wisdom and always sought
his input when she had concerns or decisions to make. She felt
sad that Michael didn't have a *familia* watching out for him
at this time in his life.

Michael was holding the envelope in his hand. Perplexed,
she tried to understand how it could have possibly gotten to

Joan. Who would have her old address? Somebody up at the Cerro Obscuro mine? Was it fate working in strange ways? She tore open the envelope while standing in his entry hall, read it silently to herself, then read it aloud to Michael. She was flabbergasted. She had practically given up hope that anything would ever come of her very long search, and now this news had arrived in this strange way.

"Pick up the phone, call them immediately," Michael said, walking into his living room.

"I will call," Otilia said, taking in a deep breath.

"What time would it be in Lima?" Michael asked.

"Two hours ahead. How did this letter ever get to you?"

"Thanks to the U.S. Postal Service," he said. "They were so kind as to track Joan down. Since she had moved to an assisted living residence, I'm sure they felt sorry for her."

"When did she receive it?"

"It came in yesterday's mail. Go ahead, use my phone—I have a good long-distance plan."

"I think I need to go home and compose myself. I've waited for this moment for so long that an hour or two won't make a big difference. And besides, how can we really know this letter came from my son. But first, have you eaten? Let me see what I can prepare for you before I go. I think you are losing weight."

"*Hola*," she said, when she heard a man's deep voice answer the phone. "*Yo soy* Otilia."

There was silence. "I received a letter…" Overcome by emotions she choked up.

"*Soy* Salvador," he responded, and at that moment she burst into tear.

A few minutes later she apologized, saying how sorry she was that her emotions were taking over, and how sorry she was that they were apart. Circumstances had forced their separation and she had always feared for his life. "I was sure you were being cared for by your father. I never stopped searching," she stammered. "Is Manuel there with you?"

There was a long silence. "No, I never saw him again."

There was so much to say.

"*Mijito*, my dear boy, how happy I am to have found you."

"Not so fast," Salvador said. "We must be sure we're related before we go there. I'm not prepared to disclose further details on the phone."

Otilia was frankly surprised. This was the first of many leads that clearly approximated her story and he was on guard?

"I'm attending a conference in San Francisco and will meet you when I come," Salvador said.

"You're coming?" she gasped, her head spinning around. "When?"

"March."

"That is wonderful news. Let me give you my address and phone number; where will you stay? You can stay here with me."

"I'll be in touch when I get there."

"Can I pick you up at the airport?" she asked.

"I'll be busy with others. I'll let you know when I'm free."

Otilia was hurt by his detachment. He'd taken the time to track her down and wanted to see her, but would not release further information until they met. He was unwilling to reveal anything about himself. Would a longer phone call not have assuaged his concerns? He wanted proof she was his mother, yet their stories appeared to be so intertwined. He seemed cold and dismissive. Why would he have so many doubts? Was that how he dealt with life? Was this the result of things gone horribly wrong at a moment's notice when he was a young child? Otilia felt grief.

Weary and confused, she decided she needed someone to talk to. She picked up the phone to call Michael and be comforted by his usual words of advice.

"He was curt and suspicious, he doesn't trust me. I expected my son to be caring," she cried.

"Don't worry," Michael replied, noting the alarm in her voice. "He doesn't want to act abruptly, only to be disappointed if your stories diverge. Caution is good. Try not to overreact, don't overanalyze."

"I see what you're saying. He might have the right attitude," she said.

"You have both gone through incredible hardship; try to see where he is coming from."

"I was under the illusion that once I found him, my nerves would be calm, that my anxieties would stop and we could reunite. I didn't expect it to be so hard."

"Don't hold a grudge. Spare yourself the frustration until you're face-to-face."

These were good words of advice and she felt more relaxed. She would have to wait patiently until Salvador showed up. She would try not to resent that she'd been thrown for a loop by his attitude and simply rejoice that they would soon be together again.

29

M ETAL RAILINGS GUIDED the crowd funneling into the
immigration lineup. When, after a long wait, Salvador
was finally called up to an officer's booth, the large man took
his passport and asked, "Reason for your visit, sir?"

Twice the officer looked at the passport picture then at his
face, as Salvador responded, "Work." When Salvador presented the letter he carried, advising that he would be attending a
conference sponsored by Interpol, the officer's frown turned
into a smile. "Welcome to the United States," he said.

Salvador proceeded to gather his luggage from the baggage
claim and walked out of the airport to find a shuttle to take
him to his hotel. The driver loaded his suitcase in the back
and told him to sit up front. Stepping into the idling van,
he noticed that all the passengers were engaged on their cell
phones. Before pulling away, the driver reminded Salvador to
secure his seat belt. As the vehicle merged onto the highway,
Salvador watched the landscape unfold. The road was lined
with large hotels and tall buildings with global company names.
En route, as the city came into view, he noticed a variety of
homes nestled into the hills and the clouds lingering above the
skyscrapers that emerged in the distance. Once they reached
the downtown core, a light rain started to fall.

Otilia was nervous, patiently waiting to hear from Salvador.

He had told her he would be in the city on the twelfth, and it was now the fifteenth of the month and he still hadn't called. Today she felt her mind slowing, and her thoughts interfered with her actions all day. Ineffective at work, the numbers in the ledger jumped all over the page, until she decided she needed to put her thoughts and her hopes to the side, and just concentrate on the tasks at hand.

Late that night, before going to bed, she checked her answering machine one more time after showering and then became angry—angry that the events in her country had warped her role as a mother, and denied her the ability to care for her son. Who had been there to love him? To protect him? Why did he have to face childhood alone? As an orphan, had he been bullied or made fun of? Had somebody spit in his face? She was mad at a world that had taken her son from her. But perhaps it was he who was procrastinating, coming up with excuses not to see her, arguing that she was really not his mother, avoiding the promised encounter. She reminded herself that she'd experienced years of disappointment and this could well be one more. In the past, every time she had hit upon a piece of useful information, all she'd gotten was frustration. This might be no different, just another false alarm.

At ten thirty that evening, after the phone rang, she began to relax. Salvador told her he could meet her the next day in the late afternoon. Now all she could do was wait. What was his history like? Did he have a family? Many friends? What fears did he have? What cheered him up? What activities gave him pleasure? Was he in pain? Was he able to enjoy life? So many questions popped into her mind. Would she find traces of her little boy on his face? She couldn't have slept more than two hours, as hundreds of brief thoughts burst through her mind, but when she awoke, her sheets were damp and sweat trickled down her face.

At five o'clock in the morning, she rose from her bed and opened the door to her closet to look for something appropriate to wear. Not black. Something casual and tasteful, appropriate for her age. Something bright, for after all they were both alive. She walked over to the dresser and picked up the picture frame to contemplate the only photograph she had of her son, his image frozen in time. The more details she noticed, the harder it was for her to imagine him as a mature man. She should have taken the photo to one of those places that projected how a person would look when they grew up. Regardless, she would welcome him with open arms. Would they argue? Would she be compelled to ask for forgiveness for having dragged him into this lengthy separation? She had no doubts he was struggling with similar ghosts from the past. She was also aware that her beliefs and her view of life wouldn't necessarily synchronize with his.

She had bought a bunch of lovely cut flowers and prepared little Peruvian snacks; the Pisco Sour sat in a pitcher on the tray, with two glasses at either side. What if he didn't drink alcohol? She'd offer him lemonade; she had plenty of fresh lemons to squeeze. She went to turn up the volume of the instrumental guitar ballads playing on her device; anticipating a knock on the door, she went to open it. The footsteps she'd heard in the corridor were the next door neighbour's.

Tears sprang into her eyes as she thought about whether she'd be able to catch up with the rest of his life. She was hoping to be calm when she caught the first glimpse of her son; feeling unsettled in her mind, with a great deal of apprehension, she went to a mirror to check how she looked. Michael wasn't the only one who had aged. Would Salvador even recognize her?

When Salvador arrived, he was carrying a flowery paper bag under his jacket. She became emotional when she accepted his gift and, with difficulty, spoke her welcoming words to let him know this was also his home. Placing the package on the coffee table, she turned to face him. She stared into his face and smiled. How handsome he looked in his suit and tie.

Standing next to each other, they let a moment go by; then they embraced. Clinging for a few minutes, she smelled his skin, then reached out to feel his warm cheeks. Making a great deal of effort not to cry, she lowered her hands down to her sides. His manner felt so familiar; she sensed him so near to her heart. He was much taller than she, but she was sure she could see the family resemblance in his eyes. *Tristeza*—wistfulness is not distributed equally, she thought; how unjust it is to fall only on some.

Salvador had a drink and a few nibbles and was showing no desire to be on his way too soon. They conversed about his trip, her apartment, their likes and dislikes, unhurriedly discovering some common preferences. Before she knew it, Otilia felt calm, and little by little, through their interchange, her story came to light.

"I never imagined that when you left, I was saying good-bye forever," she said. "Separations are akin to death. You must believe me when I say I felt wretched inside. It was a struggle; Michael stopped me from drowning, showing me support and standing by me endlessly. He offered me work at his sister's home until I got the language under my belt; then I was able to work somewhere else and that family encouraged me to pursue my education. Without him, I wouldn't have had the strength to carry on. You must understand I was suddenly facing and negotiating a system I knew nothing about, away from my family, desperately trying to find you from afar. I was reluctant to remain in this country, but was told it wouldn't be safe to go back home. Every time I heard there'd been a change within the administration, or pressure placed on the government by some foreign agency, I had flickering hopes. My only wish was to unite with you and your dad. I never lost faith; deep in my heart I knew that, with time, more information would show up. Honestly, in the last months I was beginning to feel worn down."

"Why was Michael so intent on helping you out?" Salvador asked.

"*Mijo,* there are still a few good people around—Michael is one of them. You have no idea how hard he fought to obtain support for my case."

She took a deep breath to calm herself, to stop the words from tumbling out too fast. "Through the church, I joined a community of others in similar predicaments, and we lobbied actively to get information on our loved ones who were gone. I filed appeals contending that everything was lost—my home, all my possessions—and, of course, my husband and you.

"I heard nothing. During the Fujimori years, the authorities spurned my requests, denying any claims of wrongdoing. I wrote letters to a myriad of organizations—the Organization of American States, the United Nations, United States congressmen. At times some newspapers published stories of how people were disappearing in Latin American countries, but soon after, the issue would fade from the spotlight, and I continued being left empty-handed. I feel I worked hard, dedicating practically my entire life to trying to find you, but nothing was ever disclosed."

She looked deep into his eyes. "What more was I to do? I just waited and waited until it was safe to travel back for a few months."

Sitting still, Salvador listened.

"There's been so much pain, so many nights of lying awake, thinking about that *maldito* day—the day we got separated. I still see clearly how your father took you to safety; not knowing where you were made me go crazy. You were everything, son. I felt crippled. To be so powerless.... From one moment to the next you were no longer with me, I had no child at my side, and you had no mother, God forgive me. I've been looking for you for so long.... How many times, with envy, did I watch mothers playing with their sons in the park? The events shortchanged us both."

"The burdens of history—how hard it must have been for you to see Dad take me to safety." Salvador stretched his hand to lay it on top of hers.

"I'm so sorry," she said. Looking at him, she gave a sigh. "Aren't you hungry? I could put a little dinner together. I wasn't sure of your plans."

"Sure, why don't we go see what you've got in your fridge?"

Otilia walked over to the kitchen and he followed behind her. She opened the refrigerator and took a few dishes out. "Avocado, tomatoes, bread—why don't I fry up some eggs?"

Salvador loosened his tie, and removed his jacket, placing it on the back of a dining room chair. "Son, will you pick some basil?" she said, pointing to the container on the windowsill.

After retrieving the frying pan from the cupboard, Otilia poured in some oil. "I kept copies of all the letters I wrote."

"I'd like to see them sometime. Perhaps they could help in our search for my dad."

"I went back to Lima a few months ago. I wish I had known where you lived. I tried to find my brother, but could find no record of him. He wasn't listed in the phone book. I went to the main post office, but found no address under his name. I spoke to a lawyer and made depositions; the days slipped away and I didn't get much accomplished. When I went up to El Milagro, I had a lot of wool pulled over my eyes. I met Doña Alba, one of our acquaintances, and was surprised when she reported that your dad had been killed in a blast."

"A bomb? When?"

"Her explanations were vague; she said he came back to our home, and that a few days later there'd been a car accident. I'm trying to determine if that is in fact what happened, but I haven't been able to get any confirmation of these facts."

Salvador remained silent as Otilia abandoned herself to her story, explaining that nothing back then could have predicted the mess that was generated. Listening to her words unlocked a certain compassion in him, which led to his opportunity to open up. Sitting erect at the dining table, placing his hands on the back of his head, he turned his neck from side to side, then began to reveal the story of his years growing up.

She learned all about his first months alone and the care he got from the child he befriended at the time. "A street urchin?" she gasped. "How did you manage? Was your friend a good girl?"

"I followed her up to a cemetery. We lived in the graves."

"I'm so sorry," she said, feeling her heart beating fast.

"We wandered around the city and managed quite well."

"You begged?"

"Shopkeepers at the market were kind."

"Did you have enough to eat? You must have been exposed to all kinds of things."

"It wasn't too bad."

"And what about your clothes? You must have outgrown the ones you were in."

"We stole some." He told her how when the weather turned cold they had picked up long pants from a laundry line. "We had fun."

She didn't know what to say. Could this have been considered a crime? If anything, she was the one to blame, for she was guilty of not offering continuity, stability, love—all the responsibilities of a parent. She noticed how dignified he looked sitting there; perhaps he wanted to make her see how far he'd come.

"We were kids; we didn't mind. By the time I met my *tío,* my shoes had grown small, and they had holes. One day I decided to paint a face on the sole, stick a couple of fingers through the holes, and put on a puppet show. One well-groomed little boy at the market stopped by with his mom and placed a few coins on the curb where I performed. I got the idea that I could entertain others, and although I didn't collect enough money for shoes, it helped pass the time."

He was too young for social pretentions, and treated his

displacement as a game. But he was at risk nonetheless; there must have been many dangerous elements around him. "You were smart, so very resourceful for somebody so young. I'm impressed. Weren't you afraid?"

"Sometimes, but mostly I didn't have time to be scared."

And who was this *tío* he was referring to? She held her tongue when he mentioned his name.

"I figured I'd better find a relative to move in with. I remembered you talking about Tomas, driving a taxi in Cajamarca. I didn't remember ever meeting him; I didn't know where to find him, but one day I stumbled upon him."

"You grew up with him?" She gasped. She felt envy that her brother had been able to see him growing up. At least her son appeared calm; he didn't seem to have quarrelsome tendencies.

"Tomas thought he was keeping me safe by not helping me find you," he said.

"And you became untraceable," she mumbled, staring into the distance, lost in her thoughts.

"Yes, he changed our names. I fought him on that, but now I realize I was too young to do much. I needed to trust him— what else could I do? In my teenage years, when I wanted to find you, *al tío se le subia el Indio*. He'd become mad; the native in him would arise."

"Don't say such a thing," Otilia said, horrified to hear him use those terms.

"When he got the forged birth certificate we became Rosas, you see, and he appeared as my legal guardian."

"You mean to say he nullified Perez?"

"Campos and Perez. He didn't want those names appearing on any legal documents. He said that since my dad was responsible for getting the family in trouble, keeping those names was dangerous."

"Manuel had nothing to do with the events." Otilia's body stiffened and her voice rose.

"He thought the terrorists were the only people disappearing, and since you were gone, you had to be one of them."

"Oh my God, Salvador, he was so wrong. He acted like a coward." She stopped herself in her tracks, not wanting to come across as judgmental. Feeling upset that her derelict brother had played such an important part in her son's life, she was beside herself. "And as for Manuel, if he was killed in a car blast, it was because he was probably at a certain place at an unfortunate time."

"Are you sure?" Salvador asked.

"If it's true that his body was burned, charred, unable to be identified, I guess no report was ever made."

Simmering inside, Otilia felt bitterness as, for the first time, she found out how dishonest and two-faced Tomas was. She must be compassionate, she reminded herself, since her brother had done what he could to provide her son with a safe home. What weighed her down was Tomas's deception, and the degree of spitefulness he showed. How could he not have encouraged Salvador to search for his parents at such a vulnerable time?

Averting her eyes from her son, she remained silent for a while. She ached with hurtful feelings brought on by the unfair events that had turned their lives upside down. After a moment she said, "We'll need to get a firmer grip on things."

As the evening went on, she learned he was married to a beautiful girl, and had pursued a career with a promising future; he was ambitious and doing well. He seemed to have coped, but how would he have turned out if he'd been offered a regular home? Could he have become an attorney if he'd had the opportunity for more education? Did he belong to Tomas? Had her brother injected his prejudices and shaped his behaviour? Had Tomas maligned Salvador's parents, instigating negative feelings, strong enough to undermine his feelings for them?

It was getting late and Salvador checked his watch and said, "Time for me to go. I want to call my wife to tell her half of my history is getting resolved. We'll continue our conversation tomorrow."

"I'll come to your hotel at eleven o'clock, son. Sleep well— *duerme bien*."

30

SALVADOR ATTENDED a workshop highlighting the case of a shrewd Peruvian member of the armed forces. The extradition process began when the U.S. Immigration and Custom Enforcement Agency received information from Interpol, indicating he had been involved in significant human rights violations back in his own country and was possibly hiding in Florida.

"What are you saying?" Carmen asked, the night Salvador phoned to keep her informed.

"I bet he remained with the help of intelligence operations who support the caring dictators of the world."

"What's he accused of?" Carmen asked.

"He ordered soldiers under his command to kill women, children, and men in a small town in Ayacucho. He was pardoned by Fuji's Congress, at the time when the amnesty laws were passed shielding military personnel involved in counter-insurgency from all prosecutions; his immunity was assured."

"A U.S. trained military officer, no doubt."

"In 2002, when power changed hands and the new Supreme Court rescinded the general pardon, he left."

"Went to the States?"

"Yes, and made a big mistake—he overstayed. Charged with visa fraud, he pleaded guilty, and while he was serving his sentence, his surviving victims sued for damages."

"Good for them."

"Now he is waiting for his expulsion to take effect."

"We must keep an eye on other similar cases."

"You are right; many remain in complete impunity," Salvador said. "But at long last there are agencies that are watching out for them."

Before turning off the lights, Salvador considered how hard it would be to uncover the facts about his father's so-called accident, for he knew there'd been little accountability for the barbarities committed in the name of national security, in its zeal to stamp out guerillas and leftist militants. He was aware that the records from those years pointed to serious irregularities, and many of the few that remained were said to have used testimonies from people paid to make false statements. They'd have to aggressively hunt down the perpetrators, search for witnesses, and think of ways to hold their ground in demanding lawful accountability for what had occurred. In his work, he was unearthing bodies day after day, but there was no knowledge of where the offenders were. He would have to press hard to see what stories, faces, and names he could disentangle in the unexpected places he was sent, then begin placing blame.

And then there would be another issue, the misappropriation of the victims' properties.

Salvador crawled out of bed to go to the gym an hour before he had scheduled room service to deliver breakfast. As he stood in front of the mirror shaving, he remembered that he must place his camera alongside his room key, for Carmen had insisted he take lots of pictures of his mother and the city he was visiting. Taking the elevator down to the lobby, he first went to see the concierge. He was unsure if his mother would care to see Alcatraz, but as an all-things-law-enforcement addict, this was one indulgence he intended to satisfy.

Embracing Otilia as soon as he saw her, Salvador said, "I hope you don't mind, I've made arrangements for us to tour Alcatraz."

"That will be fine; I'm looking forward to spending the day with you. I've got no plans in mind, but I never expected my son would be working continually."

He laughed. "Have you been there?"

"Never, I expect it's sinister," she said, as they began walking down the street side by side, toward The Embarcadero to catch the ferry to the island.

During the time they spent at the historical landmark, they acted like tourists—enjoying the sights, listening to the audio tour of the cell block narrated by inmates and prison guards. They chatted about the commentaries they heard, and when they moved from the dungeon toward a courtyard, Otilia was happy to be out of the intense dampness she'd felt inside.

They took the ten-minute ferry ride back and strolled to Fisherman's Wharf where they experienced a definite buzz of various sounds—sea lions honking, streets jam-packed with noisy tourists and vendors, street performers, all crowding the paths. Retrieving a piece of paper with the name of a recommended restaurant from her purse, Otilia found her way down the street. Salvador flung the door open and waited for her to go inside. The large waiting area was busy and loud. Otilia talked to the hostess who said it would be a short wait before a table for two would be free.

"All the same?" Salvador asked, pointing to a group of ten people, all wearing identical orange T-shirts with a family crest.

"They must all have gathered for a reunion," she said.

"We should get two T-shirts made."

"One for your wife, as well."

They were shown to a table in the back. A bus boy came by with a pitcher of water to fill the glasses and set down a basket of warm sourdough bread.

Wine?" Otilia said.

They ordered two glasses of Merlot and their conversation started to flow with great ease. He asked her to tell him about his early childhood—what stories he had liked, what songs she had sung to him as a child, and she started to chant his favourite nursery rhyme. *Salio la A, no se donde va, a comprarle un regalo a mi mamá.* ("Out came the A, I don't know where it went, to buy a present for Mom.") They crooned it quietly together again.

"You were a beautiful baby, always in good spirits, very curious; you started walking at an early age because you needed to explore your surroundings and pull everything apart."

"I have vague recollections of building stilts out of cans I found in the trash."

"Oh, yes, you asked your father to punch holes into the bottom of each one and he gave you some paint to decorate them."

"It was you who helped me tie the loops with the rope we put through the holes so I could hold on and walk."

"You liked standing on platforms and being tall; you had a blast."

She told him how he wanted to play this game after attending the circus under the tent and watching the people on stilts elicit gasps from the audience. How funny memories were—when you least expected, they brought forth unanticipated, but most pleasant recollections.

"Tell me about what you said to Dad when he took me to hide?" Salvador said.

Shifting from the happy memories Otilia would have preferred to continue evoking, she braced herself and, without her previous delighted smile, replied, "I will never forget. '*No te vayas*—don't leave,' I yelled."

There was a long silence before they again spoke about the political repression that overtook the country with little forewarning after Mr. Fujimori, trapped in his own power, was elected president. She told him about her loneliness and missing her family; about looking for him in familiar places;

and about how she would have sent for him, had she known he was alive. "Sent you money to sustain you," she whispered as tears came into her eyes.

She spoke about her time up in the mine, feeling terribly disconnected, as there was little talk about the country as a whole. "It struck me that people were in this God-forsaken part of the world to make a living, and nobody really cared much that things were otherwise out of control."

The conversation shifted to the time when she came to America. "I was fleeing from terror and, once in this country, I looked for normal, but there hasn't been any normal—everything has been peculiar ever since."

They had finished their meal, and before the waiter cleared the clutter from the table, Otilia, unable to restrain herself, daringly asked, "So, what's up with Tomas?"

"We don't keep in touch much. Last time I saw him was at my wedding. Sharp animosities arose over time."

"How come?"

"He didn't approve of me joining the police force, for starters. Then as I became actively involved in trying to find out what happened to you, he was taken aback. As I mentioned, I met my wife when she was working for the Truth and Reconciliation Committee and we both got involved in trying to obtain accurate facts. Tomas became disgruntled, and made a point of letting me know that he didn't approve, and that's when I went to live on my own. I had a suspicion that he didn't want to face the consequences of a possible aftermath."

Otilia began shaking her head. "I'm surprised he offered you a home."

"He told me he didn't approve of stray dogs on the street."

"What do you mean? He called you a dog?"

"Not to my face."

"*Hijo*, I must tell you that your father and I faced many problems with Tomas. He couldn't be trusted. I bet he didn't reveal the hassles he put us through."

"He never mentioned having spent time with you. He said that there was a lot of age difference between the two of you and there wasn't much contact."

Salvador tried to recall the clues he'd missed when he lived with Tomas, but it was pointless, for he had been too young to understand the subtleties of how his uncle operated. "One day a man came around saying he was from Cajamarca and offered me a chocolate bar. He started asking some questions, but when Tomas found him talking to me, he scared him away. Tomas forbid me to bite into the candy, scolding me for accepting it, saying it could be poisoned and I could die. He warned me not to expect people to be nice out of the kindness of their hearts."

"He was one to talk. He took advantage of your father's business, compromising our reputation," Otilia said.

"He was sly."

"Unscrupulous. Your father and I had cattle; sometimes we put them out to graze with a rancher; at other times we would have to buy feed to get them to a certain weight more rapidly, before we could sell. When Tomas drank too much and ran out of money, he'd come to us for help. We were against feeding his habit and giving him handouts, so we put him to work. One time we sent him to negotiate the price for a hundred pounds of cattle feed and noticed he'd been willing to pay much too much. When we questioned him, he responded that the rate had gone up that month. We were somewhat surprised, but knew there were variations in the market, and perhaps feed was actually commanding a higher price, so we let it go—we didn't want to say much. Later, after some time had passed, we heard rumours that he was taking advantage of us. We became suspicious that he was making deals on the side."

Salvador was intrigued by this strange man who'd shown shameful behaviour, yet also a great deal of generosity while he was growing up.

"One time he threatened one of the merchants who came to inform us that Tomas had insisted he make out invoices to include kickbacks for the both of them."

"He was working both ends? Plotting and planning behind your backs?"

"Other vendors came forth with similar stories and we confronted him about collecting commissions. Tomas was twisting their arms and making deals on the side; we were told in no uncertain terms that if we didn't terminate Tomas, they'd cease their relationships with us."

"What was wrong with the jerk?" Salvador said, dumbfounded, taking a sip from his wine glass.

"He wasn't married, and played around with pretty girls. He had met a young one in a bar in Lima and needed to pay for his indulgences."

"A rotten egg."

"My brother felt that your father didn't respect him and never treated him well," Otilia continued. "He claimed Manuel talked down to him. He had a certain charm, but deep inside he was jealous. Manuel and Tomas never saw eye to eye."

"You parted ways?"

"His involvement with dubious business schemes, his alcohol addiction, his use of vulgar language, made us feel ashamed. He felt entitled to share in our good fortune when he didn't do his part; Manuel got fed up and didn't want him around. Tomas had a lot of resentments, didn't feel any remorse for his bad conduct, and never apologized. By the time he left, he was irate at both of us."

Salvador looked at the facial lines creasing his mother's cheeks and felt saddened by yet another event that had been a cause of strain for her. Was Tomas solely to blame for his parent's absence from his life? Maybe so; but he had to resign himself to the facts, for it was too late to right the wrongs done to him in the past. We must make up for stolen time, was the thought that now crossed his mind, and he reached out to pat her hand.

"Salvador, I am, however, so grateful, so appreciative that he took you in and cared for you as his own," Otilia said, tears trickling down her cheek. "I would never have expected that kind of goodness in him and for that, I forgive him everything."

They got up from the table and walked back to Otilia's car. When he climbed into bed, he felt greatly comforted by the stories he had heard, and fell deeply asleep.

The following day was Sunday and Otilia was back at Salvador's hotel. She had come into town with Michael, who was settled in a chair in the lobby, reading the newspaper while she went up to Salvador's room.

"*Hola,*" she said, leaning forward to plant a kiss on his cheek.

Salvador's suitcase lay open on top of the bed where she could see his suit neatly folded inside. "Can I give you a hand?" she asked.

"I'm all organized. Did I exhaust you yesterday?"

"I felt tired, slept in, and couldn't rise at my usual time. But I am well and it was good to be with you, son."

"That's a pretty chain," he said, looking at her tenderly.

Otilia smiled. "Knowing that I found you, my brain has relaxed, blocking out thoughts and worries." Going into her bag, she handed him a plastic bag. "I brought you your stuffed animal. I have carried it with me all this time."

"You keep it," he said, giving it a good look, "for good luck."

"Okay, I'll keep it for your child."

Realizing that good memories couldn't exist separately from the unsettling realities of life, she decided not to refuse his wish. Otilia felt safe in Salvador's company, and he so much reminded her of Manuel. Vowing to begin restoring herself now that she had her son back, she would worry less and spend days finding peace of mind. But full serenity would only truly come once they learned what had transpired with Manuel. So much had come to pass and yet there were facts still to be explained. Killed in a car? Perhaps.

31

THAT NIGHT, Otilia dreamt she heard Manuel calling her name in an unusually high-pitched tone of voice. Before she could answer, she noticed her husband had been having a heated argument with their adult son, Salvador. There was something disjointed in their dialogue, but she listened closely, trying to grasp what was being discussed. When she walked into the room she saw Manuel showing Salvador a page from the newspaper, pointing out the warning signs to watch out for in the days to come. Salvador's expression was stunned. Manuel's hair had turned grey, and he was a little bit chubbier; however, his skin still was taut. Otilia responded enthusiastically when Manuel rose to hug her and, brushing his face against hers, planted a kiss on her cheek. Then, in shock, she woke up.

Sighing, trying to dispel the deluded images in her dream, she rubbed her eyes. Pushing away the thoughts that entered her wandering mind, she looked at her watch and wondered if Salvador was still asleep in her guest room next door.

Salvador had decided to postpone his trip back home so they could spend the rest of the week together, to continue talking at length and sharing their stories. They had to free themselves from needless worrying and put to rest their ghosts from the past. Besides, they had important decisions to make. How to proceed to find out Manuel's whereabouts?

After breakfast, they sat in the unadorned room where he had slept; with the single bed made, Salvador sat at her desk and told her how happy he was to have found her, for up to a few months ago, he didn't know she existed and he was haunted with questions. "I always expected you'd come to the door to fetch me. But as the years went by, I lost hope."

"Trying to find both of you got so dark, I wasn't sure this was ever going to get solved," she said. "I tried to play mind games, focus on you rather than on your disappearance, but it didn't always help."

Holding his pen and clicking it twice, Salvador said, "I want to make a list of all the agencies you've been in touch with."

Otilia went into a closet and took out a box containing her folders and notes. "Here are the records. Some of these organizations are responsible, while others seemed complicit in their silence. Some seem underfunded, lacking direction. Generally I found little effort was made to bring answers to my questions. Some agencies said they would be writing reports, but in the end few were willing to disseminate their findings."

"Challenging justice? We get plenty of data, but statistics are one thing, an individual's account is another."

"At least it created opportunity for reflection and discussion," Otilia said.

"It also erupted into controversies. As you said, agencies were under pressure from groups wanting them to muzzle the results. Did you know that the Truth and Reconciliation Committee, for example, has been charged with advocating terrorism?" Salvador said.

"You don't say."

"Opponents argue that by giving the victims a voice, they are inciting the traumatized population to fight back. One day, the commission criticized the failure of the Catholic Church, saying they were derelict in taking a stand against the abuses; some suggested the members of the committee were pro-left."

"Such criticism is truly misplaced," Otilia said.

"Of course it is. Every citizen has rights and the state has the duty to uphold their rights."

Otilia told him that she had spent time last night thinking about the matter of Manuel's identification, and felt that if they were to get a glimmer of information, they should try to find out where he had last been seen.

"I agree. I'll arrange to make some public appeals for information. We can put posters in the villages surrounding Cajamarca and in the city itself, and make use of radio and television," Salvador said.

Otilia questioned whether, at this late stage, an urgent request for help would be heard. But Salvador felt sure there were those that would be disposed to follow any leads they could to track a perpetrator and bring the criminal down. She urged Salvador to find someone to help, who didn't play games.

"Don't worry. I know a few trustworthy detectives," he said.

Otilia felt blessed. She'd given her life to finding her husband and son, and Salvador was now, at last, at her side. Though there were still bitter parts of her past she'd have to delve into, she would be able to piece them together alongside her son.

"I have two priorities on my to-do list as soon as I get back home. One is to change my name, and the other is to obtain a DNA profile," Salvador said.

Otilia knew about the *Yo Existo*, I Exist, campaign, set up to help half a million undocumented war survivors regain proper papers. In essence, these people didn't exist in the eyes of the state because they had lost their personal legal documents.

"They're making it easier to correct an identity card," Salvador said.

"I shall be very glad." Otilia could feel a wave of excitement washing over her.

"I'm proud to be a Perez," Salvador tilted his head slightly backward and looked at her keenly.

"And this DNA profile?" she asked.

"In case they uncover Father's body, to determine right away whether there is a genetic match."

The weeks after Salvador left, Otilia began to feel that, once again, she could get pleasure out of life. She tried to find time to be outside to soak up the summer sun and visit friends without a particular agenda in mind. Now that her nights, which had previously been filled with stretches of wakefulness and nightmares, had become more restful, she woke feeling energized. It brought her serenity to know that if anything were to happen to either one of them, she or Salvador would rush to each other's side.

Mother and son spoke diligently once a week, and since Michael had given each of them a tablet to Skype with, they engaged in video calls. Their conversations delighted her spirit and she marvelled at how all of a sudden she'd gotten so lucky. Sometimes they spoke of the past, for Salvador was thirsty for stories about their family life to fill in his own gaps; other times, they shared what they were up to. Sometimes they laughed at their distorted images or their cracking voices while Carmen walked around their apartment with the tablet in her hand, showing Otilia bits and pieces of the renovations she had in mind. One day she pointed the camera to the photo montage displayed on the wall, where several pictures of Otilia now hung.

Salvador urged her to return to Peru, and live the rest of her life close to them, but Otilia resolved to depart California only once she gave up working. With a pension in hand, she'd be able to take care of herself and not rely financially on her son. "I've built my life, established friendships, and so much of what I have is here, but the time will come," she said, the next time he asked.

After years away from her country of birth, Otilia had changed. She didn't behave the same way; she didn't know the same things as her fellow Peruvian residents. Some things she missed, while others irritated her to no end. What irked her most about Peru was that many people continued to deceive each other in socially acceptable ways, conveying varying amounts of truth, depending on who they were dealing with. She didn't appreciate being fooled, unwilling to live with that kind of uncertainty. Having lived for so many years in the U.S., she had come to appreciate the way in which Americans were direct, dependable, and this gave her a sense that she always knew where she stood.

Salvador kept Otilia abreast of events taking place in Lima. One day, he shared news about the Campo de Marte; this park, located in a residential neighborhood, contained monuments commemorating heroes from Peru's past. On August 28, 2005, a new sculpture would be unveiled, the first along a memory path. This carving by Lika Mutal, a Dutch artist, was cut from a black granite stone she'd found in a pre-Colombian ransacked grave. It represented Mother Earth crying for the violence and suffering committed by its children throughout history. The obelisk-like rock, with an embedded smaller stone on top, was named *El ojo que llora*—The Tearing Eye—for water constantly trickled down its side. Located at the centre of a large maze, every circular pathway surrounding it contained tens of thousands of stones with inscriptions of names, ages, and years of death of those who'd lost their lives in the recent conflict.

Salvador had asked his mother to fly down to spend Christmas with them, and Otilia was planning her trip accordingly. Last time they talked, she had let Salvador know that she'd like to make arrangements to have Manuel's name inscribed in a stone to be placed along the Tearing Eye path. She was perplexed and a little annoyed when Salvador said, "I understand how you feel after not hearing from Dad in such a long time, but there's still no proof of his death."

Nevertheless, even if he were alive, he'd been forcibly displaced and would be sustaining a vulnerable life that none should have to endure, suffering from the brunt of the conflict. Didn't he deserve to have a space bearing his name? She needed to honour him, to keep his memory alive, and make it public, while educating others about the serious offences that had taken place. Toxic behaviours needed to be righted for dignified choices to win through.

"Memory makes us." She liked this phrase that she had recently read. Her world had been shattered, but now that she was willing to assemble it again, there was no doubt that, for her own peace of mind, she would place an order for the commemorative stone to be displayed with her husband's name.

Epilogue

In 2006, the Truth and Reconciliation Committee recommended that reparations be paid to immediate family members of people who had been killed or forced to disappear in the conflict. In 2007, the recommendations remained unimplemented.

Wanted on charges of corruption, Alberto Fujimori maintained a self-imposed exile until his arrest during a visit to Chile in November 2005.

On September 22, 2007, the former Peruvian president was deported and flown back to Peru to face charges of grave human rights abuses.

In a historic trial on April 7, 2009, a three-judge panel of Peru's Supreme Court found Fujimori guilty, and sentenced him to twenty-five years in prison.

In November 2015, then President Ollanta Humala (2011-2016) signed a decree creating a national registry for victims of forced sterilization. In 2016, he also signed a bill to search for victims of disappearances. In May, a court ordered that the government pay reparations to victims of abuses committed by both sides of the conflict, overturning the limits on reparations established by the Peruvian legislature.

Reparation programs continue to be implemented unevenly with some programs receiving funding and attention, while others go unattended.

In February 2017, a Peruvuan court issues an international warrant for the arrest of former President Alejandro Toledo (2001-2006) on suspicion of accepting millions of dollars in a bribe from a Brazilian company to win a contract to build a highway between Brazil and the Peruvian coast.

In July, the same judge orderedthe arrest of ex-President Ollanta Humala for related charges.

Acknowledgements

Thank you to Sylvia Taylor for your enthusiastic guidance and believing in me.

Thank you to Patricia Anderson for your careful reads and thorough editing.

To Susan Swanson, Charlotte Coombs, Myriam Waissbluth, Marcos and Susana Cogan for your offer to read the manuscript, your kind words and valuable feedback. Thank you Marina Sonkina, Silvia Karsten, Annette Fasteau, Marilyn and Jackie Rudolph, Suzie Grossman for your friendship and your useful suggestions.

To my husband Nate Zalkow who patiently endured my obsession with this story and generously offered to read and re-read the pages which over time became this book, thank you for your endless encouragement and support.

I express a great deal of gratitude to my daughters Daniela Mantilla and Natania Mathany who fill me with love and always cheer me on. To Alejandro and Emilia, you are the best! Ale you worked hard bringing the story to life by producing a wonderful audio-visual trailer.

Thank you to the anonymous South American taxi driver for sharing his memories which became the catalyst and inspiration for my story.

I am grateful to Inanna Publications for giving *In the Belly of the Horse* a home. Thank you Luciana Ricciutelli, Editor-in-Chief, and Renée Knapp, Publicist.

Photo: Kate Cross

Eliana Tobias was born in Santiago, Chile, to immigrant parents who escaped the Holocaust. She graduated from the University of Chile then completed other degrees in early childhood and special education in the United States and Canada. After working in this field in various capacities, including teaching at the National University of Trujillo in Peru, she moved to Vancouver, where she has lived for thirty years and where she discovered her love of writing. Her rich experience of political turmoil, of listening to stories of the Holocaust when Jewish communities in Europe were shattered, of losing family in Chile under military dictatorship, and living in Peru during a time of intense civil conflict, fueled her passion to write about the ways in which people caught in devastation rebuild their lives. Eliana Tobias lives in Vancouver, B.C.

WINDS
OF THE WORLD
AND THE
MANY CLOUD FORMS

Palmer W. Roberts

VANTAGE PRESS
New York

Published by Vantage Press, Inc.
516 West 34th Street, New York, New York 10001

Manufactured in the United States of America
ISBN: 0-533-11198-6

Library of Congress Catalog Card No.: 94-90351

0 9 8 7 6 5 4 3 2 1

To my wife, Bea, who encourages me in my many ventures, and
to Gloria Green, whose guidance helped produce this tome

Contents

Illustrations

Figures

Tables

Foreword

Captain Roberts has written a wonderfully clear and concise book on *Winds of the World and the Many Cloud Forms.*

Meteorologists, in their forecasting, are concerned very much with the causes of certain weather; most of us, from accountants to airline pilots, care more about how the weather will affect our daily lives.

This book strikes a very happy medium between cause and effect. Most weather books are sleep-inducing. This one certainly is not.

I must say, I was surprised and delighted to read the proofs. I know Bill Roberts as a naval historian, author on several different subjects, and expert on the D-day landings, in which he was involved, but had no idea of his deep knowledge of this subject.

It takes a certain flair to take a difficult subject, make it easy and interesting to read and understand, and put it on paper. This he has done admirably.

I recommend it to anyone with even a passing interest in the weather.

—Capt. W. J. Reid
Trans World Airlines
New York, 23 July 1994

Introduction

Anyone who reads these pages can scarcely miss the excitement of the winds and clouds that permeate our atmosphere. Let us see how and where they form and their effect upon us and on the Earth. Included is a glossary of their names and their locations, the winds' many strengths, and all the unusual shapes of the clouds.

Winds are the movement of air that blow good or bad. The prime movers are the heated air from the tropical areas near the equator, where temperatures reach up to 180°F, which then move north or south toward the frozen polar areas, each some 1,200 miles away. There is an increasing interchange among the winds through the medium of the atmosphere, which causes varieties in the wind and the weather.

The wind can blow as softly as "the breath of life," and at other times with great strength, creating havoc.

The pattern of circulation is primarily determined by the unusual heating of the atmosphere at various levels or altitudes above the Earth, by different latitudes, and by the Earth's rotation. When heat rises, winds occur; when air is cold, the wind sinks toward the surface. Global or prevailing winds extend around the Earth and are part of the overall circulation of the atmosphere. The prevailing winds over the United States blow from west to east. Local winds depend on local temperature differences, with warm air rising over hot areas or falling over cold regions.

Clouds are patches of water content made visible; they form their many shapes by the movement of the air in the atmosphere. They may rise to heights of 25,000 feet or higher above the surface of the Earth. Other clouds form near or along the surface and are moved by the winds. As clouds transit across the sky, they stir our imagination as they create many shapes: magnificent castles, faces of charging animals, flying fish, whales, dragons, birds, and other exotic forms. Yet many of these shapes, as they darken, often predict bad weather, bringing storms that damage property, injure wild life and forest growth, and lay waste everything in their path.

Trade winds are large-scale, global convection winds that always blow over the great ocean areas in the same direction.

Doldrums occur on both sides of the heat equator; they rise straight up, then turn north and south.

Horse latitudes are so named because of the horses that died in Spanish ships heading for the Indies when the ships were becalmed for weeks.

Polar air winds deliver most of each hemisphere's dry, cold winds, bringing blue skies and good weather.

Atmosphere is an invisible, protective, stable mass that blankets the earth. Without it, the Earth would be a dead planet. The sun's rays would scorch the Earth during the day, and it would be deadly cold at night.

Weather is the state of the atmosphere. It is always changing. The impact of weather strikes deeply and cannot be measured in its regularity, toll, or damage. Factors creating the changes in the atmosphere are many, with winds and clouds being the most predictable ingredients and those that we are best able to describe. The Earth contributes to the weather by means of its annual orbit around the Sun and its rotation from west to east. Mountains, too, determine the prevailing direction of ocean currents and the persistent direction of winds.

Temperate climates are those that do not have tropical or polar extremes. The two varieties are the maritime and continental climates. Maritime is strongly influenced by the oceans, which remain relatively warm in winter and cool in the summer; it is characterized by its cold, wet, and dry spells. Continental is where the influence of the ocean decreases and summers become warmer and winters more severe.

Polar climates are regions perpetually covered by snow and ice. During the long, six-month summer days, it is daylight twenty-four hours. The long six-month polar night is a period of intense frost, where low temperatures in the Arctic are down to -70° and in the Antarctic well below -100°. In the Arctic and Subarctic, soil is permanently frozen into a state called permafrost.

NORTH POLE

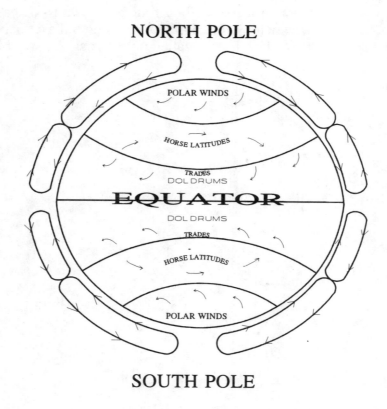

POLAR WINDS

HORSE LATITUDES

TRADES
DOL DRUMS

EQUATOR

DOL DRUMS

TRADES

HORSE LATITUDES

POLAR WINDS

SOUTH POLE

GENERAL PATTERN OF WORLD WINDS

PART I

Winds and Weather

Wind

The Wind is energy, air in motion. It performs many tasks essential to the maintenance of the activities of the atmosphere. Uneven atmospheric pressures cause the wind to blow, pushing air from high- to low-pressure areas. It fills the air with clouds and then sweeps it clear again, blowing entire storm systems around the world, moving heat and moisture from one region of the Earth to another. We refer to this as weather. Often, the wind drives cool, moisture-laden fogs onto the land from the ocean or other large bodies of water. It helps push ocean currents on global journeys, as well as sculpturing sand and snow. It scatters seeds and spores as well as clearing the heavens of smoglike conditions created by aircraft, vehicles, housing, and industrial activities. Air, which is what we call the atmosphere around the Earth and which is always moving, protects the Earth from the strong rays of the Sun. Air masses are large bodies of air, whose physical properties, temperature and moisture, form over land and water coming out of polar and tropical regions.

Polar Winds blow from the poles, bringing cold temperatures, usually with dry and mild weather. *Tropical Winds* blow from the southeast, bringing cloudy, damp, warm weather and often rain. The rotation of the Earth keeps winds from blowing in a straight line (north or south).

In the northern hemisphere, the prevailing winds are westerly, beginning in March. Such winds are barely predictable and sometimes vary violently. They are mostly capricious, irritating, damaging buildings, blowing down trees, wrecking small watercraft, bouncing aircraft about, tumbling umbrellas inside out, and injuring people.

Fronts are zones or adjacent air masses with different degrees of temperature and humidity that do not mix readily. Since cold air is heavier than warm air, when the two masses meet, the warm air tends to rise over the colder air, thus forming a front. A warm

3

front is a zone where warm is replacing colder air at the surface. Here, cloud forms develop along a southeast to southerly wind direction, with a falling barometer. A cold front is a zone where cold air is displacing warmer air, accompanied by storm cloud formations. A stationary front is a zone where neither air mass along the sides of a cold or warm front shows any tendency to displace one another, and cloud forms may be similar to those typically found in a warm front.

Pressure Areas

High- and Low-Pressure Areas control wind direction. Air pressure is the force produced by the weight of the air pressing down on the Earth. These were first described by the Dutch meteorologist as Buy's law, published in 1857. Now they are also referred to as Baric wind law.

Air Pressure is measured by a barometer, which was invented by Torricelli in 1634. Barometric pressures are vital in the forecasts of weather conditions and studies of storms.

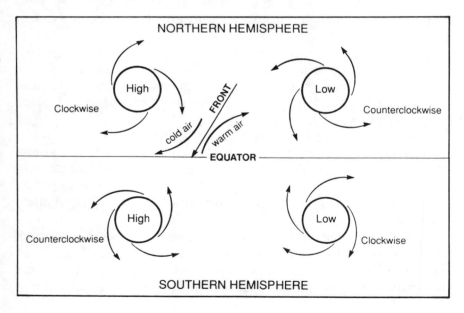

Highs are areas of high pressure, sometimes called anti-cyclones. In the northern hemisphere, winds blow in a clockwise direction. In general, a high is a region of fair weather.

Lows, or extratropical cyclones, are areas of low pressure. In the northern hemisphere, winds blow in a counterclockwise direction. Lows are considered to be a region of poor weather, with the barometer falling. Usually, cirrus, high feathery clouds appear and often thicken and form cirrocumulus and nimbus, which are often storm clouds.

Wind directions are described by the direction from whence they come: north or northerly winds come from the north; south or southerly winds come from the south. The compass shows the direction the wind travels; winds from the north, east, south, or west are referred to as "The Four Winds." Their direction is also indicated on a weather vane, which is usually located near the ground and points the direction from which the wind comes.

The speed of the wind is determined by the *Pressure Gradient*. Strong pressures cause strong winds, which are measured by an anemometer, a device that is rotated by the wind and indicates the rate or speed at which the wind moves. This is then measured by a speedometer in miles per hour or MPH. Winds higher above the Earth's surface are measured by tracing balloons released by meteorologists, who watch the flight of a balloon through a theodolite, which tracks the balloon and measures the speed and direction of the wind. Such information is needed by pilots and weather forecasters.

A system to record wind speed over water was originated in 1805 by Rear Admiral Sir Francis Beaufort, a British scientist. It is called the Beaufort scale and shows that the faster a wind moves, the more dangerous it becomes. Such information is used by mariners and others who report weather conditions and forecasts at sea.

Beaufort Scale

Beaufort Number	General Description	Sea Criteria	Velocity In Knots	Landsman Criteria	MPH
0	Calm	Mirrorlike sea	Below 1	Calm, smoke rises	0
1	Light air	Ripples	1–3	Smoke drifts	2
2	Light breeze	Small wavelets	4–7	Wind vanes moves	5
3	Gentle breeze	Large wavelets	8–12	Leaves in motion	10
4	Moderate breeze	Small waves	13–18	Raises dust	15
5	Fresh breeze	Moderate waves	19–24	Small trees sway	21
6	Strong breeze	Large waves	25–31	Large branches move	28
7	Near gale	Breaking waves	32–38	Whole trees sway	35
8	Gale	High waves	39–46	Twigs break off	42
9	Strong gale	High waves spray	47–54	Buildings damaged	50
10	Whole gale	Very high waves	55–63	Trees uprooted	59
11	Storm	Extremely high waves	64–72	Widespread damage	59
12	Hurricane	Visibility poor	Over 73	Violent destruction	Up to 500

Strong Winds Make Big Storms

Storms represent weather disturbances that vary in intensity and kind. Thunderstorms, tornadoes, hurricanes, and winter storms are the most important.

Thunderstorms usually come from inside a thundercloud. They are the most common and familiar of all weather distur-

6

bances. These are very dense, dark clouds and are usually formed in the summer, when the ground gets hot, causing winds to rise and creating a tremendously violent upsurging draft. This also builds up a field of electricity, resulting in bolts or flashes of lightning, the most powerful electrical storms in the atmosphere, and thunder, producing heavy rain, hail, squalls, and strong winds.

Lightning occurs when a great discharge of negative electricity builds in a thundercloud or cumulonimbus cloud and meets a large positive charge; then a great spark occurs, creating lightning. Such can leap from one cloud to another or to the Earth. There are many forms of lightning: forked, chain, streaked, sheet, or flash, which appear in their many ways as bright lights across the sky. "Balls of Fire" drop from thunderstorms and sometimes run along the ground. "Saint Elmo's Fire" is a continuous, luminous electrical charge of weak or moderate intensity, occurring on elevated objects of the Earth's surface, such as lightning conductors, wind vanes, masts of ships, or the wings of aircraft in flight. Lightning is beautiful, but it is also frightening and dangerous. It often causes fires or injures people, sometimes resulting in death. However, it is helpful in making changes in the ozone layer; the latter screens out harmful ultraviolet rays from the sun. Lightning also changes the nitrogen in the air as it becomes part of the rain, which in turn soaks into the soil, which plants then absorb. This is helpful for the growth of vegetables that are eaten by humans and animals and which are vital to the health of both.

Thunder is a sound caused by tremendous strokes of electrical currents, which make the air around them very hot, instantly expanding as the air molecules fly out in all directions. These bump into cold, making the noise we call thunder. A very loud clap or crash of thunder is caused by sound waves echoing among the clouds. As light travels faster than sound, the lightning flash is seen immediately, but the clap of thunder is heard later, depending on how far away the lightning is. Thunder often follows lightning by twenty to thirty seconds.

7

Rain and Snow

Rain and Snow are formed from water rising from warmer parts of the world's seas, rivers, lakes, and tropical forests and then evaporating into the air, condensing, and dropping down in the form of rain, dew, drizzle, showers, hail, or snow. Freezing vapor, sleet, is usually a mixture of ice, snow, rain, hail, and large ice pebbles.

Rain is the great atmospheric equalizer. Its cycle of evaporation, condensation, and precipitation provides a global transfer of two vital qualities: heat and moisture. The highest rainfall recorded was 905 inches in 1861 in Cherapunji, India.

Snow is formed by the massing together of ice crystals. Ten inches of newly fallen snow is equal to one inch of rain. Hail may be between one-fifth and four inches in diameter and can often weigh up to four pounds, beating crops into the ground, injuring large animals, killing small animals, and damaging buildings and equipment. No section of the United States is totally free from the damaging variety of hail. However, this is most frequent in an area extending from Montana south to central Texas, sometimes called "Hail Alley." It may also occur from Missouri up to the Mississippi Valley and to the foot of the Rocky Mountains.

Windchill is the ability of strong winds to combine with low temperatures to rapidly cool warm-blooded animals, humans, heated buildings, etc. It can be very dangerous if not protected against.

Colors in the Sky

A *Rainbow* is a bow or arc of prismatic colors formed in showery weather by the refraction and reflection of rays of light from the sun passing through drops of rain or ice as it appears in the heavens away from the Sun. A similar natural display of prismatic colors may be seen in the spray of a waterfall.

Polar Lights, Northern Lights, or the *Aurora Borealis*, are streams of luminous meteoric phenomenon of varying brilliancy seen in the heavens of the northernmost regions of the northern hemisphere at night. These are their greatest magnificence in the arctic regions. They are believed to be electric in origin. *Southern Lights*, or *Australis Borealis*, are located in regions of the southern hemisphere.

Whirling Winds

Tornadoes are the most violent, concentrated, and destructive of all storms, with winds reaching two hundred to seven hundred miles per hour and starting deep in a thundercloud, where a column of strong, warm air rising in the air is set spinning by violent winds through the top of the cloud. Tornadoes can go by many names, such as twisters or whirlwinds, etc. As many as five hundred to six hundred of these occur each year throughout the world. These winds whirl clockwise, growing larger and larger, and are extremely fast as they squeeze into small circles similar to an elephant's trunk or an hourglass figure. This then builds downward from a large gray to a black cumulonimbus cloud, forced by a tremendously strong wind, with lightning and thunder. Their paths are narrow, usually less than one-eighth of a mile across. As the funnel travels along a path of several hundred feet up to one hundred miles, the pressure within is very low, acting like a vacuum cleaner, usually bringing with it extremely high temperatures, reducing humidity, and sucking up moisture as it passes. It sucks up everything in its path from dust, sand, water, wood, small trees, even tearing off roofs of buildings, wrecking small structures, exposed machinery, automobiles, and killing animals and humans before traveling on and then dropping the debris, leaving much destruction in its wake. It comes smashing and twisting, while making a roaring noise, then narrows and vanishes. In 1936, in a Civilian Conservation Corps camp, a building was lifted off of its base by the wind, lifted over a flagpole, and dropped on a building over three hundred feet away. Fortunately, no one was injured. At sea, it is known as a *Water Spout*. These are not as violent and are composed of water droplets formed from condensation. However, they often capsize boats and then damage property as they move ashore at speeds of over fifty miles per hour.

Cyclone is a name given to a whirling storm disturbance, which was named by Capt. Henry Paddington in 1830 from the Greek word *kyklon*, which means "whirling around."

Tropical Cyclones are hurricanes named from *hurakans*, a term given by the people of the West Indies. A full-grown hurricane is an awesome spectacle, with clouds rising upward. In both the Atlantic and Pacific Oceans, they are called *typhoons*. In other parts of the world, they may have other local names. Hurricanes are the strongest and the deadliest of storms and rotate counterclockwise in the northern hemisphere and clockwise in the southern hemisphere. Whatever they are called, wherever they are, they have common features in formation, behavior, and destruction, and their paths are unpredictable. However, they are large, strong, intense, fierce whirling winds, reaching speeds of over twelve on the Beaufort scale and often bringing heavy rains and extremely high tides, sinking craft, washing beaches away, and bending or pulling up trees. They form when very warm air continually rises for several days over tropical waters, usually in the summer. They are called by names such as *willy-willies* in the sea north of Australia and Hurin or *killer wind* in the West Indies. Waves associated with these intense winds may reach thirty to fifty feet in height or more. They are tracked by radar. The hurricane intensity force is identified by numbers on the Saffir-Simpson scale.

Saffir-Simpson Scale

Scale Number	Winds (MPH)	Wave Surge (Feet)	Damage
1	74–95	4–5	Minimal
2	96–110	6–8	Moderate
3	111–130	9–12	Extensive
4	131–155	13–18	Extreme
5	156 and over	19 and over	Catastrophic

The U.S. government agencies responsible for disseminating weather and related information have used female names to identify tropical storms since 1953. However, in 1979 the United States proposed that male and female names be used to identify tropical storms; this was accepted by all world meteorological organizations.

The *Eye of a Storm* is the central region of an intense tropical cyclone, where winds spin in a circular pattern around a low-pressure center. The eye may be from five to fifty miles in diameter and may take minutes to hours to pass while traveling from sixty to one hundred knots per hour.

PART II

Winds of the World

References

Ford Times. 168, no. 3, March 1975.

The Guinness Book of Weather Facts and Feats. Cecil Street, London, England.

Herschke, Ralph E. *Glossary of Meteorology*, 1972.

Knight's Modern Seamanship, 8th Edition, U.S. Navy.

McIntosh, D. H. *The Meteorology Glossary*, 1972.

Meteorological Glossary, 6th Edition. London, England: Meteorological Office.

The National Severe Storm Laboratory. Palo Alto, Calif.: American West Publishing.

The National Weather Service, U.S. Department of Commerce.

North Country Living, no. 7 (July 1975).

U.S. Weather Bureau Circular M, 9th Edition, 1954.

Weather. Life Science Library, 1970.

The International Cloud Atlas, volumes 1 and 2. Geneva, Switzerland: Meteorological Organization.

You may combine cloud forms and make your own as you view the heavens. The imagination may produce faces, animals, castles, and other varied shapes such as a thundering chariot, like time racing across the sky to disappear behind a low-lying cloud, heralding the close of day.

They represent the thickest layer of instability to be found in the atmosphere. The immediate implication of the cumulonimbus is that it develops into "showerheads," or the thunderstorm stage, with heavy rain, lightning, thunder, gusty winds, and often hail. They are the most dangerous type of cloud because of their turbulence, which may cause damage to aircraft flying over.

Fog is a condition that occurs when warm air drops off to a dew point, 60°F, combining minuscule water droplets that, moisture rich, may number 25,000 to a square inch. Fog is formed low to the ground in damp pockets at night and usually covers a wide area.

Smog is a condition where the natural, pure atmosphere is constantly contaminated by foreign substances where the fog contains smoke, burned gas, or pollutants from aircraft, automobiles, and industrial activities.

Arctic Sea Smoke is a steam fog in the polar region that occurs when intense cold air off the ice pack or snow slopes flows over open stretches of warmer water.

The basic cloud forms often join together to form the sky into many shapes. They are found within certain ranges of elevation.

Cirrostratus is a whitish, thin, high cloud that gives the sky a milky appearance. It is usually very stable and can change to altostratus then to nimbostratus, bringing rain.

Cirrocumulus is considered the most beautiful arrangement of clouds, forming ripples of lines of clouds, sometimes called a "mackerel sky."

Altostratus is a high, gray, uniform sheet of a cloud which lowers and thickens and may cause rain.

Altocumulus is a very thick, high, gray sheet of a cloud and often changes to nimbostratus, bringing rain.

Stratocumulus is usually a patchwork, flattened layer of gray clouds.

Cumulonimbus is a thundercloud mass rising high in the air, 30,000 to 50,000 feet. It is mountainlike in appearance and may cover the entire sky, often accompanied by rain, hail, lightning, and thunder.

Nimbostratus is a low, dark, threatening layer of rain or snow clouds.

NIMBUS

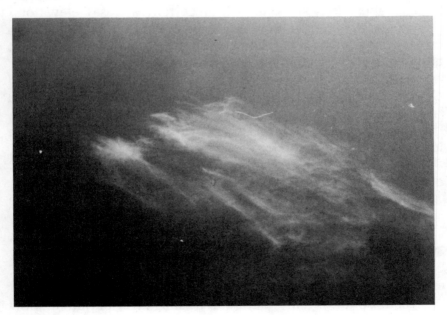

CIRRUS

FOG

VAPOR TRAILS

CUMULUS

STRATUS

SMOG

RAINBOW

Forms

Clouds are a visible collection of particles of water, vapor, or ice suspended in the air, usually high above the Earth's surface. Clouds are the visible bearers in the atmosphere of weather news telling what tomorrow's weather may bring. Clouds have a great variety of forms. Some clouds are also formed from smoke, flying dust, or from volcanoes. The shapes of clouds are, for the most part, the result of the horizontal motion of the wind. The principal cloud forms, which are easily recognizable, are:

Cirrus, the highest cloud in the sky, which means "curl."
Stratus, which means "uniform layer."
Cumulus, whose name means "heap."
Nimbus, called the "storm cloud."
Fog, a stratus, hazy cloud formed near the ground.
Smog, is a fog condition containing smoke.

The word *Cirrus* comes from the Latin word for curl, lock or tuft of hair. Cirrus clouds are the most delicate of clouds and may be found in many different forms, such as those which are distinctly wispy and windswept, similar to "mares tails," others like feathery "silky strands" stretching high across the upper atmosphere, 20,000 to 50,000 feet above the Earth. They are formed from water vapor and ice crystals rising from the ocean.

Stratus are layers or sheets of clouds that form more or less in a uniform gray mass over most of the sky, usually below 8,000 feet above the Earth and often form into altostratus, stratocumulus, or nimbostratus.

Cumulus are thick, heap-shaped, rounded, or domelike clouds with clear tops and flat bases. They are caused by heated rising air currents. Once formed, cumulus clouds may form from 8,000 to 20,000 feet above the earth. Single cumulus clouds pile majestically upward in towering castles and sky mountains. There are usually clear spaces between such clouds.

Nimbus are big, towering, black storm clouds that bring rain, dew, sleet, snow, and hail. They may extend from near the Earth's surface to 65,000 feet as they form into cumulonimbus clouds.

26

Clouds

Although there are no two alike, clouds are one of the key components of the Earth's intricate weather-making machine.

The clear blue sky becomes the background for clouds. Clouds are of all kinds as they float across the sky. A system of classification could never give them justice, yet nothing has been found to improve the system derived in 1803 by Luke Howard, an English pharmacist and a student of weather, all of which are variations of these basic cloud forms: *cirrus* meaning "curl," *cumulus* meaning "heap," *nimbus* meaning "violent rain cloud," and *stratus* meaning "layers." This system proved so simple and effective that, with some variations, it is still used by meteorologists today.

Name	Miles above Sea Level	Description
Cirrus	7.2	Made entirely of ice crystals
Cirrostratus	6.6	May spread into thin, milky sheets
Cirrocumulus	6.0	High bubbles or mackerel sky
Altostratus	5.4	High layers of clouds
Altocumulus	4.8	A puffy group
Stratocumulus	4.2	Layers of puffy clouds
Cumulus	3.6	May spread into broad sheets
Cumulonimbus	2.4	May rise to great heights
Stratus	1.2	Layers of clouds
Nimbostratus	0.6	Layer of high, dark rain clouds

PART III

Clouds: Are They Windows to Heaven?

squall reaches Malacca Strait from the Indian Ocean, there is a sudden drop of temperature.

Maestro is a northwest wind on the westerly shore of the Adriatic Sea on the coasts of Sardinia and Corsica and also in the Ionion Sea of the Mediterranean. It occurs most frequently in the summer.

Ponente, also *Tramontana* and *Levanta*, is a soft, dry wind that can turn into a fierce, damaging wind throughout Sardinia and Corsica.

Sea Mis is a violent, strong, cold, westerly wind blowing in a menacing, eerie, gigantic gray curtain. It sweeps swiftly across the horizon from the Atlantic Ocean easterly into South Africa. It comes two or three times a week and smothers everything during a period of a few hours to several days. It is like being buried in a swirling field of light, blowing cotton. Its vacuum makes it almost impossible to see anything until it completely passes over and lifts in a dissipating fog.

Leveche is a hot, dry southerly wind blowing southeast across Spain. It frequently carries sand and dust. The approach is warned by a brownish cloud on the horizon.

Karema is a violent east wind on Lake Tanganyika, Africa.

Kosava is a raving wind occurring on the Danube in southeast Bulgaria.

Desert for over fifty days a year in Malta and in the late spring in Egypt. The Egyptians call it "sel al Kasmin," their name for fifty days. In Spain, it is called "leveche."

Berg is a hot, dry easterly wind blowing over South Africa.

Simoon is a dry, whirling, sand-laden, suffocating desert wind that blows across Arabia, Syria, and North Africa. It often lasts for many days. It arrives suddenly, choking and smothering people and animals in great clouds of drifting sand.

Euraquilo is a string of northeast and north-northeast winds that blow across Arabia and the Near East.

Harmattan is a hot, dry wind that blows southwest from Central Africa across the Sudan. It usually occurs in December through February.

Karif, also *Kharif*, is a strong southwest wind that suddenly comes from the Gulf of Aden. It usually starts at about 9:00 P.M. and blows until noon the following day.

Seistan is a hot, dry, strong, sand-laden wind blowing from the northwest and north-northwest in the Seistan region of Iran and Afghanistan, with speeds reaching seventy miles per hour and carrying corrosive sand. All buildings are constructed without windows on the windward sides.

Peesash is a hot, dry, dust-laden wind that blows across India.

Depeg is a very strong westerly wind that blows over Sumatra and Indonesia.

Monsoon is a persistent seasonal southwest wind that starts in May and continues throughout the summer into October. The name is derived from the Arabic *mausim*, meaning "season." It comes with torrential rain and blows off the Indian Ocean over southern Asia, India, and the Arabian Sea. The wind may change with the season as it blows northwest in the winter.

Shamal, also *Shmaal*, is a strong, hot steady northwest wind that may blow in the lower valley of the Tigres River in the Persian Gulf. It blows constantly in June and then for over five days all summer. It often dies down at night.

Kachain, or *Kachean*, is a hot, dry wind that blows from the west or southwest toward Ceylon from the Indian Ocean in June and July.

Sumatra is a squall blowing southwest or northwest. When the

Poriaz is a violent northeast wind that blows from the Black Sea near the Bosporus into southern Russia.

Marin is a very warm, moist southeast wind blowing from the sea on to the southern coast of France and up into the maritime Alps during the spring and autumn. In the Rhone River valley, it blows from the south.

Mediterranean and Indian Ocean Areas

Solano is a southerly and easterly hot, humid wind blowing along the southwest coast of Spain.

Spanish Plume is a plume of warm air flowing from Spain toward France. It often leads to the development of violent thunderstorms over northern France and southern England.

North'wester is a violent convection type of storm that is accompanied by light squalls occurring in Bengal and Assan from March through May.

Leste is a Spanish term for "from the east." It is a hot, dry, dust-laden wind that strikes the Madeira Islands from the northeast or southeast and often reduces the relative humidity to 20°. It sometimes does not blow in the summer.

Levanter, or *Levante*, is a strong, humid easterly wind that creates great problems for ships and other craft in the Straits of Gibraltar.

Ponente, Tramontana, Greicate, and *Levanta* are usually soft, dry winds, which can turn into fierce, damaging winds, throughout Sardinia and Corsica.

Sirocco, or *Scirocco*, is a hot or warm, dry, dust-laden, dreaded cyclonic wind, which blows from the Sahara Desert and throughout North Africa. It is accompanied by a macabre sound that can drive people and animals out of their minds or crazy. This wind also affects parts of southern Europe and blows across the Mediterranean Sea.

Libeccio is a strong, squally southwest wind in the central Mediterranean. It is common in the winter.

Khamsin, also known as *Camsin, Kamassen,* or *Khemsen,* is a hot, dry, dust-laden southerly wind blowing from the Sahara forty to seventy-five miles per hour without letting up. It forces all trees in the French Provence to bend to the south. The wind arrives without warning and suddenly streams down from the Alps into the Rhone River valley and on down to the Mediterranean Sea. Boats, yachts, and barges are knocked about on the river. Persons aboard stay below deck; if they are topside, they are knocked down and often injured. This strong wind causes house builders not to construct windows on the north side, or the windward side, of a building.

Bordelais is an east of southwest wind that occurs during all seasons in southern France. It occurs most often in the summer when it is mild and rainy. It often brings violent thunderstorms.

Boulbie is a violent, cold, dry north wind of southern France. It occurs most often in December and January and is often accompanied by snow and creates a blizzard. The wind is very strong, causes much damage, and often uproots trees.

Secard is a warm dry wind that blows over Lake Geneva in Switzerland.

Marget, also *Moregeasson*, is a light breeze on Lake Geneva, Switzerland. It blows from 5:00 to 7:00 P.M. and then from 7:00 to 9:00 A.M., when it becomes a powerful breeze. It blows throughout the day in the fall and winter.

Austru is an east and southeast strong wind centered in Romania.

Bora is a fierce, cold wind that blows from the north or northeast from the Adriatic Sea across the Dalmatian coast of Yugoslavia. Its speeds reach 15 on the Beaufort scale or over land at near one hundred miles per hour.

Meltem, or *Meltemi*, is a strong northeast or east wind that comes in suddenly during the day in the summer into Bulgaria from the Black Sea and also into Turkey through the Bosporus Straits.

Prester is a whirlwind waterspout that is accompanied by lightning throughout the Mediterranean and Greece.

Porlezzena is an east wind on Lake Lugano, Italy, and in Switzerland. It blows from the Gulf of Porlezza.

Lodos is a strong southerly wind from the Black Sea onto the coast of Bulgaria.

19

Chubasco is a violent, dangerous thunderstorm with vivid lightning flashes and squall blowing throughout Central America, mostly Costa Rica and Nicaragua. It occurs most frequently in May and October.

Pampero is a strong westerly wind that blows across southern Chile or Argentina.

Papagayo, also *Papogais*, is a violent northeast fall wind on the Pacific coast of Nicaragua and Guatemala. It is strong in January and February, lasts three or four days, and is weaker in the morning. In the evening, it freshens to gale force and continues into early night.

Solatan is a very strong, dry, southerly wind blowing through the Celebes in the Philippines and the Netherland East Indies.

Baguio is a tropical cyclone occurring in the northern Philippines in July as well as in November.

Barat is a strong squally northwest or west wind that blows from the Celebes Sea onto the coast of Celebes near Manado. It occurs from December through February.

Crachin is a heavy drizzle rain with low mist or fog, occurring in July through April along the coastal areas of southern China and Cambodia.

Bali Wind is a strong east wind that blows across the east end of Java.

Black Northeaster is a northerly gale occurring in southeast Australia in summer, with low pressure in the northeast and high pressure off of New South Wales. It sometimes blows for three days with thick overcast and heavy rain.

Tenggara is a strong hazy east or southeast wind during the east monsoon in the Spermunde Archipelago.

European Area

Mistral also *Migistral*, is often referred to as "the master wind." It is an infernal, cold, dry, wind that blows only when the sky is clear, bright blue, and cloudless, and when the sun is blazing. As it occurs, the sky turns white and obscures the sun. The wind blows strong and steady from three to nine days at speeds of from of the air is enjoyed, mountains can be seen ninety miles away, and citrus growers watch the weather for possible freezing.

Chinook is a very warm, dry wind of the fohn type that blows down the western slopes of the Rocky Mountains. It is often referred to as "the snow eater." In Washington, Oregon, and other parts of North America, it is a warm, moist southwest wind blowing toward the coast.

Williwaw is a violent, destructive wind blowing westward along the Aleutian Island chain and coastal Alaska. It damages shipping and low-flying aircraft as it passes over ocean waters and land areas. The wind registers 9 to 10 on the Beaufort scale and comes without warning.

Wasatch is a strong, gusty east wind blowing out of the mouth of canyons in the Wasatch Mountains onto the plains of Utah.

Texas Blue Norther is a winter wind in the Texas Panhandle and nearby areas. With winds up to fifty miles per hour, it comes from the north and brings cold arctic air, dropping temperatures as much as 30° within one hour. The wind occurs quickly and without notice in a cloudless sky.

Norther is an ugly north wind that blows in the winter. It sweeps across the southern United States and then out over the Gulf of Mexico. It originates in Canada and moves down the Mississippi River valley.

Etison is a strong wind that blows throughout the Pacific Ocean area.

Kona, which means "a leeward wind," is a very strong gale-strength wind. It registers 7 to 9 on the Beaufort scale and blows southwest to south-southwest. The wind is a stormy ocean wind with heavy rains throughout the Hawaiian Islands and blows five times a year.

Zonda is a hot, dry, westerly wind blowing from the Andes in Argentina. When the wind blows easterly, it is called a *puelce*.

Buster is a sudden cold, squally, violent wind that blows across the coastal plain of southern Australia. It is also referred to as a *Southerly Burster*, a *Pamero*, or a *Brickfielder*.

Willy-Willies is a large, swirling wind reaching speeds of up to 12 on the Beaufort scale. It blows across Australia and New Zealand.

17

Jet Streams are very fast winds that blow high in the atmosphere above the Earth, usually about four miles or over 21,000 feet, and may travel at speeds of up to one hundred miles per hour. Similar winds higher up, from six to eight miles, may reach speeds of up to three hundred miles per hour. These extremely strong, high winds blow generally from west to east in the northern hemisphere. Aircraft flying these routes utilize them, as it gives them great added speed. Flying east to west the aircraft avoids them.

Tornadoes are common over the great central parts of the United States. When cold air from Canada meets warm air from the Gulf of Mexico, thunderstorms occur. When conditions are right, they then create tornadoes. Tornadoes, also known as *twisters*, extend from Texas, Oklahoma, Alabama, Georgia, and Louisiana, moving northward, NNE, to Illinois, Iowa, Wisconsin, Kansas, Nebraska, and North and South Dakota, areas often referred to as "Tornado Alley." They also occur in Australia and other parts of the world three or four times a year, usually in the late fall or early winter. Tornadoes leave the land dry and parched, greatly damaging orchards and farmlands.

United States and the Pacific Ocean

A *Northeaster* is a strong northeast wind blowing across New England. It brings wet weather and gale-force winds between thirty-four to fifty-five miles per hour. A similar, but not as strong wind blows across the Great Lakes of North America.

Santa Ana is a truly local name for an unpredictable, dry, hot, and often violent wind that rises in the desert areas, the mile-high Great Basin of the western United States, and plunges through canyons in its rush to the coastal areas of Southern California. It is named after the Santa Ana Canyon. The old mariners called it "the devil wind," because it raised such havoc with operations. To all, it is a very destructive, high-velocity wind. Whenever it comes, it strikes swiftly, supporting or creating fire-swept areas, creates havoc, and then quietly departs. After its departure, the clearness

The following is a glossary of the names of winds in various parts of the world. Now that we know what they are, where they come from, and how winds, and water, shape the Earth. It is noted that there are many different kinds of winds, which have many different names. Winds of extra force may not occur everyday; yet winds affect some part of the world each day.

Fohn, or *Foehn*, is a very dry, warm wind that blows down valleys on the lee side of a mountain range. Such winds are found in the Alps in France, Scandinavia, and Switzerland as well as in North and South America, Asia, and Japan.

Squalls are very dangerous and form over the water all over the world. They are made up of dozens of thunderstorms linked together, often described as "a line of soldiers advancing abreast." Some are very strong and may reach twelve on the Beaufort scale; they can last for hours. They move extremely fast, shifting, and are often accompanied by violent winds and torrential rains, upsetting small craft as well as doing heavy damage as they move ashore.

Arwind is a German term for a wind blowing off a glacier.

Doldrums are a belt of calms and light variable winds and squalls that may form over any part of the oceans situated between 30° south and 30° north of the equator. They often abound in tedious calms. These areas are often referred to as "the horse latitudes."

Gust is a rapid increase in wind strength blowing intermittently, usually without warning and continuing through a windy period.

Gales are strong winds of 8 to 10 on the Beaufort scale. Ships at sea are warned of their location, direction, and force.

Savanna, or Savannah, is a term applied to a tropical climate with a wet and dry season. This is usually from May to August in the northern hemisphere and from November to February in the southern hemisphere.